D0339067

THE GIRL
IN THE
SHADOWS

BOOKS BY MARION KUMMEROW

Not Without My Sister

A Light in the Window

From the Dark We Rise

MARION KUMMEROW

THE GIRL IN THE SHADOWS

bookouture

Published by Bookouture in 2022

An imprint of Storyfire Ltd.
Carmelite House
50 Victoria Embankment
London EC4Y 0DZ

www.bookouture.com

ISBN: 978-1-80314-217-3
eBook ISBN: 978-1-80314-216-6

1

NEAR BERLIN, SUMMER 1943

Margarete picked up her cup of coffee and sipped it as she looked out over the grounds below the terrace. It was early morning, her favorite time of the day, because the air was still fresh and smelt of moist grass and earth.

Later in the day, the sun would be scorching down on Gut Plaun, the farmland and stud she owned, about one hundred miles north of Berlin. But in the mornings, there was always hope that positive things might happen, that for another day she could keep her charges alive, and not be found out herself.

Because one and a half years ago, she had switched identities and the Jewish maid Margarete Rosenbaum who she had once been, had become Annegret Huber, the daughter of a high-ranking SS-officer, who'd died in a bombing raid along with his wife and said daughter.

She glanced at the pile of mail that lay on the table. It was a task she relished and dreaded at the same time. Mostly the mail came from suppliers she dealt with in order to procure what was needed not only for the stud and farm, but also for the ammunition factory she owned a few miles from the manor, hidden deep in the woods.

Taking up the letter opener that had belonged to Annegret's father, SS-Standartenführer Wolfgang Huber—a despicable man who'd exploited her as his maid before a twist of fate had sent him to meet his maker and made her his daughter, and sole heir of the vast Huber estate—she sliced the first envelope open.

A requirement from the Wehrmacht for more horses. After the disaster at Stalingrad this past winter, they wanted anything with four legs to help the war effort—trained or untrained. She put it on the pile for Piet, the stud manager.

Another few were from suppliers for the factory. Those she put on another pile for the new factory manager, Franz Volkmer, to deal with.

"More coffee, Fräulein Annegret?" Dora, her trusted maid asked. She was a Ukrainian worker and would soon get married to Oliver, the estate manager. She and Oliver were the only people on the estate who knew about Margarete's real identity, but for security reasons they still addressed her as Fräulein Annegret, even when they were alone.

Nobody wanted to risk a slip up or an accidental eavesdrop, because if anyone ever found out they all would be hauled away, first to the Gestapo dungeons and then to a camp in the east.

"Thank you." Margarete nodded absently. Not even the rich or famous could get hold of real coffee these days and she would much prefer to drink tea. But to prefer tea over coffee, even *Ersatzkaffee*, was as un-German as it got and might even be reason to be suspected as a friend of the English, who were mocked for their habit of constant tea drinking.

Dora poured her another cup and then disappeared as silently as she had arrived. Margarete glanced up from the correspondence to look after her as she vanished into the house.

She and the housekeeper Frau Mertens kept the manor in excellent condition, with the help of two or three girls from the village for preparing the meals for several dozen workers on the farm and stud.

With the upcoming harvest a few weeks from now, she would have to get more help, but able-bodied men were in short supply these days, since most males were shipped to the Eastern Front as soon as they turned eighteen. She sighed. The shortage of civilian workers was a huge problem, not only for her estate.

When she came to the bottom of the correspondence, she had three neat piles: one for Piet, one for Fritz and one for Oliver, the estate manager, who oversaw the others and the manor. Once again no letter for her. She felt a familiar knot in her stomach, because even though she and her favorite aunt had agreed that it was better not to write letters, she always wished for news from her.

Heidi was a Christian who had married Margarete's father's youngest brother Ernst many years ago. She was the one Margarete had gone to for help after switching identities with the deceased Annegret Huber. Without Heidi's help, she wouldn't be here and alive.

She yearned to hear that her aunt was well and safe. After the air raid in March this year, setting part of Leipzig on fire, it had become all too clear that the British bombers were able to reach Central Germany and wreak havoc there the same way they had done over the Western parts for years.

In her mind she sent a prayer to her aunt, imagining how the two of them once sat on her sofa in Leipzig, chatting about this and that. She also gave thanks for the serendipity that Uncle Ernst—whom they'd both believed had been killed in some Polish camp—had miraculously appeared, although almost worked to death, in Margarete's newly inherited munitions factory.

She took up the last envelope and frowned at the sight of the familiar and dreaded Imperial Eagle. It was from the SS district headquarters in Parchim and she wondered what they might want from her.

Usually they never bothered writing letters, but instead ordered Oliver to come into town if they wanted something from Gut Plaun. Thankfully that didn't happen often, but, like every producer in Germany, the Gut and the factory were prone to receiving control visits.

She opened the letter and skimmed the words, not impressed at all with the compliments and accolades the writer tossed her way. If he knew how much she detested the Nazis, the SS and everything he stood for, he'd spare himself the ink for these words. But then, if he knew who she really was, she wouldn't be here anymore receiving his letters.

Her eyes jumping down to read the second paragraph, she held back a gasp as a chill coursed through her veins.

The Reichsführer SS Heinrich Himmler has decreed that all concentration camps in Germany have to be cleaned of Jews. All remaining Jews are to be deported to the Auschwitz Camp or to Lublin-Majdanek. This order extends to any and all Jewish prisoners on work details throughout the Reich.

Her hand with the letter sank to her lap. About half of the one thousand forced workers in her ammunition factory were Jews. Did this vile bureaucrat actually expect her to send all of them, including her uncle Ernst, to their sure deaths?

Contrary to popular belief that they were just concentration camps, she knew exactly what was going on in Poland. Not working camps, but death camps. Her former employer Wolfgang Huber had bragged about the atrocities going on and she'd heard first-hand about the plans to exterminate her entire race by starvation, exhaustion, disease, and, if all else failed, by gassing them right off the train ramp and burning their remains in the huge crematoriums erected for the sole purpose of handling the never-ending influx of corpses.

> *We appreciate that to keep the factory producing sorely needed ammunition for our great Wehrmacht, this cannot be done all at once. Therefore we see fit to begin the deportation with all Jews deemed non-essential by the end of next week. This will give you the necessary time to replace them with prisoners of war and other subjects available.*
>
> *We have arranged for new workers to be sent to your factory this coming Monday to be trained by the subjects they are to replace. We hope to meet all your requirements to keep producing the best possible quality for the war effort with this arrangement.*
>
> *Most cordial greetings,*
>
> *Unterscharführer Lothar Katze*

Desperate, she crumpled the letter in her hands. She knew Lothar Katze well, an unpleasant, sadistic man who made up in brutality what he lacked in intelligence. He'd been the one who'd whipped her friend Lena to death, and he'd also been the one who'd taken the punishment of Margarete's former, corrupt and cruel, estate manager into his own hands. A punishment Gustav Fischer hadn't survived. Not that she pitied him, since he had deserved multiple times whatever came his way.

Unfortunately Katze wasn't one to beg for clemency, since he found too much joy in making others suffer and was convinced the Jews were no better than a cockroach he could crush under his jackboot.

Her mind frantically searched for a way to ignore the order and save "her" Jews without breaking her cover, but came up empty. Annegret Huber, the spoilt heiress of Gut Plaun, was a staunch Nazi supporter who wouldn't have a problem sending five hundred men and women to their deaths.

And she would have done it with a smile on her face. Hatred not only for the Nazis, but also for herself, trapped in this predicament, rose in Margarete's chest. The decision to switch identities with Annegret had been done on the spur of the moment—to save her own life. But, as it had turned out, it had been only the beginning of a charade with implications she'd never foreseen.

Wilhelm Huber, the second son, who'd discovered her ruse and had protected her anyway, had opened her eyes to the bigger picture. It wasn't just her life at stake. Not only one Jew who wanted to cling to life. When he'd sacrificed himself to save her, he'd given her a mission to fulfill: do good with all the money you'll inherit. Transform dark to light, evil to good, and hate to love.

And she had tried. But time and again fate put a spoke in her wheel, setting her back in her efforts to save her fellow Jews.

She longed to scream the injustice to the skies, rant about the vileness of this letter, about the horrors of the Nazi regime, but even that she couldn't afford to do, because there were eyes and ears everywhere.

Somehow she needed to figure out what to do. *The end of next week.* That gave her a bit of time. But without a plan, time was in vain.

2

"Those two are coming along nicely," Oliver told Piet as they stood at the corral fence and watched the horse trainer put two young horses through their paces.

When Fräulein Annegret had promoted him to estate manager more than six months ago, he'd reluctantly had to give up his work with the horses. But he never missed an opportunity to visit the stables and watch the training, or take a horse out for a ride.

It wasn't that he distrusted Piet, who had worked under him as a stable hand before he had been promoted to Oliver's previous position as stud master. Piet was a good man. The sixty-year-old horse lover could sometimes seem gruff, but despite his bulky stature, he was gentle to the horses and had accumulated a wealth of experience over decades.

"They are. I'm just worried the Wehrmacht will press us to give them even more and we will have to send them younger horses. We can only do so much training when they're not ready," Piet said.

It was a constant threat. Oliver cared for his equine charges and wanted to give them the best training possible to withstand whatever was thrown at them on the battlefield, but the Wehrmacht seemed to care exclusively for replenishing their stock.

Oliver shook his head. He'd been at the front himself, in a cavalry unity during the early stages of the Russian invasion. In hindsight he'd been lucky to catch a bullet that had shattered his lower leg. After the doctors had patched him up, he'd been left with a limp—and a medical discharge from the Wehrmacht.

"We are going to need more hay before summer's end," Piet interrupted his thoughts.

"I know," Oliver replied. "We have several acres that are almost ready. Provided the weather cooperates we should be able to cut the hay in a few weeks and, once it's dry, we can bale it. That should suffice to get the horses through the winter and into next spring."

"Good, good."

Oliver nodded and pushed off the top rail of the fence. "I have to tackle my other duties. Let me know if anything comes up."

"Will do, boss."

Oliver chuckled at the jaunty salute Piet gave him and shook his head. "Save it for someone who cares." Then he left to take a tour through the stables, which, strictly speaking, wasn't his responsibility anymore, but he enjoyed being with the horses too much to let go.

Sabrina, his favorite mare, whinnied when he entered and he approached her to give her a pat on the neck. She'd given birth to a beautiful foal in the spring and it broke his heart to know that the cuddly bundle would be trained much too soon to be a cart horse and sent to the front. His only hope was that two years from now, the war would be long over.

Next, he checked up on Snowfall, a gorgeous gray mare he'd chosen for Fräulein Annegret, back then when he still believed her to be the real Annegret Huber. A capricious, nervous and temperamental animal, Snowfall would have been the perfect horse for a seasoned rider like Annegret.

Margarete, in contrast, had never been near a horse before coming to Gut Plaun, and when she'd asked him to give her riding lessons, he'd chosen a brown gelding for her. He was the most sweet-tempered horse Oliver knew and during his younger years had been the first companion for each of the Huber children. Pegasus might not be the obvious choice for the expert rider Annegret was supposed to be, but they'd agreed to explain it with the need for keeping the more temperamental mares for breeding.

Pegasus whinnied when Oliver approached.

"Sorry, Peg, not today. I know how much you hate standing in your box, but I promise, Annegret will take you out soon." Unfortunately with the huge demand for cart horses from the Wehrmacht, the stud was bursting at the seams, and a non-productive old horse like Pegasus often came up short.

The horse brushed his muzzle against Oliver's shoulder, who removed a carrot from his pocket. Before Annegret had come to the Gut, he'd never thought anything about giving the horses such a treat, but these days he always felt a twinge of guilt, since the workers at the factory never received enough food. How much one of the skeletal women and men might relish this carrot!

He left the stables and walked to the manor, his limp more pronounced than usual. Looking up into the sky he frowned at the dark clouds rolling in from the north. Some rain was welcome to water the meadows, but too much could damage the harvest coming up soon.

"Good morning, Annegret," he called out to his employer, who was sitting on the porch.

"Good morning, Oliver. Do you have a moment?" she answered with a serious frown on her face.

"Sure. Anything wrong?" He walked up the few steps, acutely aware of the dull pain in his injured leg.

She didn't say a word, but simply passed him a crumpled piece of paper. He wondered what had possessed the calm woman to do such a thing, and smoothed it out to read the contents.

After the second paragraph he understood her reaction, because she cared so much for the well-being of the workers and went out of her way to provide them with the basic necessities.

"That's bad news. It just came today?"

She nodded. "What are we going to do? I can't possibly allow them to deport all the Jews working for us." Her voice was no more than a feeble whisper.

His mind went into overdrive and he said the first thing that came to him. "We could ignore the letter, pretend it never arrived."

"That's ridiculous. I'm sure the mailman keeps a list of everything he delivers, especially if it bears the Imperial Eagle. Even if they believed us, they might just come here and choose the prisoners to deport themselves."

"You're right. What are we going to do then?" Oliver took a seat opposite her.

Only moments later Dora hurried outside and asked, "Would you like a coffee? And perhaps a bun? They are fresh from the oven."

"Yes, please," he replied. After Dora had received her paperwork, verifying her German ancestry and was allowed to be "Germanized", he'd proposed to her. But they still never exchanged endearments in public, because he knew how much Frau Mertens, the housekeeper, valued strict morals.

Dora hurried back into the kitchen and Annegret spoke. "I have no idea what to do. I've been sitting here all morning trying to come up with a solution."

"There's really only one way out of this," Oliver offered.

"We need to declare all the Jewish factory workers as essential for the war effort and get exemptions for them."

"For all of them? Won't that seem suspicious?"

"It may. But production is up and we are always slightly above the Wehrmacht's quota. If we convince the district office that without the essential workers our output will drop considerably, I'm sure they won't oppose."

"You make it sound so simple." Annegret sipped from her coffee and stared at him intently, as if she knew he was hiding something from her.

"Well, it might not be as straightforward." He sized her up, pondering how best to break the news. She was an upright person and hated corruption with all her heart, especially after the experience with Gustav Fischer, the former estate manager.

"I thought so. So what if they don't want to sign the exemptions?" Her beautiful brown eyes lingered on him and once again he was in awe of the inner strength this woman possessed. She was a Jew, someone who'd been persecuted and harassed all her life, and yet here she sat, impersonating the spoilt daughter of a rich, and very anti-Semitic Nazi officer. He couldn't fathom how she did it. Personally, he would have given himself away a thousand times already.

"We might have to grease some palms."

Her eyes widened in surprise. "Bribery?"

"Sometimes you have to do immoral things for the greater good."

"As if I didn't know..." Her shoulders sagged, but it took only a few moments until she straightened her spine once more. "And who would we be bribing?"

"Unterscharführer Katze. Since his boss was transferred to the capital, he's the acting head of the district office in Parchim."

"Katze..." She made a pensive face. "A man who's as cruel and sadistic as he is surely doesn't have any integrity and will be open to bribery." Her face scrunched into a grimace. "Those

Nazis don't have an honest bone in their bodies! All the talk about the Aryan Master Race, gallantry and serving the Fatherland, is just that: empty talk. They trample their own values the moment they can line their pockets. I'm fully convinced that ninety-nine percent of them don't even believe the rubbish they spew about us Jews. They use us as a convenient scapegoat for all ailments in Germany, and eagerly profit from our suffering."

"Annegret!" He'd never seen her in such an agitated state, and neither had he heard her mention Judaism. She usually was completely composed, exuding an air of haughtiness. It was the first time that she'd fallen completely out of her role as Annegret Huber, and he wondered whether there was something else that was bothering her. Something closer to her heart than the deportation of complete strangers.

"Please excuse my improper outburst." She took a napkin from the table and dabbed at her face. "I'm afraid this oppressive heat is getting to me."

"We all are on edge. If you wish, I'll travel to Parchim first thing in the morning and talk to Katze."

"That would be perfect, thank you." She leaned back in her chair, looking her usual haughty self once more.

Despite having become close friends over the past months, they both carefully avoided appearing anything more than employer and employee. If anyone ever found out about her real identity, it was vital for Oliver and Dora's safety to believably claim they hadn't known anything.

3

Margarete ventured into the kitchen to talk with her housekeeper Frau Mertens about ordering household supplies, because after discovering that her former estate manager had been stealing from her, she now took a personal interest in the workings of the estate and the factory.

"Frau Mertens," Margarete announced herself as she entered the cozy room. How often she wished she could sit at the kitchen table and have her meals together with the household employees, instead of alone in the dining room. But it would be completely inappropriate for the lady of the manor to do so.

"Fräulein Annegret, you should have called me if you needed something," Frau Mertens scolded her. She couldn't fathom how much Margarete hated using the house telephone to bark her orders and wait like royalty in her room until Dora or Frau Mertens delivered whatever her heart desired.

Even after living for almost a year at Gut Plaun she hadn't adapted to living the high society way.

"I was about to order supplies and wanted to check with you and see what else you might need."

Frau Mertens cast her a disapproving gaze as she put the kettle on the stove to heat water. "Your mother would be shocked. This isn't appropriate work for a young lady."

In the late Frau Huber's opinion no work was appropriate for the likes of her and she had spent her time gossiping with her society friends over coffee and cake. The closest she'd come to doing any actual work was organizing social events either to impress other Nazi bigwigs or to collect money for the *Winterhilfswerk*, the winter relief charity that supposedly cared for all poor citizens—excluding the Jews, of course—under Hitler's directive *no one shall be hungry, no one shall freeze*. In reality, though, it mostly provided for Wehrmacht soldiers these days.

"We all have to make sacrifices for the war effort," Margarete brushed her off, unwilling to discuss the topic of whether a lady should work. "Mind you, I'm not saying I will be able to get whatever we are short of, but I can try."

"If we at least could buy what the ration cards allow that would help a lot. If we didn't have the gardens, I don't know how I would feed all the farmhands."

"What do you need most urgently?"

"Cooking oil, because butter goes only so far." While Gut Plaun didn't own cows, they traded hay from their meadows with nearby farmers for milk, cheese and butter.

Margarete sighed. "That's almost impossible to get. But I'll try."

"And a new colander, the old one has holes as big as a fist."

Another thing that was impossible to buy, since any and all metal was used for the production of armaments. In Hitler's war economy there was no room for the housewives' mundane need for kitchen utensils.

"I'll see what I can do. Let's go over the inventory in the cellar to see whether we need anything else."

"That's a good idea. Winter is still a long way off, but it's never too early to stock up. Let me just get the coffee ready."

Frau Mertens took the kettle from the stove and poured the boiling water through a filter filled with *Ersatzkaffee* into a huge Thermos, before she called, "Dora! Will you bring the coffee out to the field workers?"

Seconds later the maid rushed into the kitchen from wherever she'd been working, her waist-long black braids flying behind. She stopped short when she saw Margarete standing in the kitchen. "Fräulein Annegret, did you need me?"

"Not at all, Frau Mertens and I are going to check the provisions in the cellar storerooms."

"That's a good idea." Dora took the huge Thermos and a basket with freshly baked buns to carry them out to the field. Most of the farm workers were women from the nearby town, or prisoners of war from *"racially valuable"* nations like France, the Netherlands, or Belgium. Without them, the estate wouldn't be able to harvest all the produce they did.

It was such a shame that per regulation she wasn't allowed to use Jewish workers on the fields, because they supposedly posed a threat to the Aryan women helpers. Otherwise she would have been able to employ so many more and give them much better living conditions than in the factory.

Despite her efforts to alleviate the conditions, work in the factory was backbreaking and the prisoners never got enough food or rest. Nevertheless, the prisoners didn't complain, because the alternative was so much worse: transfer to another factory under a less benevolent owner or deportation to the east.

Frau Mertens kept meticulous lists of all the supplies stored in the cellar and thus it didn't take long to get an overview of what was needed to ensure the people working for Gut Plaun, including the factory workers, could be fed over the winter months.

"I'll talk to Oliver about how best to source what we need," Margarete said.

"One more thing, Fräulein Annegret." In contrast to her

usual brusqueness, the housekeeper seemed reluctant to broach the subject.

"Yes?"

"It's just... The women in the district committee have been talking about you."

Margarete had difficulty staying calm. Didn't these society ladies have anything better to do than gossip about her? "What about?"

"Well, they think it's been much too long since Gut Plaun hosted a reception or party of any kind. They are wondering if you have something to hide."

Margarete's breath caught in her chest, even as she tried to make her face neutral.

"I hate to tell you this and I wouldn't even know if it weren't for Frau Bracke."

"What does she say?" Inwardly, Margarete groaned. The owner of the haberdashery possessed an evil tongue.

"Well, there are rumors that Gustav Fischer led the estate to the brink of bankruptcy, and now you cannot afford to buy a new dress, let alone host a party. Some have even suggested you might have been in cahoots with him."

"How dare they!"

Frau Mertens gave a terse smile. "You know how fast rumors spread. There's been plenty of talk and it's not good. Some even question your allegiance to the Reich, because you haven't been seen at party gatherings or meetings of women's associations."

Margarete's gut twisted. She'd avoided those gatherings like the plague because there were few things more awful than a room full of Nazi wives droning on about how exceedingly handsome and charming Hitler was. It infuriated her to realize that apparently people assumed she had a duty to invite the important party members in the area to her house, just because they loved social events so much.

"Do you suggest we host a reception?"

"If you want my opinion..."

Margarete eagerly nodded a response.

"I think it's long overdue for us to organize something. Your mother threw some kind of social event every time she came here."

"Those were different times, the war..." Margarete protested weakly.

"The war certainly has made things more difficult, but it's still important to show that Gut Plaun supports the Reich."

That was exactly the answer Margarete had been afraid to hear. Just the thought of inviting a bunch of Nazi officers and their gossipy wives to Gut Plaun made her stomach lurch. "I'll consider it."

"If that's all, Fräulein Annegret, I need to return to the kitchen."

"Yes, please do attend to your duties. I'll take it from here."

She climbed up the stairs and was about to head for Oliver's office on the ground floor, when a group of men from the factory arrived, dragging handcarts.

They were the kitchen aides who came to the manor every week to load up the deliveries destined for the factory. It was one of the easiest work details in the factory and under Gustav's rule the most unscrupulous inmates had been given this task as a reward for helping to keep the other prisoners under control.

But as soon as she'd installed Oliver as estate manager, she'd also changed the rules. Troublemakers, sadistic capos and relentless criminals had been removed from the camp hierarchy and instead fair and kind individuals had been nominated barrack elders.

As for the kitchen duties, she'd chosen the oldest and weakest prisoners for this job, among them her uncle Ernst, Aunt Heidi's husband. It had been such a surprise to find him toiling at her factory. Having had little hope that he was still alive after his arrest many months before, she'd been overjoyed to see him again, but at the same time she'd been shocked at his awful appearance.

It had been one more reason for her to do everything she could to keep the Jewish workers safe. While she tried to be impartial, she knew full well that she favored him over others who might need the respite of working in the kitchen even more.

But she owed it to Aunt Heidi, who'd welcomed her with open arms—regardless of the risk to herself—when she'd needed refuge after switching identities with Annegret Huber.

She lingered in the hallway until the four men passed on their way to the storage room, and when she was sure nobody would see, she gave Uncle Ernst a wink and a brief smile, which he acknowledged with a nod.

As much as she yearned to talk to him, there was no way she could risk being exposed. She watched his back as he shuffled down the stairs in that energy-conserving gait the prisoners adopted after a few short days in the Nazis' hands.

Despite her doing everything to alleviate their suffering, she couldn't go against the regime and had to carefully work within the existing rules. Giving every prisoner a mattress and a blanket might not sound like much, but it could mean the difference between life and death during a cold winter's night.

As she observed her uncle's back in the striped prisoner garb, she suddenly realized that he would never be considered an essential worker. Even if Oliver got exemptions this time for all the Jews, it was only a matter of time until someone came here to verify the claims and then they would notice that none of the people who worked in peripheral areas, such as the kitchens or the gardens, qualified.

Her heart constricted violently even as her brain jumped into overdrive, trying to come up with a solution. The only thing she could think of was to transfer him back to a production line

—tedious, backbreaking and dangerous work, for which he was too old and frail. He wouldn't last long either way.

She and Oliver had discussed ways to improve the living conditions without drawing unwanted criticism or questions from the SS. So far, it appeared to be working, but the conditions remained deplorable, no matter how one tried to justify it.

Under Oliver's management and Margarete's new rules, the death rate had plummeted, although for her liking too many of the emaciated people continued to die. Even young and strong people sometimes became victims of horrible accidents while cooking the explosive nitropenta. No, she couldn't transfer Uncle Ernst back to that work.

There had to be another solution. Just what?

4

LEIPZIG

"Don't look so glum. It's only for a short while."

SS-Unterscharführer Thomas Kallfass wanted to protest his latest assignment, but knew there was no use in doing so. Still he tried. "But why Parchim of all places? It's a tiny town in the Mecklenburg Lake District, and there's nothing worthy for the war effort there."

His boss shook his head. "That is where you are wrong. Parchim itself may be inconsequential, but the many studs and farms in the area provide horses for the Wehrmacht and food for the people."

The mention of horses softened Thomas' resolve. He was a huge horse lover and had worked as a groom before he'd joined first the party and later the SS. He was incredibly thankful to the party, because it offered a boy with a working-class background like him a career that he had never dared to dream about. Hitler truly had changed the rules of life and created equal opportunities for everyone.

"The way I see it, it's the perfect opportunity to recommend you for more important tasks," his boss added.

"I know, and I'm more than willing to do whatever my

Führer wants me to... I just had hoped my next post would be in a bigger city. Someplace where I can make a real difference." Thomas tried not to look gloomy. Despite Hitler's best efforts, the old ways hadn't been fully eradicated and the best postings were reserved for men with connections. Someone working his way up the ranks by merit alone, had to be twice as good to prove himself.

"Well, it's decided then," his boss said jovially, punching him on the shoulder.

"When am I due to leave?"

"Since Berlin thinks it's important, you'll start on Monday. But if I were you, I'd go there before the weekend to familiarize myself with the area."

Since it was Thursday already, Thomas didn't have much time to pack his things and say goodbye to his mother, with whom he lived. "I take it everything has been organized?"

Finally his boss smiled. "The party takes care of those who serve her. An official residence is ready and your new subordinate Unterscharführer Lothar Katze is waiting to hear when to pick you up at the train station. He'll help you get your bearings. But never forget: you're the boss over there."

"I will do my best to follow your example." Thomas had never been the boss anywhere. Suddenly the posting didn't seem so glum anymore.

"One more thing."

"Yes?" Thomas said hesitantly, waiting to see whether his own boss had another unpleasant surprise up his sleeve.

"Katze has the same rank as you do."

"Oh?" Thomas hadn't thought about that detail, which he knew from experience would make his life so much more complicated. The SS was an organization strictly based on hierarchy and obedience of those lower down to the ones higher up, but among those of the same rank a fierce competition prevailed.

"We can't have that, now can we?" His boss grinned like a fat cat who'd just killed a mouse.

"It would certainly complicate things." Thomas didn't dare hope for a promotion, since he wasn't due for one for at least a few months.

"Here are your new papers. Congratulations, Herr Oberscharführer." His boss handed him a certificate stating his new position.

"Thank you so much," Thomas stammered, overwhelmed with the sudden turn of events.

"Thank me by not disappointing my trust in you."

"I certainly won't, Herr Hauptscharführer. I'll make you proud and will let Berlin know that I closely followed your example to become a valuable asset to the party."

"Heil Hitler." His boss saluted, effectively dismissing him.

"Heil Hitler!" responded Thomas, clicking his heels in the perfect manner, before he walked out of the office, wallowing in self-pity over his transfer to the middle of nowhere. The one good thing about it was getting away from his mother, who could be a bit too smothering at times.

She was in the kitchen when he arrived home. "You're early, Thomas, dinner is not yet ready."

He knew she would be sad and worried, but he preferred not to wait for a better opportunity to break the news to her, for it might never come. "I've been transferred."

She dropped the wooden spoon into the pot, leaving dark spots on the tiles behind the stove and turned around with an amazing swiftness. "Transferred? Where to?"

"A town called Parchim, in the Mecklenburg Lake District."

Her eyes became big as saucers. "When?"

"Immediately."

"But where will you live?"

"I've been assigned an official residence, and apparently my new subordinate is waiting for me already."

She beamed with pride. "Oh, my little Thomas! If your father were still alive, he'd be so proud of you. The son of a simple coal miner, making a career in the SS. People can say what they want, but without Hitler none of this would be possible and we'd still live like servants under the ruling class."

"Yes, Mother." Thomas was grateful for the opportunities the party gave him, although he'd experienced firsthand that there were still advantages for those with the right background and connections. "I also have been promoted to Ober-scharführer."

"This is so wonderful!" She approached him and went up on her tiptoes to press a kiss to his cheek. "You can't imagine how happy this makes me."

A loud plop caused her to let go of him, grab the wooden spoon and stir the stew she was making.

"It smells delicious, what is it?" he asked.

"Goulash with potatoes," she answered, while moving the pot from the stove. As she spooned stew onto two plates she suddenly stopped mid-air and asked, "Who will cook for you over there? Wash your clothes? Make your bed?"

"Mother, I'm twenty-five and old enough to take care of myself. I'm sure there's some kind of canteen for the members of the SS and if not, I can eat at a restaurant."

"Oh dear." She carried the plates over to the table. "I always forget how grown up you are. My sweet little boy."

"I am, Mother, there really is no need to worry about me. I'm sure I will be perfectly fine." He settled at the table.

"I'm sure you will." She tousled his hair, a habit he utterly detested, since he always took such great care to slick back his natural waves with pomade. "At least there are no bombings in the Mecklenburg Lake District, so you'll be much safer, which is a relief for me."

"Mother, you shouldn't say such things. It is very un-

German to be concerned for one's own safety when we should wholeheartedly embrace the war effort."

"Bah," his mother waved away his concern. "I am allowed to want my son safe. That doesn't mean I don't support Hitler. He's done so many great things for the country. You don't remember, because you're too young. The depression after the last war was horrible. People died like flies because they didn't have money for food."

"I should start packing," he said after finishing his dinner.

"You're not leaving right now, are you? Surely they'll let you stay overnight and leave in the morning for your new post?" She jumped up as if she'd been bitten by something. "I must wash your clothes and press your uniform, so everything's ready for you in the morning. You go and rest."

Thomas rolled his eyes, but dutifully said, "I will, Mother." As much as he sometimes loathed her smothering love, it was very convenient to have someone take care of all the menial work, so he could concentrate on his career. The Führer said it himself: women were in charge of the small world at home, so men could go out and achieve great things in the big world of politics and science.

He withdrew to his room and removed a map from the drawer of his desk. Parchim was a small town about four hours' drive up north, with Berlin marking the midpoint between Leipzig and this godforsaken area in the Mecklenburg Lake District. It wasn't near enough to the Baltic Sea to be of strategic importance for the Navy, and too far away from Berlin in the south or Hamburg in the west to be of importance for the industrial sector. As far as he knew, up there only farmers and horse owners resided.

It wasn't even located on the shore of one of the lakes, of which the Müritz was the biggest one. He drew a line with his finger from Parchim to the nearest lake and stopped in a town called Plau am See.

The name jogged his memory. Last year, he'd been on a business trip to that area, searching for an underground organization supposedly smuggling Jews to the coast and across the Baltic Sea to Sweden. Unfortunately they hadn't been successful in locating the culprits and had returned to Leipzig empty-handed.

Perhaps this was the reason why Berlin gave the post in Parchim any importance at all. If he was able to make a raid on said organization, he'd be showered with praise, another promotion and most probably a transfer to a bigger city. Berlin maybe, or at least someplace like Stralsund, Rostock or Lübeck.

He whistled with delight. His day had just become a lot brighter. There was another benefit too, he realized. Something he hadn't even dared to dream about. Next to Plau am See lay an ammunition factory, owned by none other than the lovely Annegret Huber, heir to Gut Plaun and all that came with it.

He'd had the pleasure of being her guest during that business trip and he could well see himself getting married to such a charming and beautiful woman. It would be a match made in heaven. She must be loath to run such a big estate all on her own and would welcome a handsome, honest, and intelligent SS-officer like himself with open arms.

Being the daughter of the late SS-Standartenführer Wolfgang Huber, there was no doubt she'd pass with flying colors the rules and tests future wives of SS-men had to go through. Her standing with the Nazi elite, together with her riches, would ensure a faster career path for him. With her by his side, he'd finally have the social backing to propel him to the top.

Yes, he'd pay her a visit as soon as he'd gotten his bearings. Given his track record with women, it would be an easy task to charm her into falling in love with him.

5

PLAU AM SEE

Margarete was sitting in the front parlor with Dora, looking through the dresses the late Frau Huber had left behind.

"What about this one?" Margarete asked, holding up an off-white long dress with small, appliquéd roses scattered across it.

"Oh, Fräulein Annegret, that's much too fancy for the likes of me," Dora said with a wistful glance at the elegant gown.

"Nonsense. Since Oliver is now the estate manager, folks will expect him to get married in style. We can easily have the seamstress alter this dress for you. You'll look absolutely stunning." Margarete felt a fondness toward the shy, Ukrainian girl, almost if she were a daughter to her, when in fact, she was only four years younger than Margarete herself.

Despite her shyness, Dora possessed an inner boldness and had shown her loyalty and devotion for her mistress many times in difficult situations. She'd been the one to help her hide Lena, an escaped Jewish prisoner, who was later killed by the Nazis. Finding Lena had been the nudge needed for Margarete to find her true vocation in life: using the inherited Huber fortune to help those who couldn't help themselves.

Since finding out she owned an ammunition factory that used slave labor, she'd done everything in her power to make the lives of the prisoners more bearable. She'd doubled daily rations, had installed working shifts of no more than twelve hours, access to clean water at all times, and a blanket and straw mattress for each prisoner to protect them from the harsh cold during winter nights.

"That is much too kind of you, Fräulein Annegret," Dora interrupted her reminiscence.

"But I insist." When she noticed that Dora still wasn't convinced, she added, "It would make me look bad if my estate manager couldn't even afford a proper dress for his bride. You wouldn't want that, right?"

Dora opened her eyes wide and returned to the annoying habit of curtsying whenever she felt anxious. "No, Fräulein Annegret. Of course not. I would never..." She blushed. "I will take the dress, and thank you so much."

"Then it's done. I'll ask Frau Mertens to send for the seamstress so she can get to work."

Another curtsy. "How can I ever thank you for all you've done?"

"Thank me by doing good for those who are oppressed." Even with Dora, who was one of the three people at Gut Plaun who knew her true identity, she never spoke frankly and avoided criticizing the Nazi rulers.

"I will." The maid nodded with a serious face, her waist-long braided hair popping up and down. "Thanks to your help in getting my Germanization papers, I'm now in a much better position than my compatriots and I want to follow your example."

This time it was Margarete who blushed. She, the former Jewish maid who'd known only harassment in her life, served as an example to another girl. It was perhaps the praise she most cherished, certainly more than the shallow compliments of the Nazi suitors in Paris who'd tried to sweet-talk her into stepping out with them.

"Here you are, Dora. There's work waiting for you." Frau Mertens stepped into the parlor, a disapproving gaze in her eyes.

"Excuse me, Frau Mertens., I'll attend to it right away." Dora jumped up in a hurry.

"It was my fault for keeping Dora from her work," Margarete said and held up the dress for the housekeeper to see. "Won't Dora be a lovely bride in this dress?"

Frau Mertens' expression softened. "She certainly will. Your late mother wore this dress when she went to the inauguration party of the SS headquarters in Parchim."

Margarete suddenly wanted to throw the dress to the floor, its connection to yet another Nazi event making it a lot less lovely. But she held her fingers still and put a pleasant smile on her lips. "She had exceptionally good taste. I miss her very much."

Frau Mertens raised an eyebrow, giving Margarete the feeling she'd said something wrong. Dealing with the housekeeper who'd known Annegret from the cradle, and her parents even longer, always made her nervous, since there were so many potential pitfalls. What worked to her advantage though was that Annegret hadn't returned to the country house for a decade prior to her death, and Frau Mertens had never doubted Margarete's identity, even though she often raised her eyebrows and had commented in private how much the spoilt girl had changed.

Gratefully everyone seemed to accept unquestioningly that the dramatic experiences of losing her parents and her two brothers in two separate bombings, was more than enough reason for a person to change.

"Could you send for the seamstress to alter the dress for Dora?" Margarete asked Frau Mertens.

"Certainly, Fräulein Annegret." Frau Mertens paused for a few seconds before she continued. "Are you planning to attend the wedding?"

"Me? I guess so." To tell the truth, Margarete hadn't thought about this yet. Oliver came from a modest family and Dora was a Ukrainian foreign worker, so she had wanted to pitch in and help her co-conspirators at least with a proper dress.

Suddenly she had a fantastic idea. It would help her fulfill expectations, while giving the perfect excuse for a social occasion and keep the focus off her. "Actually, I thought we could offer a reception at the manor and invite all the important people in the district."

"Whyever would you do this?" Another rise of Frau Mertens' eyebrow.

"Didn't you recently tell me that people are complaining because we haven't organized a single celebration, aside for the dinner for our Gestapo guests last fall? The wedding is as good a reason for a party as any other, isn't it?"

The housekeeper cocked her head, and then slowly said, "That's actually a wonderful idea. We could have the wedding in the morning, and a big official event in the evening."

Dora paled slightly, showing how much she loathed the idea of having her own wedding party swarming with Nazi officials. Margarete thinned her lips though; as much as she understood the feelings of her maid, she couldn't show consideration. It was too important to keep up appearances.

Margarete knew it, Oliver knew it, and Dora must know it, too. All three of them were stuck far too deep in subversive activities to risk the slightest cause for suspicion.

With a side-glance at Frau Mertens, who'd also noticed Dora's unease, Margarete said, "I know you expected something more intimate, perhaps only Oliver's family and a few close friends."

Dora immediately caught on to what her mistress was insinuating and shook her head so that her braids bopped around. "Please, Fräulein Annegret, don't consider me ungrateful, I am merely overwhelmed by your generosity. I had never expected all of this." She pointed at the elegant dress in front of her.

"Don't worry. We were overdue to host a party and your wedding is the perfect occasion to kill two birds with one stone." Margarete paused, afraid she might have been too matter-of-fact, but Dora nodded.

Frau Mertens beamed with agreement. "Your late mother loved hosting parties and"—she lowered her voice—"it might be about time you stepped up to your task."

"What task?"

"Supporting the war effort."

Margarete squinted her eyes. Wasn't she supporting that damn war every single day by producing explosives in her factory?

"Everyone understood you were mourning your family, but whispers are growing... you must show everyone that you're happy about your sacrifices and fully support our Führer in everything he does."

She forced a thoughtful expression on her face. "You're right, Frau Mertens. I was selfish in my grief. My father would want me to be proud of his hero's death, and avenge it by doubling up my efforts to bring justice to our Fatherland. We can't allow our enemies to win by letting them sap our motivation."

Frau Mertens looked pleased and once again Margarete wondered where exactly her housekeeper stood politically. The strict but fair woman was never cruel or disdainful, not even to the foreign workers under her care. She showed empathy with the plight of the forced workers, but then she also always made sure to mention they were subhumans or criminals who deserved their treatment.

She always praised the Führer, but never went as far as actually participating in a rally or attending a speech, claiming she had too much work. Giving her another scrutinizing gaze, Margarete concluded Frau Mertens was a simple follower who kept her head low and did what the ruling class told her to do.

And, truth be spoken, what else could be expected from a woman who'd served as a maid and housekeeper throughout her life? She was used to obeying orders without questioning their sense or viability.

Hadn't Margarete herself acted similarly before she became Annegret? Growing up as a harassed Jewish girl, she'd never once considered the possibility of resistance. She'd taken the rules for granted and, while she hadn't been happy about the treatment she received, she had accepted it as her fate.

Only when she'd switched identities with the late Annegret Huber during that momentous bombing, where the girl and her parents had died, had she begun to see things differently. But it had taken several more nudges for her to finally fight against the system.

First her troubled relationship with Wilhelm Huber— Annegret's brother—who'd protected her, the Jewess, despite his disdain for the Jews in general. He and she had never seen eye to eye on so many things, and she'd been torn by guilt for having tender feelings toward him, the kind person, who at the same time was a Nazi.

He'd ultimately redeemed himself by sacrificing his life to save hers. But not even the promise she'd given him to do good with the Huber fortune had propelled her into action. It wasn't until she'd found Lena, the escaped prisoner, that Margarete had finally begun to resist.

"Have you settled on a date yet?" Frau Mertens asked.

Dora blushed slightly. "We were just talking about that

when you came in, and Fräulein Annegret suggested by the end of the month."

"May I suggest something?" Frau Mertens seemed not at all pleased all of a sudden.

"Of course, Frau Mertens," Margarete said.

"We might wait until December. Then we won't have the day workers milling about and can take better care of the guests." The older woman raised her hands as if ashamed. "This never used to be a problem, but with the ever-tightening restrictions on food..."

Margarete nodded. "I think that's an excellent idea. And it gives the important guests enough time to clear their schedules." Although she had hoped for the exact opposite: that the event would be too short-notice for many of the party officials to attend, due to their other obligations.

Dora seemed to have the same thought, because she looked disappointed. Or perhaps it was only because she'd wanted to get married as soon as possible?

"It will be the perfect time. A white wedding, with snow on the ground, would be so romantic," Margarete suggested.

"Do you have a guest list in mind?" Frau Mertens asked.

"Partly," Margarete lied. Of course she had to invite the town nobility, along with the important functionaries and industrialists in the district. A shiver ran down her spine. She wouldn't be expected to invite people from Annegret's former life in Berlin though, would she? People who would recognize that she was an impostor? "But I want to keep it to regional guests only."

Frau Mertens' eyebrows shot up. "Your mother always invited guests from Berlin."

"And I'd love nothing more than to do the same, but with travel restrictions and everything, we need to be frugal. I certainly don't want to give the impression that Gut Plaun is squandering resources."

Frau Mertens nodded. "It used to be so much easier before the war."

Both Dora and Margarete pricked up their ears, because this was the most criticizing sentence that had ever come out of the housekeeper's mouth.

6

Oliver jumped from his saddle and let his mare drink from the fountain, before he tethered it to a fence.

"Here you go," he said, giving Sabrina an apple and patting her on the neck. He could have used the automobile, but gasoline was strictly rationed. Furthermore, he enjoyed riding as it gave him time with his beloved horses. Time he had too little of after taking on his responsibilities as estate manager for Annegret.

Not that he regretted taking her up on her offer, because first of all it came with a very generous salary, and secondly he could actually help people. Ever since his deployment to the Eastern Front, he'd been discontent with Hitler's politics. The atrocities he'd witnessed, and had been forced to participate in, were something he never talked about and refused altogether to think about. Nevertheless, the queasy feeling in his stomach about the direction Germany was headed had been increasing.

Annegret's plan to help the forced workers had come at the right time to soothe his conscience. Even a country boy like him who had no idea about the greater issues in the world, knew it was wrong to treat people this badly. Jews, Gypsies or Russian prisoners of war, they were human beings just like himself and Dora.

Thoughts of Dora warmed his heart, but at the same time it tightened with worry. Ukrainians had been considered allies so far, but this seemed to be changing and if the rumors were to be believed, they'd soon join the ranks of "barbaric and subhuman" Slavs.

It was one more reason to marry her as soon as possible. Equipped with Germanization papers and his last name, surely nobody would dare touch her, even if her entire nation somehow became considered an enemy.

He took a briefcase from his saddlebag, squared his shoulders and entered the SS district headquarters. Being inside the majestic building that played host to the sinister organization, sent a shiver of fear down his spine.

Nobody was safe from the SS. They could basically do whatever they wanted, no questions asked. If they ever found out who Annegret really was... he didn't delude himself into believing they would let him go unpunished. Not when he'd known her back then as a child. Nobody would believe he hadn't noticed. Heck, he barely believed it himself. In hindsight, the signs were glaring and he wondered how he'd not seen them.

"How can I help you?" the young woman behind the reception desk asked as he slipped through the heavy door into the foyer.

"I'd like to see Unterscharführer Katze."

"Your name?"

"Oliver Gundelmann from Gut Plaun."

"About what?"

He had no intention of letting her know that he was planning on bribing her boss, so he simply responded, "A business matter concerning the nitropenta factory."

She pursed her lips, apparently not content with the

amount of information he'd given her, nevertheless she took up the receiver of the black telephone on her desk and dialed a number. "Herr Unterscharführer, there's a Herr Gundelmann to see you... About the nitropenta factory... Thank you." She turned to Oliver and said, "He's waiting for you in his office. Second floor, first door to the left. Don't knock. Wait until he comes to get you."

Inwardly, he groaned, as he dutifully thanked the receptionist and climbed the stairs to the second floor, where he stopped in front of the door, with the label "Manager". It seemed Katze had been promoted to district leader, and Oliver mused whether this would make future dealings with him easier or more difficult.

Katze was a sadistic brute, not very intelligent, and greedy to the core. He could be bribed without fearing repercussions, which might get a lot more costly in his new position.

The last time he'd been here he had been with Annegret. They had informed Katze, then deputy manager, about Gustav's treason to the Reich and Gustav had been bestially slaughtered mere days later. Even though it was never confirmed that this was Katze's doing, it was too much of a coincidence to his mind.

There was no bench or chair to sit down on, so Oliver waited standing up. About fifteen minutes later he heard steps behind the door and shortly after the Unterscharführer's chubby face with the small eyes peeked out. "Heil Hitler!"

"Heil Hitler!" Due to his limp, Oliver couldn't click his heels the way Katze had done, but he stretched out his right hand to the exact angle.

"Herr Gundelmann, what brings you here today?"

"I'm very sorry to take up your precious time, but we have a slight problem at the factory."

"You're not falling behind on your production quota, are you?" Katze motioned for him to sit on a wooden chair in front of the monumental desk, before he walked around to sit in a huge office armchair, towering over him.

Despite feeling browbeaten, Oliver squared his shoulders and kept his voice steady as he answered. "Certainly not, but we might, if we're to follow these orders." He removed the deportation order from his briefcase and handed it to Katze.

"Jews? And?"

"I'm afraid to say these people aren't just any Jews, they are essential workers and without them the factory won't be able to keep up production at the current pace."

"They aren't people, but vermin! And how can rubbish like them be essential?" Katze leaned back and lit a cigarette.

"Herr Unterscharführer, we wouldn't normally resort to employing these subjects, but unfortunately we're short of skilled workers. Most of the expert men have joined the Wehrmacht to serve Führer and Fatherland, and the foreign workers are, between us, substandard. At least these Jews speak our language and most do have a work ethic, drilled into them by years of living among Germans."

Katze took a few puffs from his cigarette, before he offered one to Oliver. "Want one?"

"Yes, please."

The other man threw him the packet and pointed to a lighter on the desk. Oliver leaned forward and lit himself a cigarette, inhaling deeply. The tangy taste of the smoke filled his lungs and calmed his nerves. Lothar Katze might be a sadistic pig, but he knew what was good for him, and causing one of the biggest ammunition factories in his district to miss its quota certainly wasn't.

"So what do you suggest?" Katze asked.

"An exemption."

"For everyone on the list?" Katze all but choked on his next puff.

"We do see the necessity to rid Germany of all Jews, but

under the current restrictions, we are afraid that our efforts to
support the war effort have to take precedence."

Katze rolled the cigarette in his hand, as if weighing his
options. "I have my own quota to keep, if you understand."

Oliver understood all too well. "You might find the missing
subjects from other places maybe?" The words tasted sour in his
mouth, and he grappled with his conscience. It was a very cruel
thing to suggest, but he'd learned that he couldn't save everyone,
thus he focused on those under his care.

"That means a lot of extra work," Katze mused. "Issuing
exemptions, having to find replacements..."

"I agree, it's a lot to ask, given that you're already swamped
with work." Oliver bent forward and lowered his voice. "But it
wouldn't be to your disadvantage. I'm authorized to offer a
token compensation for all the extra effort." Oliver hoped he
hadn't been too bold, since one could never be too sure a bribe
wouldn't offend the receiver.

He needn't have worried, because Katze licked his lips.
"That would certainly be appreciated."

Oliver reached into his pocket for the envelope Annegret
had handed him earlier that morning. He slid it across the
table and watched as Katze opened it and thumbed through
the bills. There was an identical envelope in the other pocket
should the need arise, but he was hoping he wouldn't have to
reach for it.

Katze gave a contented grunt and tucked the envelope
inside his desk drawer, before he said, "Well, let's take a look at
your essential workers."

Oliver handed him a typewritten list with the names of
every single Jew in the factory. It was several pages long and
Katze raised an eyebrow as he thumbed through the sheets.

Oliver waited with bated breath for the inevitable questions
because the list purposely didn't mention the task of the supposedly essential workers, since it included unskilled cart pushers,

kitchen staff, and medics, in addition to those actually working on the production lines.

"Quite a lot."

"Yes, and we request more prisoners every week." This was mostly due to prisoners dying from bad health, despite the improvements Annegret had implemented.

Katze nodded. "I can give you an exemption for current staff, but not for future ones."

"It won't be needed, because we'll heed your advice and request non-Jewish workers from now on. We at Gut Plaun are good Germans in full support of Hitler's policies."

"Yes. Yes." Katze was stamping first *Exemption* and then *Essential worker* across every single sheet of the list, before he returned to the first page to stamp it with the official Imperial Eagle stamp carrying the words *SS-District Headquarter Parchim*. Finally he signed each sheet with his name and rank.

Looking at his work, he grunted with satisfaction and used another stamp with the current date. Then he placed the list on top of other papers on his desk. "I'm afraid this is a one-time exemption for workers currently on your staff."

"Thank you. You have done a great service to the Reich and the war effort." Oliver suddenly was in a hurry to leave the office, fearful Katze might change his mind and rip the precious exemption list into pieces. He got to his feet. "Heil Hitler."

Katze followed suit. "Heil Hitler."

Once his business with the SS was completed, Oliver wanted to get away from the headquarters as fast as possible. He rushed down the stairs and almost bumped into a man in a black uniform rushing up at the same speed. Quickly sidestepping to avoid a collision, he said, "Excuse me, sir. I didn't see you." Only then did he raise his eyes to look at the officer's face. Recognition hit both of them at the same time.

"If it isn't Oliver Gundelmann, from Gut Plaun?" the man about Oliver's age said seemingly delighted.

"Thomas, what brings you here?" Oliver had made Thomas' acquaintance last year when he and some of his colleagues had lodged at the manor for a few days. Unterscharführer Thomas Kallfass was a keen horse lover and had offered him the familiar first name after several drinks.

His gaze fell on Thomas' collar, adorned with two new and shiny silver collar pips, and he wondered whether he should better address the man with his new rank. But before he could correct himself, Thomas said, "I wasn't expecting to see a familiar face on my first day in office."

"You're being stationed in Parchim?" Oliver inquired as both stepped to the side to leave access to the stairs open for others.

"Yes. Following the transfer of my predecessor, I'm the new man in charge around here. Or, I will be by tomorrow," Thomas offered.

"Congratulations. On your promotion, too, Herr Oberscharführer."

"Honestly, I would have preferred a bigger town, but the promotion is very much appreciated and I am happy to serve my country wherever I'm needed most."

"I'm certain you'll do magnificent work here," Oliver said, although he wondered whether this new development actually was an improvement. Katze was brutal and incompetent, but at least he was open to bribes and not bright enough to find out when he was being played. Thomas, though, was intelligent, ambitious, and correct. He might not bend the rules for a bit of extra cash. But on the plus side, he was a rather decent chap instead of a cruel sadist.

"Perhaps once I've gotten settled, I might make another visit to Gut Plaun?" Thomas suggested.

"You are always welcome," Oliver answered. Thomas had phrased his statement as a question, but he was the new district commander. Coming from him, the question was in fact a command.

"How about this coming weekend?" Thomas continued. "We could go for a ride together. If I remember correctly, you have some beautiful horses on the estate."

"That we do. I'm sure I can find you a suitable mount. Advise me of your arrival time and I'll have everything prepared."

Thomas looked as if he were to ask something more, but then almost imperceptibly shook his head. "Perfect. Now, I shouldn't keep you any longer. Heil Hitler!"

Oliver responded in kind and turned around to head for the exit. On the way back to the estate he whistled a tune, completely at peace with himself and the world for the two-hour ride through fields and forests. It gave him time to unwind and forget about all the bad things happening around him.

7

Dora was waiting impatiently for Oliver to return from his trip to Parchim. She always worried about him when he was away. It was a strange sensation because before rescuing Lena and finding out about Fräulein Annegret's secret, she had never done so.

In her mind he'd been safe. A respected stable master on a German farm. Back in the Ukraine her family had showed little interest in politics, except that everyone in her village hated the Soviet occupiers. She was the fifth of twelve children. Her older four siblings had gotten married and left the house. But even then her parents, poor farmers with German roots, constantly battled to feed that many mouths.

When the Wehrmacht came to liberate the Ukraine, her parents had been overjoyed—and had sent her away to work in Germany. She still didn't follow politics, but the things she heard through the grapevine indicated that life in the Ukraine had deteriorated immensely once the cherished liberators had shown their true colors. Apparently these days nobody welcomed them anymore.

Some of the other Ukrainian *Fremdarbeiter* she knew in

Plau am See worried they'd soon end up the same way the Russians, or the Poles did. Worked to the bone, humiliated, starved. Dead.

She'd been so happy when her Germanization papers and later the marriage permit arrived. Being Oliver's wife was not only her heart's deepest desire, but also a way to keep her safe. Although recently she had second thoughts, that she might be tying herself to the wrong side. Not because Oliver wasn't the man she wished to spend the rest of her life with, but because the rumors indicated that Germany might not win this war.

If the Soviets came, they wouldn't be kind to her. A Ukrainian girl, who'd gone out of her way to become a German and had married a German. What would they do to her? The same things Gustav had done to Lena, the Jewish prisoner he'd brutalized and whipped to death?

She shivered violently and fought off her morbid thoughts. Things were as they were, nothing she could do about it. She had made her bed, quite literally, and would have to sleep in it until her end.

The door of the gardener's house where Oliver lived opened and she fell around Oliver's neck, even before he crossed the threshold. Since their official engagement, she had moved in with Oliver, despite Frau Mertens' disapproval. The housekeeper had grudgingly agreed to Fräulein Annegret's suggestion that the couple in love would be very discreet and Dora would keep her room in the manor for the time being.

"You missed me fiercely," he said with a laugh and pressed a kiss on her lips. He smelled of horses, sweat and tobacco. Dora didn't smoke, because it wasn't something women were supposed to do, but she liked the smell of tobacco on his skin.

"I was worried about you. It's late."

He moved her away from him, stepping into the house and shutting the door with his foot. "It was just a trip to Parchim."

"But..."—she knew it was irrational, or perhaps not—"I'm always afraid when you leave the estate."

"I know, my darling. But don't worry. Nothing will happen to me."

She didn't believe him, but let his words lull her into that cozy feeling of assurance she craved so much. "I saved dinner for you."

"Thank you so much. It was an exhausting day."

He could have walked the few hundred yards to the manor and eaten his dinner in the kitchen, but Dora knew he preferred to stay in the small house, drinking a beer with his meal.

Bursting with curiosity she could barely wait to ask her questions. But first she went down on her knees and yanked his heavy riding boots from his feet, putting them on the mat beside the door. She'd polish them later, wanting him to look impeccable at all times, because she was so proud of him. Then she served his meal and sat down on the opposite side of the table.

"Aren't you going to eat?" he asked between ravenous bites of the hearty rabbit stew.

"I already ate with the others at the manor." Seeing how he slowly relaxed, she finally asked, "Did you get the exemptions?"

He smiled. "Yes, I did. It was costly, but Katze stamped them all. For now they're safe."

"All of them? Fräulein Annegret will be so pleased." Dora had never set foot in the factory and hadn't talked to a single prisoner except Lena. Nevertheless, she felt sympathy for them. Even with all the extra food Fräulein Annegret bought, the ones who came up to the manor to retrieve supplies were thin as sticks.

"I'll have to walk over to the manor to tell her."

"You haven't done so already?"

"I wanted to see you first."

Dora flushed with joy and love. Oliver wasn't a romantic

man who showered her with poems or love letters, but wanting to see her before reporting back to Annegret was all the proof she needed to know he truly and deeply loved her. Whatever might happen after the war, being by his side was definitely worth it.

He ate in silence and suddenly said, "You remember Thomas Kallfass? From the SS in Leipzig?"

Dora squinted her eyes thinking hard, but the name didn't jog her memory, so she shook her head.

"He stayed at the manor with Reichskriminaldirektor Richter's colleagues last year."

Still, no face connected with the name, but she nodded and said, "I guess I do. What about him?"

"He's the new district leader."

"Is that a good thing?"

"I don't know. He seems to be a decent guy, but also ambitious and very loyal to the Führer." He paused, a vertical frown appearing on his forehead. Glancing at his plate she wanted to ask whether he'd like another serving, but decided it was best not to interrupt him. Seconds later, Oliver continued, "When I ran into him, he immediately recognized me and... he has invited himself this weekend to go riding."

"He invited himself? To Fräulein Annegret's estate? How rude!"

Oliver looked up and laughed. "Can I have more stew, please? Yes, it's rude, but he's the district leader and phrased it as a suggestion. I had to accept."

She scurried off to refill his plate in the small kitchen. She never cooked there, because it lacked even the basic ingredients, but it served to warm up the meals she brought from the manor or to make coffee in the morning.

"Here you are." While Oliver dug into the food, she said, "You'll have to tell Fräulein Annegret about his visit."

"Yes. I hope she won't be too upset about it."

"It's not your fault. This man basically commanded you to invite him."

"Don't worry. I guess it's a good thing to stay on good terms with the authorities." He finished off his plate, but when she wanted to take it away, he caught her wrist. "Wait. I'll have to go to the manor in a bit and tell Annegret about today's errands, but first I need to thoroughly kiss my future wife."

After he devoured her mouth until she ran out of air, he wrapped his arms around her and asked, "How was your day?"

It was the moment she'd dreaded, because she knew that he —just like her—had wanted an intimate wedding ceremony with only his family and a few close friends. "Fräulein Annegret arranged to have one of Frau Huber's evening gowns altered into a wedding dress for me."

He sighed, clearly expecting more to come.

"And she and Frau Mertens agreed to host a reception in the evening." She looked at him with pleading eyes.

"What are you not telling me?" His hand stroked her hair.

"It'll be a very big event."

"I was afraid so."

"Fräulein Annegret said people would ask questions if we didn't celebrate it in style. It might encourage rumors about my heritage."

"But you got your Germanization paperwork done..." They both knew that even with the paperwork there was a slight taint on her person, because papers could be faked, and exemptions bought. In this case, attack—presenting her to the world—really was the best defense for possible problems down the road. Oliver sighed, obviously coming to the same conclusion. "It may be for the best."

She snuggled up against his broad chest. "She also said she was long overdue to host a social event and that would kill two birds with one stone. Lending credibility to us, but also taking the heat off her. That's why she'll invite all the top brass in the district."

He groaned. "Thomas will be so pleased. He loves that kind of festivity. You should have seen him today in his uniform, boots shining and grinning all over his face."

"We don't have to stay through to the end. Isn't it customary that the newlyweds retire early?" She said it with a teasing smile and as she'd intended, he pressed another passionate kiss on her mouth, murmuring, "I guess there are worse things than to marry you."

8

Margarete had been sitting on pins and needles all day, awaiting Oliver's return. When he hadn't arrived by dinner time, she'd started to worry.

Unsure whether she should retreat to her rooms or linger downstairs she took up a book from the library. It was *The Maid of Orleans* by Friedrich Schiller. She knew the story in broad strokes but had never actually read it. Back when Jews had still been allowed to go to public libraries she'd been too young for adult books, and then... her fingers caressed the old linen binding.

It was a beautiful exemplar: A brown cover, the black title printed in a black circle, adorned with arabesques, curved lines and a Pegasus with the roman letters MDCXL beneath. She opened the book reverently and found it had been printed in 1909, more than thirty years ago, as a school edition.

She thought back to the time when she'd worked in the university library in Leipzig after usurping Annegret's identity and how much her life had changed since. Completely immersed in her memories, she didn't hear the door open and jumped, when someone said, "Here you are. Good evening, Annegret."

She turned around. "Oliver, you scared me."

"I'm sorry."

She tried to read his expression, wanting to brace herself for the news he brought, but he didn't give anything away. When she'd first come to Gut Plaun, she'd detested him, had even been afraid of this brooding, tight-lipped and serious man, who seemed to warm up exclusively in the presence of his beloved horses—and Dora.

But she'd soon come to appreciate his reticence and aloofness, since they were ideal character traits for a co-conspirator, because the enemy always listened. Or, as the British liked to say, loose lips sink ships. Although on occasion she wished he could be a bit more talkative.

He closed the library door, before he walked up to her and said, "The visit to Katze was successful. He generously granted me exemptions for all essential workers."

Her hand shot to her chest as she exhaled all the anguish she'd been feeling ever since the deportation order had arrived. "That's wonderful news. Was it difficult?"

"Not really." Finally one end of his mouth quirked up into a half grin. "Your envelope helped." He removed the second envelope from his pocket and handed it to her.

"Well done." She wished it could have been done without because the money would be sorely missed when buying extra food for the prisoners.

"He insisted this was a one-time event. There won't be exemptions for future workers. In fact he advised me to request only non-Jews for essential work and leave the Jews for tasks too dangerous for anyone else."

Her eyes glared daggers at Oliver, although he was only the messenger. "I'm certainly not going to do that."

"Annegret." He stepped closer. "You need to stay reasonable, there's only so much we can do. Perhaps it's time to accept that we can't help them and instead focus on the foreign slave workers?"

As much as she understood his reasoning, her heart opposed. "Never. We will find a way."

"For now the people we employ are safe, but"—her head jerked up at his undertone—"we might have another problem."

"What kind of problem?"

"You remember Thomas Kallfass? One of the officers who stayed here last year?"

She nodded. Of course she remembered him. He'd been the one to almost blow her cover by asking about that cursed equestrian competition Annegret had won and Margarete had no idea about.

"He's the new district leader."

"He seemed an upright man."

"I guess he is. He also loves horses." Oliver rubbed his chin. "But he kind of forced my hand to invite him over on the weekend."

"He did what?" Margarete knew she had to entertain high-ranking Nazis to keep up her cover, but she did so as scarcely as possible.

"He suggested a visit, but it wasn't really a suggestion. Therefore I told him he's always welcome and I'll have a mount waiting for him."

She could see Oliver was as unhappy as she was, but there was nothing they could do. "It might turn out to be beneficial in case we need more exemptions."

"I cannot say for sure, but he doesn't strike me as corruptible."

"In any case, we shall have to make sure he feels appreciated. I'll let Frau Mertens know and arrange a luncheon to welcome him. What do you think?"

He nodded. "As long as he doesn't get too cozy and decide to visit us every weekend."

"I should hope he has other obligations. Don't worry about that."

Oliver took his leave and after a quick glance at the clock, she decided it was early enough to inform Frau Mertens. She took up the bell on the coffee table and rang it. Normally Dora would show up, but since she had moved into the gardener's house with Oliver—under Frau Mertens' disapproving gaze—they'd employed a second maid. Gloria was a skinny girl from Eastern Poland who spoke little German, much to Frau Mertens' chagrin. Margarete had insisted on her because she wouldn't have survived much longer toiling in the factory.

In the factory some fortunate Jew who would have been deported otherwise replaced the girl. It was a pact with the devil and every day Margarete doubted whether she was doing the right thing. The work in the factory was by no means—even with all the improvements—a walk in the park, and every other day someone died from the hardships.

"Fräulein Annegret, what you need?" Gloria curtsied.

"Please get me Frau Mertens."

"Frau Mertens. Yes. Now." Relief and worry at the same time passed across her juvenile face.

Minutes later Frau Mertens arrived. "You needed me, Fräulein Annegret? Gloria couldn't tell me what for."

Margarete smiled. "That's because I didn't explain."

"With all due respect, but we need someone who speaks German."

"I'd prefer that too, but you know how impossible it is to get staff these days. And Gloria is quick to learn." Due to the similarities of their native languages Dora and Gloria communicated surprisingly well, and Dora often translated for her. "The newly appointed district leader Oberscharführer Kallfass will visit us at the weekend."

"This weekend? What did you have in mind? A reception? How many guests?" Frau Mertens was in her element.

"Nothing of the sort. It seems he wants to ride out with Oliver, but I thought a special luncheon would be appropriate to welcome him at Gut Plaun and show our desire to serve the Reich in every way we can."

"Oh yes, the poor man, he must be flooded with work. I'll have everything arranged for a semi-formal lunch. Will it be just the two of you?"

Margarete thought for a moment. "No. Include Oliver and the factory manager Franz Volkmer as well. I don't want it to look romantic."

Frau Mertens nodded. "Four people then. How about poached fish with potatoes on the side?"

"That's a good idea. Nils can talk to the fisherman." The old handyman Nils ran most of the errands in town in addition to his duties on the estate. "Oh, and one more thing. I don't know if the Oberscharführer plans to stay the night but see that one of the guest rooms is freshened up, just in case."

"Everything will be done to your satisfaction, Fräulein Annegret."

"Thank you, I would expect nothing less."

The next morning Margarete went to find Nils who was fixing something in the dining room.

"Good morning, Nils."

"Good morning, Fräulein Annegret."

He didn't stop what he was doing, so she added, "May I talk to you for a moment?"

"Sure, just let me tighten this screw or everything will fall down."

Frau Huber would probably have been shocked at his insubordination, but Margarete was much more practical and waited patiently until he was done and climbed down from the ladder.

"What can I do for you?"

"We're having a guest this coming weekend and Frau Mertens would like to prepare fish. Can you talk to the fisherman?"

His face fell. "Sorry, but I can't make the trip. The *Reichswehrersatzamt* summoned me for some kind of exam. Can't believe they want to draft such an old man."

Margarete suppressed a shocked gasp. For all she knew Nils was closing in on sixty years. Was the Wehrmacht that desperate to consider sending men like him to the front? No, that must be a mistake. Some bureaucrat writing down the wrong birth year. "Well, then... what shall we do?"

"Why don't you go yourself, Fräulein Annegret? I can give you a ride into town and drop you off near the wharf."

"Agreed." She would have to let Oliver know that she couldn't attend their riding lesson, since pleasing Oberscharführer Kallfass was currently her most important task.

A worrisome thought struck her. If this man was such a horse lover and wished to visit more often to ride their horses, he might ask her to accompany him on one of these occasions. All the more reason to double up on the secret lessons with Oliver instead of having to cancel them.

After Nils dropped her off, she walked down the cobblestone street to the famous lift bridge on the Elde River, but didn't cross. As always she was fascinated by the technical masterwork, constructed during the First World War. It opened up whenever a ship needed to pass into the Plauer See, an important fishing area.

Walking along the riverbank she eyed the picturesque wooden boathouses located on the other side, wondering what they looked like inside and why people bothered to put their boats into houses instead of leaving them out on the water like she'd seen elsewhere.

At the end of the road was the beacon signaling the entrance to the Elde waterway from the lake. There, the fishermen moored each morning to sell their catch of the day.

Nils had given her the name of the fisherman he usually dealt with. She spotted the small green boat without difficulty, but the man didn't fit the description of a gray-haired, elderly person. On the contrary, he was quite young, about thirty years old, with a broad upper body, sturdy legs and flaxen hair that contrasted sharply with his tanned skin.

After reviewing the entire dozen boats once more, she was sure it must be the right one, even though the man wasn't.

"*Entschuldigung,*" she called out to him. "Are you fisherman Stober?"

He turned around, scrutinizing her with interest in his eyes. "Yep. What's it you want?"

"I'm from Gut Plaun. I mean, Nils sent me here to order fish, but he said you were much older..." She wondered whether she should tell him her name, but decided against it.

The man broke out into laughter, flashing the cutest dimples. "I'm standing in for my grandfather."

"Oh, I see. Has something happened to him?"

His expression closed up with suspicion. These days people didn't answer questions about the whereabouts of their relatives from strangers, since too many were arrested or simply disappeared to never show up again. Everyone closed their eyes, intent on not mentioning them accidentally, fearful the whiff of affiliation with a traitor to the Reich might cast suspicion on them as well.

"Just old age." He sized her up, making her fully aware of her clean, expensive dress with the matching shoes and hat, while he was clad in dirty old dungarees that reeked of fish.

Despite his appearance, he exuded a down-to-earth ruggedness that was refreshing to say the least.

"Send your grandfather my best wishes to get well." Again, she had let her upbringing say a polite thing that people of Annegret's social status usually didn't and she added, "I am in need of fish for a special luncheon on Saturday."

"Entertaining the Nazi elite?" he asked. Well-versed with the sub-tones in people's voices, she got the impression that he condemned her for doing such a thing.

Somehow she felt the need to defend herself, although she shouldn't have cared what a stranger thought of her. Choosing her words carefully, she let him know without pronouncing it that she too didn't care much for the Nazis. "There's a new district leader in Parchim and he's paying an official visit to Gut Plaun. Entertaining him the best I can is a duty expected from a good German citizen."

The arms crossed in front of his broad chest, he relaxed the slightest bit. "A duty, but not a pleasure?"

She gave him an innocent smile. "I'd rather feed the fish to those in need, but will gladly serve where I'm needed most." She couldn't say more without risking trouble if this man was more loyal to the regime than she instinctively believed him to be.

"How many fish do you need?"

"To feed four persons well. Although," she sought his gaze, wanting to see his reaction before she continued, "if you can sell me more, I have many people to care for."

"Who don't have ration cards," he stated.

Under no circumstances could she openly admit such a crime, so she slightly bowed her head as a sign of agreement. Every item of food was rationed and the fishery was subjected to the *Reichsstelle für Fische*, the department of the Agricultural Ministry responsible for fish. It was the organization in charge of distributing the catch, but Nils had explained to her that the fishermen had some wiggle room for personal use. Which probably meant some were willing to catch more than their allotted quota and sell them on the black market to people who could pay.

For a second, a wave of disdain crashed over her for the man who was nothing more than a common thief, enriching himself by selling fish on the side. But two seconds later, she realized how ridiculous that thought was, since she was doing the same. Buying food on the black market to give to prisoners. Compared to her crime, his was petty.

"I do have ration cards." She showed them to him, knowing full well they wouldn't cover even half of the amount she asked for.

"That'll do." He stated a price per kilo that was about double the official price and she agreed.

"Thank you. Can you bring it to the manor or shall I send someone to pick it up?"

His eyes twinkled with mischief. "Aren't you coming yourself?"

"I'm afraid I'll be too busy preparing the luncheon." She took a second glance at his broad shoulders and strong tanned arms.

"Then I'll come up to the manor." He wiped his right palm on his thigh and extended it to her. "We have a deal?"

She was mesmerized by the length of his fingers. His fingernails were dirty from a long day out on the lake, but cut short and round, making his hands look strong and capable. He certainly was a man who knew how to work as was evidenced by the callouses she felt on his palm as she shook his hand. "Saturday morning then?"

"Fresh from the lake into your mouth."

She made a disgusted grimace. "I'd rather eat it cooked."

He broke out into laughter. "You truly are one of a kind, beautiful Fräulein. The name's Stefan by the way."

"Annegret."

He clucked his tongue. "The young Miss Huber herself deigning me with her presence?"

The real Annegret would never have walked down to the wharf, so she couldn't hold his surprise against him. Yet, for some reason she wanted him to know that she was a better person than her alter ego. "Whatever you believe to know about me, it's wrong. I've become a completely different person since losing my family."

A flash of sympathy lit up his blue eyes. "My condolences." He tipped his chin at her and winked. "I'll be up at the manor on Saturday, hoping to catch a glimpse of you. Goodbye, beautiful Annegret."

She should have scolded him for his insolence, but she couldn't well annoy the man who'd sell her the fish needed to entertain Oberscharführer Kallfass. Or so she tried to convince herself, as she answered, "I'm looking forward to seeing you again too, Stefan."

9

Saturday arrived in the blink of an eye. Thomas stood in front of the huge mirror in his bedroom and revised his gala uniform. It was impeccable, freshly washed and pressed, thanks to the cleaning lady that came with the official residence.

He flicked away a speck of dust from his shoulder and studied his reflection. Nobody could say that Oberscharführer Thomas Kallfass didn't look jaunty. The silver SS-runes on one side and the two diagonal pips on the other side of his black collar patches competed against the sun with their brilliance.

The single silver star on his shoulder straps meant he was on his way to a position of true power within the SS. If nothing else, his transfer to this outpost had brought about a promotion and—finally—the command over several subordinates, even if they were as inept and dumb as Lothar Katze was.

Satisfied with his appearance, he put on his cap, the Imperial Eagle enthroned above the skull, the symbol of belonging to an elite troop that had its roots in the *Preußische Leibhusaren*, a cavalry unit in the Prussian Army.

Meeting Oliver had been a stroke of luck, because it allowed Thomas to spend his, admittedly meagre, leisure time riding horses, while at the same time working on advancing his career.

Not even a day had passed since the lovely Annegret Huber had called his office and invited him to lunch on the occasion of his visit to Gut Plaun. No doubt, she remembered him fondly from his stay at the manor the previous year, because what young, well-bred woman could resist a man like him?

Matches like theirs were made in heaven: the lovely heiress falling in love with the dashing, intelligent, strong, valiant, virile, but unfortunately poor soldier. With her social status backing him, his career would skyrocket and soon he'd lead a regiment of his own, while his soon-to-be-wife stayed home raising the many children he begat upon Annegret for Führer and Fatherland.

He sighed dreamily. Long vacations at their country home, riding horses, hunting deer and fishing in the lake would alternate with shoulder-rubbing with the important people in Berlin. They might buy a house on the island of Schwanenwerder where all the Nazi greats like Reichspropagandaminister Goebbels, Hitler's personal physician Theodor Morell and Minister Albert Speer lived.

It wasn't just dreams either, because he'd watched it happen over the years. Young men who had joined up at the same time he had were several ranks ahead of him based solely on the weight of their last names. It didn't seem to matter that most of them were less capable than he was. They were given the best posts in the best cities while he, and others like him, were shipped off to godforsaken places like Parchim.

With Annegret's surname, her money and social status the game would finally be skewed in his favor. Yes, she would make the perfect wife for him.

Pushing his Mauser pistol into the holster on his belt, he nodded at his reflection the way his father might have done if he were still alive. "Well done, son!"

He liked to wear the pistol open for everyone to see. Should the shady elements freeze in fear at the sight of an honest man ready to defend the Reich. A doubt invaded him, but he shrugged it away. A good German woman like Annegret wouldn't take offence at a weapon on display.

He left the building and walked over to the black vehicle that belonged to the SS district office, but stood entirely at his disposal. He could have asked one of his men to drive him the forty-five minutes to Gut Plaun, but he enjoyed getting behind the wheel himself.

It was almost as good as galloping on a horse, especially away from town, when he pressed his foot down on the gas pedal and brought the powerful vehicle to maximum speed. Before leaving Parchim, he stopped at a house, where the woman sold flowers from her garden and purchased a bouquet for his hostess.

He set the flowers on the passenger seat and drove to Gut Plaun, enjoying the speedy drive through fields and forests. In contrast to Leipzig, the area around here was pristine: completely untouched by the bombs of the devious Allies who spat at every rule of war, targeting women and children with their bombs instead of industrial compounds as they should have.

In any case, the Luftwaffe would finish them off soon enough, not least thanks to the all but finished V-1. Like anyone in Germany he yearned for the day when the new wonder weapon would turn the tide around and bomb the arrogant Tommies into oblivion.

They could have reigned over Europe side by side with the Germans, had they not been so stubborn and refused Hitler's generous offer. Should they get what they deserved. *Traitors!* he spat out.

Even the lazy, unintelligent Italians knew what was good for them, although he didn't quite understand why Hitler considered poor Mediterranean people with olive skin to be equals to the Aryan race.

Shortly before noon he pulled up in front of the impressive manor with fenced corrals, stables, barns, and a plethora of cultivated land.

Almost instantly, Oliver exited the house to greet him with a warm handshake. Thomas returned it and took a moment to look full circle around the estate. "It's as lovely as I remember."

"Did you have any trouble finding us?" Oliver asked as the two men walked toward the front door of the main house.

"Not at all." Thomas held the flowers he'd purchased for Annegret up and said, "A small gift for the hostess. It was very kind of her to invite me for lunch."

"She wanted to welcome you to the area, and show her support for Führer and Fatherland. We are always at your service."

Thomas would have like a more personal response, but immediately scolded himself. Oliver was her estate manager, she wouldn't discuss romantic matters with him. Next, Annegret stepped onto the porch, breathtakingly beautiful in an elegant, but modest ruby-red dress with a dark trim around the collar and the cuffs. The skirt ended about mid-calf, exposing the most finely shaped ankles. Her brown hair was done into a braided put-up hairdo, which looked sophisticated and down-to-earth at the same time. She truly was the perfect German maid.

"Herr Oberscharführer Kallfass. Welcome to Gut Plaun." She descended the stairs, while Thomas watched in delight.

Shaking her extended hand, the smell of lavender wafted into his nose. He handed her the flowers. "Thank you for the invitation, Fräulein Annegret. These are a small token of my appreciation."

"How very thoughtful of you. You needn't have bothered." She smiled graciously and buried her nose in the blossoms.

"While you and Oliver take your ride, I'll see about putting these in some water. Lunch will be served in an hour. I have taken the liberty to invite Oliver and the factory manager Franz Volkmer, I hope you won't mind."

"Of course not, I'm delighted to get to know the men in charge." Thomas would have preferred to have lunch with her alone, nevertheless he gave her one of the smiles women usually found irresistible.

"Let's go to the stables then, I have a mount ready for you," Oliver said, leading him the short walk away from the manor.

"That's a nice horse, what's its name?"

"Snowfall. She's a temperamental one, but easy to ride."

Thomas patted the mare on her neck, before he expertly adjusted the length of the stirrups to fit his long legs. Like most members of the SS he was taller than the average man and towered over Oliver by several inches.

They set out for a ride into the nearby woods, making easy conversation. For Thomas, though, it was more than chit-chat because he subscribed to the idea that the topics a man talked about told much about his character. Oftentimes shady elements betrayed their sympathies by a seemingly careless remark about this or the other they didn't agree with.

Not every man who voiced criticism was necessarily a traitor, but since there was supposed to be a nest of resisters in the area, it wouldn't hurt to sound Oliver out.

"You have some beautiful foals," he commented as they rode past a paddock.

"These are the ones born this past spring," Oliver explained. "We keep them separated by age. Over there are the two-year-olds who will soon go into training."

"That early?"

Oliver grimaced. "Under normal circumstances we would wait until they are at least three, but the Wehrmacht keeps pressing for horses faster than we can train them."

"You don't seem happy about that." Thomas had picked up the note of discontent in Oliver's voice. Perhaps this was an angle he could use to find out whether the man was fully behind Hitler and his politics.

"I do see the need for more horses, especially in the Russian campaign. They can go places and in temperatures the motorized vehicles cannot, but handing them over to the Wehrmacht when they're too young and not sufficiently trained, isn't the best course of action."

"That may be true, but more horses could well be the deciding factor between winning and losing a battle. The war effort takes precedence over everything, even the health and safety of some very nice horses."

"It's not only the horses' safety, but those of the soldiers as well. If a horse bolts, it could potentially cause great damage to those it is supposed to protect." Oliver turned to look at him with a pleading face. "I just want to give our soldiers the best I can to win against the Russian threat. Although it seems sometimes the reality takes precedence over what would be ideal."

"It certainly does. We are a nation of inventors and engineers, I'm sure someone will come up with a solution."

"Agreed, but I'm just a simple horseman who doesn't have the bigger picture in mind. Still, I'm proud of every single one of my charges I send to the Wehrmacht, confident they'll get us one step closer to the final victory."

"Well said." Thomas actually felt it was *too* well said. Simple men like Oliver often had very emotional reactions when they didn't understand why something had to be done differently than they were used to. Maybe being promoted to estate manager had given him a glimpse at a bigger horizon and adjusted his worldview.

The man certainly was able to adapt, and might become a useful ally in exposing the wicked underground organization wreaking havoc in the area.

"I'm afraid we have to return or we won't be in time for lunch," Oliver said.

"We wouldn't want to make Fräulein Annegret wait." After several minutes Thomas added, "I wonder, if Fräulein Annegret would agree to take a ride with me one day."

"She's still suffering with her back injury, but I'm sure if her health allows, she'd love to accompany you."

It was all he needed to hear. If she didn't outright refuse, it meant she was interested in him. Hadn't she already done more than her civic duty demanded by inviting him for lunch? And who could hold it against her? A beautiful, intelligent, young woman all alone in that country house with a bunch of stable hands. She must be desperate for the company of a suitable, socially acceptable, handsome, charming, powerful man.

After leaving the horses to a groom, Oliver showed him to the boot room, where he could change his riding boots and freshen up. Then he escorted him into the impressive dining room with expensive-looking tapestries hanging on the walls.

His lips twitched with disappointment when he noticed an older man standing next to Annegret, and the table set for four. Although Annegret had forewarned him some part of his brain had still hoped to spend time with her alone. On the other hand, it raised his opinion of her, since it would have been absolutely against the rules of society on their first meeting.

"Fräulein Annegret, may I congratulate you on your beautiful estate and the exceptional stable of horses you have."

"Thank you so much, Herr Oberscharführer. I take it you had a pleasant ride?"

"I certainly did, thanks to your estate manager."

"May I introduce you to Franz Volkmer, the new factory manager?"

Thomas snapped to attention and launched into a perfect *Hitlergruß*, clicking his heels with a satisfyingly full thud, his right arm and hand straightened at an exact forty-five-degree angle slightly above eye level.

His counterpart showed a befuddled expression, before he sprang into action and returned the greeting, albeit his elbow sloppily bowed and the hand not reaching high enough. Herr Volkmer, it seemed, wasn't an enthusiastic follower of the Führer. His saving grace was that at least he shouted the words "Heil Hitler" with so much rigor that they echoed through the room.

Out of the corner of his eyes, Thomas noticed that both Oliver and Annegret rendered the greeting, too, and only the matronly woman entering the dining room in this instant with a big bowl in her hands did not.

He half intended to stay in the pose until she'd set down the bowl and could join them, but decided against it, since she was just the housekeeper. A young woman in a servant's dress with long dark braids followed with more platters full of delicious food.

Thomas inhaled the scent of the meal being set down, and ended the *Hitlergruß*. He wasn't here to question the loyalty of Annegret's servants, but to impress her and forge a common future.

"Please have a seat," Annegret said and took up her position at the head of the table. He was seated to her right, while Oliver and Herr Volkmer took their chairs opposite him and to her left. For a second he let himself fantasize how in the near future he would occupy the seat at the head of the table with Annegret sitting opposite him at the far end of the table when they had guests.

After finishing the first course, more platters were brought in and he stared with delight at the abundance of sautéed fish in a bed of boiled potatoes garnished with parsley.

The conversation evolved around war production, horses and then turned to the current news coming from the propaganda ministry. Annegret was a radiant hostess and he raptly listened to her every word, wishing for the other two men to take their leave.

That time finally came when the maid entered and curtsied nervously. "Please excuse me, Fräulein Annegret, but Herr Volkmer is urgently needed at the factory."

Volkmer excused himself and blessedly disappeared. Thomas grabbed the opportunity with both hands and addressed Oliver. "Please, don't stay on my behalf, since you must be very busy and I have taken up enough of your time already."

Thomas had judged him right, because the other man rose, relief over not having to attend the formal luncheon any longer visible on his face. "We're proud to serve the Reich and you're always welcome at Gut Plaun, but I really should get on with my duties."

For a moment Thomas believed to see a flash of anxiety in Annegret's eyes, but a mere second later she was her gorgeous self again.

"Would you like a drink?" she asked.

"I'd love one."

He followed her into the library, where all the walls were covered in shelves from floor to ceiling, stuffed with books. She walked over to a beautiful brass bar cart with several bottles of alcoholic beverages.

"I can recommend our home distilled fruit schnapps." She bent down to retrieve a glass bottle with transparent liquid inside and a handwritten label.

"You have your own distillery?"

"No, we make it just for personal use, and less every year since we can't in good conscience make schnapps from fruits that are perfectly edible, since we provide for so many people."

"There's nothing wrong about drinking a schnapps once in

a while." He nodded and accepted a glass from her. "To profitable future relations."

She raised her glass. "We love to cooperate with the SS in any way we can." Then she poured the contents into her beautiful mouth and he yearned to kiss the moisture from her enticing lips.

Following suit, the spirits ran down his throat, stingy but soft with a very distinct apple aroma. "Very good."

"Would you care for another one?"

"I'm afraid not at this time of day." He wondered how to take the conversation into a more personal terrain, charming her with his sophistication. "You have a very impressive library."

"This was mostly my father's doing." Her face darkened and he got the impression she missed him very much.

"I'm very sorry about your loss. Standartenführer Huber was a respected man and his sacrifice will serve as paragon for generations to come."

Noticing her forced smile, he thought it prudent to steer the conversation toward more agreeable topics for a woman and asked her about her time in Paris.

"I loved it there, it's such a wonderful city. Although..." she paused, looking at him with a forlorn expression, "it can't compare with home."

"Understandable." He'd never been to Paris, but believed a good German couldn't value the French city over a German one.

After some more small talk about movies, actresses and what other stuff women were interested in, he decided he had achieved enough for a first date and would take his leave. It was always good to make oneself scarce and leave the woman feeling bereft, yearning for the next opportunity to meet.

"Fräulein Annegret, it was a lovely visit, but I'm afraid I must return to Parchim. Duty calls."

She bowed her head slightly. "Of course. How inconsiderate of me to take up this much of your precious time."

"No, it wasn't inconsiderate at all. If I were a private man, I'd love to stay. Perhaps we may go for a ride together one weekend?" he suggested.

She seemed surprised and hesitated for a moment. "That would be lovely."

"I'll check my schedule and let you know." He absolutely knew every item on his schedule for the next four weeks, but she didn't have to know that. An important man couldn't be seen having endless time for chasing a woman, not even one as precious as she could be to him.

"I'll await your telephone call then." She accompanied him to the hallway, where he'd put his hat on the rack. Before putting it on, he gazed down into the eyes of the lovely woman before him who exuded so much poise and grace.

He longed to kiss her, but it was much too soon for that. He had to woo her into falling in love with him. To make her his wife was worth waiting for a kiss.

"Thank you again, until next time." He lifted her hand and kissed the back of her knuckles briefly. "Have a lovely week." Without further comment, he placed his hat on his head and exited the house, striding toward his vehicle.

10

Margarete slid onto the sofa, feeling as if all energy had drained from her body. Oberscharführer Kallfass had been nothing but friendly, but it was too friendly, and she hadn't missed the appreciative glance in his eyes whenever he looked over her person. A groan escaped from her throat, just as the door opened and Dora stepped inside.

"Fräulein Annegret, are you alright?"

"I'm doomed."

Dora's face contorted with shock. "Please, don't say that. Did someone find you out?"

"No. It's worse. He likes me."

"Who?"

"The Oberscharführer. He looks at me with *that* gaze. What am I to do?"

"You mean, he is sweet on you?" Dora stepped nearer and knelt down next to Margarete's feet.

"I can't possibly indulge him. He's a Nazi, for God's sake!" She put a hand across her mouth and scanned the library for listeners, but thankfully Dora had closed the door before coming inside.

"You don't have to go out with him, if you don't fancy him," the maid tried to reassure her.

"But I do! He's the man in charge of the district and could cause us a lot of trouble if he feels rebuffed."

Dora nodded sagely. "Then you will need to find a balance between being friendly, but not too friendly."

And keep his fingers off me should he become handsy. Oh dear, she knew how little the Nazis respected women and saw them mainly as a vessel for their baser needs, or as mother to their children, which basically amounted to the same thing under a different name.

"He invited himself for another horseback ride!" Margarete spat out.

"Oliver will gladly oblige, you know how much he misses working with the horses."

"He wants to ride with me! Me! How am I supposed to do this?" Margarete slumped deeper into the cushions, desperation seeping into every cell of her body. Despite having taken clandestine riding lessons with Oliver, she was by no means the expert equestrian Annegret had been.

"Don't worry so much, Fräulein Annegret, you'll do well. Oliver says you're a fast learner. It's only a pleasure ride, not a tournament. The Oberscharführer won't notice a thing. Even if he does, you can claim your back injury."

She so wanted to believe Dora, but anxiety held her in a fierce grip. If Kallfass found out that she wasn't well-versed with horses it would raise his suspicion and from there it was only a matter of time until he found out that she was a fraud.

Noticing that Dora was still waiting for her response, she shrugged her shoulders and said, "I guess you're right. In any case, I'll have to get in more lessons. None of us can afford the slightest suspicion."

"Is there anything you need, Fräulein Annegret?"

"No, you may retire now." Margarete watched her leave the

library and sunk back. She so wished she could lean her head against her maid's shoulder, if just for a minute. Having someone tell her "We'll get through this" or "It'll all turn out fine" would ease the ever-increasing anguish she suffered.

But this was just a dream. Despite having Dora as confidante, they could never develop a true friendship. Annegret wouldn't have been seen dead with a racially inferior person from the Ukraine, and her mentor Horst Richter had warned her against showing too much lenience toward the staff.

No, if she wanted to survive this war, she had to keep to herself and rise above her own doubts and worries. Her thoughts turned to Stefan, the fisherman. In the morning, before Kallfass' arrival, she'd seen him from afar delivering the fish to the kitchen.

He was so sure of himself, so grounded, seemingly without a care in the world. His blue eyes twinkled with *joie de vivre*, a zest for life. And yet, he'd clearly expressed what his thoughts about the current regime were. She sighed on a dreamy smile. Another ally. It might be time to expand her reach beyond the factory—and have a confidant who wasn't her employee.

Someone who didn't depend on her and could offer that reassuring emotional support Dora and Oliver could not.

The ringing of the telephone interrupted her thoughts.

"Yes?"

"Fräulein Annegret, Reichskriminaldirektor Richter is on the line for you," Frau Mertens said.

"Thank you, please put him through," Margarete replied, waiting until his voice came through the line. "Horst, what a pleasant surprise. To what do I owe the honor of your call?"

"I'm afraid nothing good." Horst Richter was a high-ranking Gestapo officer, who'd been a close friend to Herr Huber and had taken it upon him to mentor his friend's daughter after the demise of both her parents and her brothers.

Despite him becoming something of a fatherly friend, she

was acutely aware that he wouldn't hesitate for a second to execute her with his own hands should he ever find out who she really was.

"I hope nothing is wrong with your family?" she said, suppressing a shudder.

"No. This is not a social call."

The shudder intensified and she all but dropped the receiver. "What has happened?"

Her voice must have shown the alarm she felt, because he answered, "Nothing, yet. But I'm calling to give you a heads-up: the SS seem to think there is something odd happening at your factory."

"There was, of course. But we caught the culprit last year and I've replaced all the men in leading positions to prevent this from ever happening again." She forced herself to keep breathing. Gustav had been stealing from the Reich, and from the prisoners, but that was water under the bridge. "According to the figures, production is at an all-time high."

"And that has been applauded by the authorities. But it has come to my attention that the factory has recently asked for exemptions for supposedly-essential Jewish workers."

"Really?" She thought it best to pretend that she heeded his advice not to get herself involved with men's business and thus didn't know details where the factory was concerned.

"Yes. It doesn't cast a good light on you, especially since there's still that other problem with an underground organization active in your area smuggling deplorables out of Germany."

"I remember, but I thought the SS must have caught them by now." She didn't dare to ask any questions, although she itched to know more.

"You'd have thought so! But no! The inept SS hasn't made any progress on that issue. I have no idea what these people are spending their time doing. If they'd let us send in our people, we would have made a raid months ago and eradicated every last member of that gang of criminals."

"I'm sure you would have. You know that I hold the SS in high esteem, but truth be told, the Gestapo is so much more effective." She gave a fake laugh. "I can't believe I'm actually saying this, being the daughter and sister of late SS officers."

Horst bellowed into the phone. "Your relatives were among the few competent men in the SS, but these days they've been lowering the entry standards so much it seems like everyone can get into the organization. Have you heard that they contracted former prisoners and men from the Baltic States into the ranks of the Waffen-SS?" He droned on about one of his favorite topics, the slow decline of morals and standards within the German population, obviously blaming the vile Allies who killed too many of the precious elite soldiers.

After a lengthy monologue that Margarete used to pour herself a glass of water from the bar cart, he returned to his initial topic. "Now about those exemptions. It doesn't look good to go begging for the privilege to employ Jewish scum."

"Oh no, we would never do that. You know here at Gut Plaun everyone works day in day out to serve our Führer the best we can. I'm sure there's a perfectly valid reason for the exemptions. Perhaps the factory wouldn't be able to keep the same production pace without them?"

"It still leaves a bad taste." It was typical for the likes of him. They'd rather stop producing much-needed weapons than to admit they were wrong and Jews weren't dispensable rubbish. To make matters worse she wasn't so sure whether this was the best thing for her to do. Could she sacrifice several hundred Jews to deportation to possibly save tens of thousands by not producing weapons intended to kill?

Confused, she shook her head. This kind of philosophical problem was way above her intellectual capacity. All she knew was that she could immediately save her workers from sure death, while the soldiers on the battlefields were just numbers to her, a mass of people who might or might not be affected by her factory's inability to produce grenades and other explosives.

"Do you want me to talk to the estate manager?" She imagined Horst sitting in his home office, smoking, and moving his head slightly from left to right while pondering her question. The pause extended such a long time that she wanted to check whether the line was still working.

"Yes, you might want to talk to him, I'm sure he can come up with a solution that works without exemptions. These are tenuous times, and while your loyalty to Führer and Fatherland is above suspicion, it's better to be safe than sorry."

"Thank you so much for calling. I'll certainly heed your advice."

"I know you will. Goodnight," Horst said and disconnected the call.

She dreamed of punching his arrogant face or at least screaming what a despicable man he was at him and that every last one of the Jews working in her factory was worth a million of him.

But she did nothing of the sort. Instead she poured herself a schnapps because she was at her wit's end. Whenever one problem was solved, two more arose in its place, just like the Hydra's heads when they were chopped off.

In the morning she would talk to Oliver and together they'd find a solution. They had to. For now she retired to her rooms. But sleep was elusive and several times throughout the night she woke with a start, seeing Uncle Ernst's solemn face. He never said a word, but the sadness in his loving brown eyes slashed her heart more than any accusation ever could.

He was no longer safe at Gut Plaun. It seemed her well-meant intention to move him to the kitchen had put him into harm's way, because a kitchen worker was by no means essential for the war production.

11

Several days later Oliver watched as Annegret mounted Pegasus, before he did the same with Sabrina. After their first clandestine lessons, they had taken to riding out together almost every day. To everyone else, it was just a leisurely stroll, but as soon as they were out of sight, they changed direction and headed to a clearing by the lake.

It was a place Oliver knew from his childhood, far enough removed from roads to risk being seen. No children played in this part of the forest these days, because of the threat the nearby factory posed. As soon as they reached the clearing, he jumped down and tethered Sabrina to a tree letting her graze.

Pegasus whinnied enviously but it didn't take long for him to accept his fate and work with Annegret under Oliver's tutelage. He put her through the various gaits, amazed at the progress she'd made in such a short time. She was a fast learner, but to an expert eye she couldn't measure up to an excellent rider like the real Annegret had been, and he pondered on a believable excuse if anyone should ask.

The problem wasn't so much a technical one, because she soaked up all the knowledge he could convey and sat on the horse's back like a poster child from a textbook. No, the issue was much harder to identify, and remedy: she lacked natural ability. Everything about her poise shouted focus and concentration, not joy of riding and a casual ease that came from growing up with horses.

"How am I doing?" she asked, biting her lip after jumping across several branches.

"You're doing well."

"But?"

He sighed. "It's hard to explain. You need to stop thinking so much and enjoy more."

"Enjoy? How am I supposed to do that while trying to remember seven hundred things at the same time?"

"That's exactly your problem. Annegret never thought about where to put her hands or her chin, she simply sat in the saddle and was."

"She grew up around horses."

"You don't need to be perfect, just good enough to fool an onlooker."

She directed Pegasus across the clearing and stopped one step in front of Oliver. "But I do. Oberscharführer Kallfass asked me out for a ride."

"He did what? Did you decline?"

"No. I didn't think I could. We need his goodwill and I was scared to rebuff him."

He muttered a curse under his breath. Thomas was a decent equestrian and, if Dora was to be believed, sweet on Annegret. That might pose a problem indeed. "Hm... When?"

"One of the next weekends, although he hasn't called to confirm the date."

"Believe me, you'll be fine. He's a decent rider, but by no means an expert."

"What if I fall off?"

"Then you pretend you had a spell of dizziness." When he

saw her frightened face he added, "Falling from a horse doesn't make you a bad rider. I can't even remember how many times I've fallen on my ass."

Annegret's eyes widened. "You? But you're such a good—"

"Perhaps good but also reckless. Although after the thing with my leg, I've calmed down." His accident had been a blessing in disguise, because it was the reason why he was unfit for service and could work at Gut Plaun.

Her brown eyes bore into his, before she straightened her back. "I guess we all need to do what we must. Let's continue our lesson."

When they rode back, he said, "Kallfass seems like a decent man. He might be sympathetic to our cause."

She turned her head toward him, a pensive expression on her face. "I don't trust him. He may seem nice enough, but many Nazis are kind when dealing with their own. Take Herr Richter, for example. He's kind to me, but absolutely ruthless when it comes to dealing with anyone he views as a traitor."

"I just meant to say that Kallfass may be a better counterpart for us than that greedy sadist Katze."

"Perhaps. At least with Katze we know where we stand. He's corrupted, which most people might not consider a positive trait, but for us it's worth gold."

"Yes. The most dangerous people are those deluded by ideology never considering they could be wrong."

She kept silent for a few minutes, before she shocked him with her next question. "What do you make of Stefan Stober, the fisherman?"

"Old man Stober's grandson?"

"Yes. He sold me the fish for lunch with Kallfass."

"Good chap. He used to live near Cologne with his parents and came here every summer to visit his grandfather."

"He seemed... let's put it this way: not overly content with the current regime."

Oliver broke out into laughter. "That's putting it mildly. If he's anything like the old man, he hates the Nazis with all his heart."

"Really?"

"Don't give me that look of shock. You of all people should understand."

"I do... I just... it's all still new for me and I'm always surprised to find other people who think the same way, considering it's not a very popular opinion right now." She took the reins tighter to steer Pegasus around some half-rotten trunks. "How come he's never been bothered by the authorities, the grandfather, I mean?"

It might be his imagination, but Oliver believed he spotted a slight blush on her cheeks. She wasn't afraid of the two fishermen, was she? "God knows, the previous mayor has tried. But if you ask me the old man is too clever, pretending that his mind is half-gone, so nobody takes his babbling seriously."

Margarete nodded. "That makes sense. And what about his grandson, shouldn't he be serving on the frontlines somewhere?"

"He's deaf in one ear. It happened about two years ago during an explosion in the ammunition factory where he worked as a chemical engineer. After spending several months in hospital, he came here to help his grandpa."

"So he's an engineer, not a fisherman? I can't believe the Nazis let him off the hook. Wouldn't he be important for the war effort?"

Oliver stopped his horse, because they were about to reach the end of the forest and he'd rather not talk about these things out in the open field, where voices carried a long way. He'd never spent a second thought on Stefan, not even after the rather strange circumstances of his return to the village, but Annegret seemed mighty interested in him.

"There's been a lot of gossip about him. I don't know

whether any of it is true or not, but you might as well know."
Her face showed rapt attention, and he continued. "That explosion, there were rumors he did it himself."

"Oh no!" Sabrina jumped at Margarete's soft cry, but the much calmer Pegasus barely moved one of his ears. "Whyever would he do that?"

"Well, that's the question. Stefan claims it was an accident, but the authorities started a lengthy investigation for sabotage. In the end, they couldn't prove anything. He was considered politically unreliable and fired from his job. So he came here and became a fisherman."

"Poor man," Annegret said, her face showing genuine compassion.

"Don't pity him. He seems quite happy with what he's doing." Oliver himself had been much happier working with horses and not having to take difficult decisions on a daily basis. It's not that he regretted having accepted Annegret's offer to become estate manager, because he could do so much good in his position, but it came at the price of never leaving the worries behind.

These days most of his waking hours seemed to be consumed with anger at the Nazis and agonizing about the safety of his horses and his loved ones. How much easier life had been before. He sighed.

"I know how you feel." Annegret sidled her horse up to him and her brown eyes burned into his, making him feel like a wimp. Despite having suffered so much, she always kept her composure and never wallowed in self-pity, reminiscing on the good old times.

"It's hard to do the right thing," he answered.

"It is. But I wonder..."

He looked at her, half-fearing what she wondered about. Knowing her, it wouldn't be anything easy or comfortable.

"... might it be time to connect with other like-minded people in the area?"

Oliver shook his head. "It's much too dangerous. The more people who know what we're doing the more we risk being exposed."

"I know that... but... I'm scared. Richter telephoned and the exemptions may not be set in stone."

He jerked his head around. "Why didn't you tell me about this earlier?"

"I didn't want to worry you."

"My job is to worry."

She smiled. "Yes, and I feel guilty putting so much on your shoulders when you should be looking forward to your upcoming wedding without a care in the world."

He shrugged. He'd been less than enthusiastic about her decision to use it as an excuse for a big reception with all the top brass in the area, but he wouldn't tell her that.

"With the war and everything going on," she continued, "you can't even go on a honeymoon, although I was thinking of giving both of you a few days off."

"Thank you, so much." He was truly moved. The real Annegret would never have shown consideration for anyone besides herself.

"It's the least I can do. We should probably head home or they'll send a search party after us."

"Can't have that, now can we?" he joked and propelled Sabrina into a light trot.

That night he had difficulty sleeping, because his head was whirling with possibilities. He wouldn't even tell Dora what caused him so much anxiety, since he had to protect her at all costs. The less she knew the better for her.

12

What she was doing would get her into hot water. Perhaps not with her mistress, but certainly with Oliver and with the authorities, should they ever find out.

But she so wanted to follow Fräulein Annegret's example, who secretly worked for the benefit of the prisoners while pretending to be a model Nazi. If the rich heiress could risk her life, so could Dora.

Information about the abysmal treatment of the people back home by the Germans they'd welcomed as liberators only two years ago trickled in and enraged her. She wanted to do something to help, however little.

She'd been given the afternoon off and wanted to chat with some of the Ukrainian girls who lived in town working in similar positions. Young girls whose parents hadn't been able to feed them and had resorted to sending them to Germany to work as maids.

Normally they met after Mass, when the entire village flocked together, even if only for an hour at most.

"Hello, Olga," she greeted the thin girl with shoulder-length brown hair, as she entered the haberdashery, looking for a hair ribbon.

"Dora, it's been such a long time. How's life treating you?"

She side-glanced at the owner of the shop, who was currently serving another customer and whispered, "Can we talk somewhere safe?"

Olga raised an eyebrow. "Sure. At the lifting bridge?"

Choosing a dark blue ribbon, Dora walked to the cashier to pay, praying the owner wouldn't engage her in a lengthy conversation. But no such luck because the nosy woman cried out, "If it isn't the little maid from Gut Plaun! What a pleasure to see you here. Is it true you snagged up the estate manager and are getting married to him?"

She nodded.

"That's a remarkable advancement for a farm girl from the Ukraine."

"Yes, Frau Bracke."

"How on earth did you pull this off? Being a Slav and all!" The woman bent forward, her huge beaked nose pointing at her with accusation.

"My great-grandmother was German."

"Ah, another one using her attractions to lull the racial board into attesting her German blood. Did you enjoy having the attention of so many men on your naked body?"

Dora blushed all over. The examination that formed part of the process to approve her Germanization had been the most humiliating affair of her life, because she'd had to stand stark naked for an entire hour in front of nine men, while a female assistant measured every inch of her body. The length of her nose, the cheekbones in comparison to her skull, fingers, arms, and legs, every bone in her body had been measured and written down on a sheet of paper, comparing her against the model of an ideal Aryan.

They hadn't told her anything about the results, but in the

end, her body had apparently fulfilled the norm sufficiently to receive the coveted stamp "racial exam passed" on her Germanization application.

"Ah, I thought so. Your kind likes to flaunt what they have. You should be ashamed of yourself! Stealing a man like Oliver Gundelmann from a proper German girl."

Dora took her ribbon and the change and fled from the shop. Normally she went to town with Frau Mertens or Fräulein Annegret and in their presence nobody had dared to talk to her like that. She turned to head back to the manor and crawl beneath the covers of her bed for the rest of the day... or week.

But after several steps pure fury rushed through her veins. She'd come to town to find a way to help, and this awful woman posed yet another reason to go through with her plan. Her head held high, she turned on her heel and walked down to the river until she arrived at the lifting bridge, where Olga was waiting for her.

"What took you so long? I thought you'd changed your mind," Olga asked in their native language.

"Frau Bracke insulted me."

"Oh dear, she does that all the time. Don't pay attention to her." Olga linked arms with her. "It's good to speak Ukrainian, I sometimes fear I'll forget our language."

"Me too. At the manor I speak German day in, day out."

"So, what's the big news you couldn't tell me in the shop?"

All of a sudden, she got afraid and said instead, "I'm going to get married."

"Really? How wonderful! When? How?" Olga knew that Dora and Oliver had been walking out for almost a year.

"In December. Fräulein Annegret said I could invite friends, if you'd like to come?"

Olga beamed with delight. "I'd love to... but... I have to ask my employer to give me the day off."

"Let's hope she'll allow it. Didn't you say she was a decent person?"

"Yes, but recently... things have become difficult."

Dora finally found the courage to ask. "There's something else I wanted to ask you about."

"Spit it out."

"There's so much troubling news from back home." She scanned the surroundings for other people, assuring they were alone. "The Nazis..."

"... are not what we expected them to be?"

"Yes. And I want to help... I mean, those who suffer. Perhaps you could... If there's anything I can do."

Olga scrutinized her from head to toe. "What would Fräulein Annegret say if she found out that her waiting maid works for the other side?"

It was probably prudent to keep her mistress out of the picture. Not even Olga had to know that she was actually on their side. "She won't find out."

"But if she does?"

"She'd tell the Gestapo, I guess."

"And that doesn't scare you?"

Dora cocked her head. "It does. A lot. I mean I'm frightened to death, but I still want to do something."

"Hmm... It might be possible, but I have to investigate first. We can't take any risks, too much is at play."

Dora understood. "See me at church and let me know."

"I will. It might take a while, though. It was great to chat." Olga winked at her and walked away, leaving Dora alone. She'd known for a long time that Olga and some of her friends were secretly criticizing the Nazis, but she'd never had the courage to join them. Now that she had laid her cards on the table, she felt liberated and anguished at the same time, although she could hardly wait until Olga told her what to do next.

13

The dreaded phone call arrived and Oberscharführer Kallfass announced he'd be delighted to ride out with her the coming Saturday.

Margarete stood at the window in her room, overlooking the front yard, wishing he would have an accident en route so he never made it. Perhaps a broken leg that would require him to spend weeks in the hospital and would not allow him on horseback anytime soon?

But her wishes didn't manifest and much too soon she saw the black automobile driving through the gate. Feeling for the pins in her hair, masterfully pinned up by Dora, she squared her shoulders and took a deep breath. *You can do this.*

She opened the door and listened to the sounds downstairs, where Frau Mertens greeted the visitor and ushered him into the parlor. For a minute she considered pretending a migraine, but then shook her head. It was best to get it done with, since he would surely return otherwise.

Just yesterday Oliver had praised her riding skills and acknowledged that she was up to the task, as long as she didn't let herself be challenged into any kind of jumping or race, which she had no intention of doing.

Putting on her friendliest smile, she entered the parlor and greeted him warmly as he kissed the back of her hand, another bouquet of flowers in his hand, this time soft pink roses. She stopped herself from shrinking back, since the roses made one thing obvious: he was romantically interested in her. This was not a social call to an affluent estate owner in his district. No, he had come here to charm the woman he had designs on.

Despite his good looks and manners, nothing could be further from her mind. For a split-second the image of the rugged, down-to-earth fisherman flashed through her mind, sending a tingle into her limbs.

"Thank you so much for the flowers, Herr Oberscharführer. I'll see that they get some water." She rang the bell and moments later Dora stepped into the parlor, gazing at the beautiful bouquet. "Would you put these into a vase, please?"

"Certainly, Fräulein Annegret, I'll bring them right back."

"Shall we? I believe the stable master has two horses ready for us." Her thought was, they'd get the ride over with and she'd send him on his way as fast as he'd dashed into the yard.

"I'd love to. What could be more pleasurable on such a beautiful morning than time on horseback in the company of the most beautiful woman in all of Germany?"

She plastered a pleased expression onto her face. "You're so kind." She motioned for him to follow her and together they walked the short distance down to the stables. To distract him from her person, she decided to make him talk about his work. Most men loved to drone on and on about all the incredibly heroic and important things they did for the Reich. "I shall hope you have acclimatized yourself in Parchim by now?"

He sighed. "Frankly, it's more work than I thought. My predecessor has lacked strictness and you can't imagine how many Jews are still poisoning the district. We're planning a concerted action rounding up all the remaining ones."

"You are?" Her heart missed a few beats.

"Yes. We're only a few men, and people around here are simply unreasonable."

"Unreasonable?" This was her chance to get some information out of him.

"Fräulein Annegret, I'm afraid to even say this, but there are still people around protecting the Jews, asking for exemptions under the flimsiest of excuses."

She pressed a hand to her heart. "What upright German citizen would do such a heinous thing?"

"Right." He turned his head to look at her, his dark blue eyes boring deep into hers. "I'll make sure this comes to a stop. I made the solemn promise to free the district from all Jews by the end of this year, including prisoners and forced workers."

Margarete barely suppressed a shocked gasp. Fortunately she was saved from having to answer by Piet, the stud manager, who stepped toward them with two horses. The spirited Snowfall for Thomas and Pegasus for her.

"Fräulein Annegret, Herr Oberscharführer, here are your horses." Piet, a man of few words, handed them the reins.

"Thank you, Piet," Margarete said, suppressing the shivers she felt at her upcoming baptism by fire. Inhaling deeply, she walked to Pegasus' side and mounted him in what she hoped was a graceful and effortless-looking movement.

Nothing awful happened and she settled down with ease, earning an appreciative glance from Kallfass, who followed suit.

"You lead the way, Fräulein Annegret, since you know the area much better than I do."

"It would be my pleasure, Herr Oberscharführer." She pressed her legs into Pegasus' flanks, who moved his ears, delighted about the upcoming ride, and took off.

Kallfass sidled up beside her and said, "Perhaps we should do away with these formalities. Please call me Thomas."

Dear God! Refusing his offer would have been exceptionally rude, so she agreed. "With pleasure, Thomas."

"Annegret..." he pronounced her name slowly and quietly, as if caressing it with his tongue, making his intentions crystal clear.

She shuddered at the manifestation of her foreboding. How on earth could she keep him at a distance without wounding his pride? From previous experiences with SS officers she knew that the more you fought them, the harder they came back to take what they considered theirs anyway.

Even in her position as owner of Gut Plaun, she was just a woman without male relatives, at the mercy of whatever the men in this world decided was in her best interest. Apparently Thomas had decided that he was to be her best interest.

Pushing the disquieting thoughts away, she steered her horse toward the lake, giving the factory grounds and the town a wide berth. She certainly didn't want the village people to gossip about her paramour.

"Have you had the chance to visit some of the villages in the district?" she asked.

"Not really. There's too much to do in the office." He smiled at her, which softened his face and made him look like any young, decent man. There were certainly worse choices than him.

Reiner Huber, Annegret's brother, came to mind. He'd been one of the worst human beings she'd ever met and she still felt a lump forming in her throat whenever she remembered the unsavory things he'd done to her.

"Isn't the nitropenta factory around here somewhere?" Thomas asked.

"It is. But I rarely, if ever, go. Reichskriminaldirektor Richter advised me that it's not a place for a woman to be."

"A very wise man. Those prisoners behave like the animals they are."

And whose fault is that? She thought of Lena, the intelligent, cultivated journalist whom she'd found hiding in the forest last year. Lena hadn't lived like an animal by choice, but because the sadistic Nazis found pleasure in humiliating and torturing her. Margarete balled her fist harder around the rein, sensing how the leather dug into her palm. "As I said, I leave the business side with Franz Volkmer, the factory manager. You met him during your last visit."

"Hm." Thomas made a pensive face. "I looked over the production numbers."

"They are way up this year, at least that's what I've been told." Her voice sounded feeble.

"The output is not the problem." He looked at her, a frown creasing his forehead. "I'm more concerned about the churn."

"Churn? I'm afraid I don't understand what you mean."

"It means turnover. The rotation of workers in and out of the facility."

Panic constricted her throat, threatening to choke her. She clenched her fists so tight that the leather string cut into her skin, causing a sharp pain. "We strive to train our workers well and keep them alive as best as we can, but unfortunately, there are still some who succumb."

"How strange," he mused.

"Oh, I don't think it's strange. There's simply not enough food and always too much work. We do everything, really, because training new workers takes time and slows down production, which we don't want."

He let out a full-belly laugh. "You're adorable, Annegret, and forgive me for being so blunt, but it's a good thing Reichskriminaldirektor Richter told you to stay away from the business side of the estate, since you got it all wrong."

"Wrong? Aren't we supposed to keep production high to

help the war effort?" Now she was more confused than panicked.

"Yes, and no. Almost as important as producing armaments is to exterminate the Jews, since they are a blight on our society. One of Hitler's most ingenious plans is extermination through labor. Instead of wasting valuable resources, we can benefit from the existence of our enemies. Put them to work to rectify at least in a small way all the havoc they wreaked on our great nation, until they succumb. Goebbels himself has said, 'Whoever perishes from this work, is not worth being pitied'." He looked at her expectantly, apparently waiting for her to applaud such a heinous and inhumane scheme.

"I never thought about it that way. But what about production?" She'd always thought fulfilling the required quota would keep her Jews safe from deportation, but apparently the war effort wasn't as important as the authorities liked to tout.

"There's more than enough replacements for the Jews. In fact, government policy these days is to employ strictly non-Jewish subjects, like foreign workers or prisoners of war in forced labor on German ground."

"I see."

He gazed over at her, his eyes full of infatuation she didn't requite. "I'm telling you this only because I hold you in such high esteem. The low churn rate in your factory has caused plenty of questions further up in the hierarchy."

"I had no idea," she hedged.

"That's what I thought. Still, I hoped you could talk to your factory manager, completely off the record, and advise him to make sure that more of the Jewish workers die. That would take care of our little problem all by itself."

She didn't think the Jewish workers were a problem and she certainly had no intention to force their demise, but she gave him a pleasant nod. "If you think it will be useful, I'll do as you suggest. Although, wouldn't that put a dent into our production?"

"It may take some trial and error, until you find a balance between output and the churn of prisoners. Consider it growing pains for running a successful business."

"Do you have any further suggestions?" Margarete felt sick to her stomach.

"Oh, there are countless possibilities to speed up the process." He animatedly counted the ways to kill Jews as if they were some unwelcome pests. "Apart from the obvious measures like reducing rations and increasing workload, your manager can get creative here. A fun thing to do would be games to cheer up the guards and reward them for their loyalty to the Führer."

"What kind of games?"

"Really, the sky is the limit. My favorite is one we call 'shooting rabbits'." His face lit up with delight. "The Jews are the rabbits, running for their lives, while honorable men hunt them down and shoot at them. It is so much fun. Like a deer hunting party, just better, because you know you're serving your country at the same time."

Vomit rose in her throat and she swallowed it down, before she answered, "That is exceptionally cruel, I would never condone such a thing."

"My dearest Annegret, they are only Jews. Have you never ordered to shoot deer in your forest?"

"We shoot animals for food, and I certainly don't intend to eat Jews," she said, hoping he'd change the topic.

"You'd be poisoned if you ate a piece of such rotten scum." Again, he cast an amorous gaze at her, before he continued. "You're such a kind-hearted woman and I admire you all the more for it. Tell your factory manager to see to it. How he does it is not of your concern."

"I will." What else could she say? Shout what a despicable man he was? Worse than the people he considered scum. At the manor she would talk to Oliver and hopefully together they would come up with a solution to the problem, albeit one that was completely different to what Thomas had in mind.

Thankfully they arrived at the lakefront and she stopped Pegasus. "From here you have a wonderful view across to the other side." She'd meant to continue their ride, but Thomas dismounted his horse, came around and held his hand up for her.

"I can get down," she assured him.

"I know you can, but I'm here and willing to assist a beautiful woman." His amorous grin was unbearable.

"Well then, how can I refuse?" She gave him a terse smile as she swung her leg over the horse. His hands closed about her waist and he guided her feet to the ground, keeping her in his arms much longer than was needed.

The second she felt steady, she stepped out of his embrace and walked toward the edge of the water, leading Pegasus to drink. Thankfully he followed suit and with the reins in his hand, he didn't make another attempt to get his hands on her.

"It so peaceful here," she said just to dispel the silence between them.

"It certainly is." He settled on a nearby rock, beckoning for her to join him.

"I'd rather not get dirty," she said with a pointed gaze at the dusty surface.

"You have changed, Annegret."

"Me? Why would you say that?" Panic constricted her throat. Had he known the real Annegret and had waited until now to rub it under her nose that he'd figured out her deceit? Was he going to propose an indecent arrangement for him to keep his mouth shut?

"Gossip has it you used to be quite the wildcat, always running with your brothers and not at all behaving like a girl should."

"Oh that." Her alleviated giggle chinked in the warm air. "I must admit, when I grew older, my mother was more successful in making a lady out of me... Although," she continued, looking down at her jodhpurs, "she would have preferred me to use the sidesaddle."

"An expert rider like you would certainly be able to and look even more elegant."

God, how she hated his way of thinking. Was a woman nothing but a decorative piece in a man's household?

"It's getting a bit chilly, shouldn't we perhaps return to the manor?" she asked, since she couldn't stand being in his presence one minute longer.

"How thoughtless of me. I wouldn't want you to catch a cold."

I bet you wouldn't care if you knew I am a Jew. She pushed the thought away. Identifying with whom she used to be only brought up memories, confusion and the risk of slip-ups. She was Annegret Huber. Full stop.

They rode back to the stables, talking strictly about the weather and the beauty of autumn, mostly because Margarete didn't trust herself to keep her mouth shut if he launched into another tirade about the evildoings of the Jewish race.

"Is something bothering you?" he asked after a while.

"No, I'm just tired. I had a horrible headache last night that wouldn't let me sleep." The lie tripped off her tongue so smoothly she almost believed it herself.

"You should have told me, we could have postponed our riding out."

"It wasn't that bad, it's just that I'm quite tired now," she lied once more. The thought of canceling on him had crossed her mind many times, but she'd considered it best to get it over with, since she couldn't well keep finding excuses not to meet him for all eternity.

As they left the horses with a stable hand and walked up to

the manor, Thomas stopped her with a hand on her arm, his face looking contrite. "Annegret, I can't help but notice that you seem to be upset with me. Please forgive me for my earlier words. I was only trying to help."

"I realize that."

"You have a kind heart, which is a wonderful thing, but in this case it's misguided. Against our enemies we need to be ruthless, locking any empathy we might have deep down in our souls in order to protect our ethnic community."

"That's what Reichskriminaldirektor Richter always says." Margarete had once asked him how he could be so kind to some people and cruel to others.

Thomas beamed with pride. "If the Reichskriminaldirektor says so, it must be true. Forgive me for being insensitive, I often forget that women don't have the strength to deal with this kind of thing."

If she had needed any confirmation that Thomas and she came from different worlds, these words did the trick. She barely kept the sarcasm out of her voice. "It's such a relief to have men who take care of everything we cannot do on our own."

"That's exactly what Hitler says. The big world and politics are for the men, the small world, children and the home are women's domain. We men can only be successful when we have a doting woman at the center of our world, making our home cozy for us and letting us forget about the evils of the world in your arms." He looked expectantly at her.

"Our Führer has such elaborate thoughts."

"It was a lovely morning," Thomas told her, still holding her arm, slowly letting his hand slide down until he was holding her hand. "I hope you know how much I treasure the time we are spending together." Margarete couldn't find any words to say so she remained quiet. He smiled warmly, lifted her hand and kissed the back of it, then turned her hand over and kissed the inside of her wrist. "When can I see you again?"

"I'm not sure. We are in the middle of harvest and there are so many things to get done. And then there's Oliver's wedding to organize. It may be several weeks before I have another Saturday free."

"How about a Sunday?" Thomas suggested, squeezing her hand.

Margarete shook her head. "I'm sorry, this is a Christian household. We attend Mass on Sundays."

"It doesn't have to be an entire day, an hour or two will suffice. Why don't I give you a phone call next week?"

"That would be nice."

He walked to his automobile and nodded his head in a small bow to her. "Have a wonderful evening and I hope you think of me, because I'll be thinking of you."

Margarete waved at him as he got behind the wheel and drove away. Once she was sure he could no longer see her, she sagged against the doorjamb and forced away the tears that threatened to spill. Thomas Kallfass was a horrible man. And he was clearly smitten with her.

14

During his drive back to Parchim, Thomas was in an exceptionally good mood. The visit with Annegret had been a success. This woman was absolutely adorable and it was clear that she was smitten with him – albeit a bit shy, which seemed to contradict the things he'd heard about her.

Although his mother always said that every wild girl would eventually grow up to become a well-behaved woman if she received the proper education. His mother would be so pleased. He knew without a shadow of a doubt that she'd approve of his choice, because what was not to like about the beautiful, charming, well-educated, and rich Annegret.

He dreamed of bearing the insignia of an SS-Standartenführer while Annegret presented their latest-born child to the Führer for his blessing, their older children standing in an immaculate line, dressed in their Hitler Youth and BDM uniforms. They would be the poster family of the Reich, with more honors and glamour than Goebbels himself.

With a bit of patience and some more visits wooing her, he'd soon be able to propose.

. . .

On Monday he was the first in the office and began working through the pile of papers needing his signature. The work mostly kept him at his desk, when he'd rather chase the bad boys out there. There was nothing like roughing up traitors, criminals and riff-raff to show one's dedication to the Reich. Nobody got rewarded for meticulous desk work, because true men earned their stripes with valiant actions.

A knock on the door interrupted him.

"*Herein*," he asked the visitor to come in.

"Good morning," his deputy, Lothar Katze said as he entered the office, a pile of papers on his arm.

"I gather you have slept well." Thomas pointedly looked at the clock on the wall opposite his desk. Katze, though, didn't have the decency to look contrite for arriving this late.

"Yes, thank you. It has been an exciting weekend, if you understand what I mean," Katze said with a salacious grin.

Thomas understood quite well and much to his surprise he felt appalled by it. Now that he'd put his designs on Annegret, he had no intention to go whoring with other women.

"What did you need?" Thomas asked.

"Here are some papers for you to review and sign."

"Put them on the desk, I'll have a look at them later." Katze made to return to his office, when Thomas had an idea. "Wait, get me the list of exemptions."

Katze seemed to hesitate for a split-second, before he said, "They have just returned from Berlin. We had to send them there for final approval, because you had not yet taken on your position."

"But I've been here for over a month already!"

"The mail is slow and our district doesn't have top priority where Berlin is concerned."

A slow-burning anger took hold of Thomas. If they didn't even consider this rotten place he'd been transferred to important enough to process the mail in a timely manner, how could he ever prove himself and get promoted? But once again, Annegret's lovely face came to his mind and he relaxed. As soon as she was married to him, they couldn't ignore him any longer.

"What do we usually do with them?" he asked.

On Katze's forehead appeared a sheen of sweat. "Well, people request exemptions for all kinds of reasons. Mostly miscategorized half-Jews, or privileged Jews protected by their marriage to a German."

"Disgusting! What racially-pure German would choose to stay married to a Jew?" Thomas couldn't find anything gracious or even likeable in those abominable creatures. He could spot them from miles away, not only by their horrible looks but also by their stink. It was scientifically proven that Jews smelled rotten, which was additionally increased by their complete disregard for cleanliness. A fact Thomas himself had witnessed in every camp he'd been to.

"It eludes me as well, but our great Führer has been lenient with them, so there must be a greater wisdom behind and I'm not to question his wishes."

Katze said it in a truculent tone that caused Thomas to perk up his ears. This man couldn't be trusted and would probably lick his fingers if he could hang out his superior to dry and put his own fat ass on Thomas' chair. He knew that kind: a bootlicker, loyal to nothing but his own greed.

He thumbed through the papers until he came across a bunch, neatly stapled together. He pulled it out of the heap. His eyes almost popped out as he saw the letterhead of Gut Plaun atop the long list of exemptions for essential workers.

"What's this? Essential workers?" He held the pile out to Katze, whose face was covered in droplets of sweat.

"Ah, let me see." Katze took the pile and scrutinized it, before he answered. "Herr Gundelmann, the estate manager of Gut Plaun, came here to request exemptions for some workers, explaining they wouldn't be able to reach their production quota without them."

Thomas scratched his chin. He'd pegged Oliver as a man mostly interested in horses and had been quite surprised to find out Annegret had promoted him to the position of estate manager after Gustav Fischer's death. Something felt fishy. Perhaps he should pay Oliver a visit and scrutinize his motives to request these exemptions. Anyone with half a brain knew that Jews were lazy, dumb and certainly not essential for anything.

A horrible suspicion crossed his mind. What if the factory manager Franz Volkmer was part of the underground organization that supposedly worked in this area, smuggling undesirables out of the country? And Oliver was too naïve to see through the scam?

He had to find out and make sure Annegret wasn't somehow dragged into this mess. The poor girl would be appalled if she knew what was going on directly under her nose. For the moment, he decided to keep his suspicion to himself and not make Katze privy to his thoughts.

"Well then," he said, assuming a light-hearted tone. "War production takes priority, right?"

"That's what I thought, even though it would have been preferable to deport the subjects." Katze seemed relieved.

"Thank you. You can archive the files."

"Yes, sir." Katze clicked his heels and fled from the office, leaving Thomas pondering about the allegiances of his subaltern. He presented the image of a fervent Hitler supporter, but he might be a bit too interested in his own benefit.

For now, he'd observe him closely.

In the evening he went out to dinner with colleagues. As usual the radio was blaring, entertaining the patrons with popular music. When the news came on, the waiter turned the volume higher, so everyone could listen to the newest information from the various frontlines.

All conversation ceased and everyone hung on the words of the speaker, whether it was out of genuine interest, or because it was the expected thing to do, Thomas could not say.

He used the time to lean back and observe the other patrons, trying to peek inside their heads, wondering what they really thought. Just a few weeks prior the news had broken that American and British troops had landed in Italy after that traitor Pietro Badoglio had signed an armistice agreement. Apparently the Duce Mussolini was no more and the weak Italians sought their luck by siding with the former enemy.

After the shameful capitulation of the Afrika Korps in Tunis, it was yet another bitter setback, opening up a second front on the European continent. According to the narrator frontlines in Italy and Russia were being straightened and strategically retracted, army groups regrouped, all to prepare for the final attack, that would bring the ultimate victory.

As much as Thomas believed with all his soul in Hitler and his military brilliance, it was disconcerting. No doubt the Wehrmacht was the best army mankind had known, but the enemy outnumbered them vastly. If eyewitness reports from the Eastern Front were to be believed, for every Soviet soldier killed, ten new ones were thrown into battle.

It seemed the Soviets had vast pools of young, unspent men deep in the Asian parts of their territory. Racially inferior Mongols, Cossacks and other Orientals who made up in quantities what they didn't have in quality.

Judging by the set jaws of several men in the audience, Thomas wasn't the only one secretly worried about the direction the war was taking.

As the music resumed after the news, a Wehrmacht soldier on leave said, "This is only a temporary setback. You'll see the new wonder weapon that will send the Allies running to their moms."

"Right. A bunch of cowards they are."

"I have it on good authority, that the V-1 is as good as ready to go into mass production."

"Whooom. It'll wipe out the *Inselaffen*."

"The Englishman should have joined forces with us when he could, now he'll pay with complete extinction of his island."

"What about the Italians, doesn't their capitulation give the Allies the upper hand on the boot?" an older civilian asked.

"Pah... getting rid of the ballast will only strengthen us. The Italians have always been sub-standard. It was only out of respect for Mussolini that Hitler didn't occupy their country."

Thomas felt a renewed urgency. If they were to implement all the glorious betterments for the German nation, they had better hurry up. Every Jew eradicated was one Jew who couldn't return to haunt the Aryan community.

Starting tomorrow he'd pursue them with more determination than ever before. As true as he was sitting here, he'd see to it that every last Jew in the district of Parchim was deported, exempted or not. If he rounded up that pesky underground organization in the process, it was an added bonus.

His actions would kill two birds with one stone. Apart from freeing the German nation from the Jewish plague, it would also recommend him to the upper echelons. Annegret would admire his swift and energetic conduct so much that she might toss all social niceties overboard and marry him right away.

"Good night, comrades," he said after another round of beer.

He entered his apartment as the telephone began to ring. With a glance at his watch he wondered who would call him this late at night.

"Oberscharführer Kallfass," he answered the phone, just in case it was an official caller.

"Thomas, there you are. I've been trying all evening."

He suppressed a slight groan, half waiting for a sermon about how a good young man should be at home early. "I had business to attend to."

"Oh, you poor boy. Isn't it enough that they keep you working all day? But this late at night?"

"*Mutti*, please. We all need to make sacrifices for the Fatherland, and if I'm needed after office hours, I'll be the last one to refuse."

His mother sighed into the phone. "Talking about sacrifices. The situation is getting untenable. They turned our electricity off again for hours on end. They say it's needed for industry, to make these new wonder weapons. But how am I supposed to cook dinner? To mend clothes at night? Do these men up there even know how much work has to be done? Knitting socks for our soldiers, collecting metal scraps? And then I have to queue up for hours just to find out there's not much to be gotten with my ration cards. And the bombing... Lord, the bombing never stops." She took a deep breath and he could sense her emotional turmoil. "I'm afraid, Thomas."

"I know, *Mutti*, I know. But we are a nation with many enemies, they forced us into this war. You wouldn't want to live under the yoke of the barbarian Russians now, would you?"

"Of course not." The shiver was evident in her voice. "But Hitler promised us good times, Lebensraum and no more hardship."

He was getting impatient. That was exactly the problem. People expected instant rewards without effort. Nobody, not even his own mother, seemed to understand that it took sacrifice to reach the final victory and all the benefits that came with it. "And we will have all of this, but it will take some time. A few months maybe, or a year at most. When has the Führer ever let you down?"

"He hasn't. It's just... So many deaths and so much sorrow.

The neighbor's boy came home last week without his legs. Can you imagine? He's twenty years old. A cripple."

"He can be proud of his service for the Reich. I'm sure he'll receive a medal for his bravery and the state will take good care of him. The Führer looks after his loyal supporters." Despite his soothing words, Thomas shuddered. Not much older than the neighbor's boy, he sensed the horror of what it would mean to live without legs.

For one thing, Annegret would never fall in love with a cripple. He shrugged off the worrisome thought. The further up the hierarchy, the lower the chances he'd be sent into combat.

"Oh, Thomas. I'm so glad you're safe out there in the countryside. There aren't any bombings where you are? Right?" Her voice became pleading. "At least, there's been nothing in the news. It seems those disgusting child murderers focus all their efforts on the big cities, where they can kill more children and women. These Allied pilots are cowards, criminals, disgusting riff-raff."

At least in that aspect he could one hundred percent agree with her. "You're right, *Mutti*. Our Luftwaffe aces would never do such a heinous thing. They only ever bombed industrial targets, and only as a last resort, after the English refused to negotiate."

The next day at lunch he headed to the SS cafeteria. It was one of the perks of his position that he didn't have to worry about where his next meal came from or what it included. He had a vast array of dishes to choose from, including meat and fresh fruit his mother had claimed wasn't available anywhere.

He shook his head, not understanding why she complained so much. He could see with his own eyes that none of it was warranted.

15

Margarete went in search of Oliver. She found him sitting at his desk and knocked on the open door.

"Do you have a minute?"

"For my employer? Always." He motioned for her to sit on the chair in front of his desk.

She closed the door behind her, which earned her a questioning gaze.

"We have a problem," she told him without preamble.

Oliver put aside the papers he was looking at and asked, "Thomas?"

She nodded. "He's concerned because not enough people are dying in the factory, which is apparently a bad thing. He even insinuated that productivity has to take second place to killing off Jews. 'Churn' he called it." She still reeled from the callous suggestion of games to reach this goal.

"That doesn't sound good at all, since we have requested the exemptions to keep up productivity."

"And there's more." Margarete frowned, remembering the warning Horst Richer had issued. "The exemptions have raised some red flags up in the hierarchy. It seems there's a growing sentiment that even essential Jews have to be exterminated."

Oliver furrowed his brow. "What are we going to do?"

"I have no idea." Desperation threatened to overwhelm her. She had fought so hard to keep her workers, including Uncle Ernst, safe, but if the exemption didn't hold... how could she make sure they survived?

"We need to let them die."

"How dare you!" Margarete jumped up in protest, but he waved her off.

"Not really, just pretend they did. That should satisfy the authorities."

"But how? And what do we do with them? We can't keep them in the factory, since we need to ask for replacements and the barracks would soon overflow."

"That would be too risky anyway. The authorities could come to inspect the facility any time without prior warning. Furthermore, we can't rely on the civil workers to keep such a huge secret. I'm sure there are quite a few willing to rat us out for an extra ration card."

Margarete leaned forward and pressed her hands on his desk. "Right. We can't have confidants. Despite being big, the factory is much too small to be anonymous."

Oliver nodded wordlessly. She knew from experience that he often needed time to think over things, and he didn't like to fill the silence with empty words. So, she sat back and waited patiently for him to speak up.

"Assuming we fake the death of someone. The next question is what do we do with him afterward?"

"He has to go into hiding."

"But where?"

"At the manor?"

"How soon before Frau Mertens or one of the day laborers finds out?"

"The stables maybe?"

"We have the same problem there." Their gazes crossed and she knew he was thinking about Lena as well. They had been hiding her down by the stables, until Gustav had found out.

"You're right. In addition, we can hide a handful of people at most. They will need to leave the estate."

He nodded, deep in thought. "If Thomas is serious about deporting every single Jew in his district, essential or not, then we have a much bigger problem."

"Do you think," Margarete asked tentatively, remembering that Lena had been hiding in the forest for days before she had found her, "that a group of them could survive in the woods? If we helped them to find a cave and provide them with blankets and regular food."

"That might work. It gets cold in winter, but sheltered in a cave, it wouldn't be too bad. Although there's always the risk they would be found."

"There's a risk to everything," Margarete said with determination.

"It is one option, definitely. We should also put out our feelers for people willing to hide a person. And our ultimate goal has to be to move them out of the country."

"Emigrate? That's not allowed anymore." She looked at him with surprise.

Oliver laughed. "I meant smuggling them out."

"Is that even possible?"

"There are rumors about a resistance organization doing just that."

"But we don't have any contacts... And where would they send them to? Aren't the Nazis in every single country around us?" She knew friends of her parents who'd emigrated to the Netherlands or France ten years ago and had found themselves in the same predicament once again after the Nazi invasion.

"England, maybe? Or America?"

"But they don't issue visas for Jews."

Oliver made a long face. "A neutral country like Switzerland?"

"They take anyone with a coffer of banknotes." She calculated in her head, how much the Swiss would consider sufficient to forego the normal visa process and for how many people she could buy freedom before she ran out of cash.

"I know. Even if the Swiss agreed, the refugees have to cross Germany all the way from north to south to get there, which is altogether much too dangerous."

"Hmm." She nodded. It seemed like an impossible under-taking. After a long silence she said, "Sweden is a neutral coun-try, too."

"Yes, it is. Close to where we are, too. But they are very restrictive with allowing refugees in."

Her shoulders slumped. It seemed that none of the coun-tries in Europe and beyond actually cared about the plight of the Jews. "If we knew someone in these countries..." She looked up. "We do know people in Sweden!"

"We do?" Oliver wrinkled his forehead.

"Not personally, but the factory buys steel from Swedish manufacturers."

His face expressed shock. "You can't just telephone your supplier and ask if he's going to help smuggle Jewish refugees out of Germany."

This time she had to laugh. "Since the phone lines are tapped, I wouldn't recommend it."

"Then what?"

"I don't know. In any case, we first have to find someone to get them to the border."

Oliver nodded. "As I said, it's just rumors, but apparently this resistance organization smuggles people out via the Baltic Sea."

She felt a giddiness in her bones. "We need to make contact with them."

Oliver shook his head. "But how? It's not like they advertise in the newspaper."

"We'll find out in due course." She wasn't about to give up, just because her proposal seemed impossible. "Let's start with planning the demises of the first batch and putting them up in the forest."

"Only the youngest and strongest ones are eligible for this plan, since living conditions will be harsh."

She nodded, thinking of Uncle Ernst. He was so frail, he would definitely not withstand a winter out there. Her heart squeezed with worry about him. She owed it to Aunt Heidi to keep him safe. Then she had another idea. "What about arranging for fake papers? They could go wherever they wanted and pretend to be a German citizen." Like herself. With the difference that her papers weren't actually fake. They belonged to a real, albeit deceased, person.

"That seems like the most viable solution, with the constraint that we first have to get fake papers, since we can't produce them ourselves."

"No." Her shoulders slumped as she remembered the many times in Paris, when she'd had to show her identification. Most times the officer had scrutinized the type of paper and the stamp on it carefully to make sure it was genuine.

She'd always been on pins and needles that they would comment on the photo, but thankfully it had been too battered after the bombing—and additional treatment with her fingernails—to give away that she resembled the girl whose papers she used, but wasn't actually her.

On her return to Leipzig, Horst Richter had helped her to apply for a new *Kennkarte*, this time with her own picture. She sighed. If only Horst was sympathetic to the plight of the Jews, he could be so useful in protecting them, including providing genuine papers.

"Are you even listening to me?" Oliver said.

"No, sorry. I was thinking about where to get genuine or at least genuine-looking papers."

"Don't do anything rash," he warned her. "We can't go asking around about these things."

"I know... what about the fisherman? Stefan."

"What about him?" He wrinkled his nose.

"Didn't you say he sabotaged the war production?"

"It was never proven, but after they kicked him out as an engineer, I would think he hates the Nazis more than ever."

"Shall I perhaps ask him?" A thrill of anticipation tingled across her skin. Stefan had made a very positive impression on her.

Oliver squinted his eyes, thinking. "I'm not sure you'd be the right person to talk to him."

Disappointment spread through her bones, since she'd already looked forward to meeting him again. "Who do you suggest?"

"Normally I'd say Nils. But since he's not privy to our predicament that wouldn't work." He looked at her, leaning his hands on the desk. "Stefan does have the reputation as quite the charmer, despite his rugged looks. The town gossips will have a field day if they get a whiff of you seeking him out."

Because of his rugged looks, Margarete thought and felt a warm feeling rushing through her veins. She said, "I can leak to the owner of the haberdashery that Gut Plaun is forging a closer business relationship with him, maybe?"

"That might work... although to get him into a talking mood, you might want to pretend to be smitten with him."

"I think I can do that." The warm feeling increased and she wanted to rush into town this very moment.

"Yes, that might work. Schmooze him up, appeal to his

manliness, get him talking and if you feel it's safe ask him, very carefully, whether he might be able to help with people who have to disappear for a while."

"No problem."

Oliver cast her a measuring glance. "Don't be casual about this. While Stefan is certainly not a Nazi sympathizer, we don't know anything about his current situation. He might have cut a deal with the Gestapo to go free after being accused of sabotage."

She refused to believe Stefan would hoodwink her. She prided herself on having gained a certain knowledge about human nature over the past year and Stefan's bright blue eyes exuded nothing but honesty. "Don't worry."

"Promise you'll be careful. The slightest doubt and you don't ask him."

"I promise."

For two days she brooded over the best excuse to go and see Stefan until she came up with a watertight plan.

She arranged to meet someone in Zislow, a small village on the other side of the lake. By boat it was less than half an hour across. The two of them alone on his boat, where nobody could overhear them, would give her the perfect opportunity to ask him about falsifying documents. All the while pretending it was a business trip.

Then she sent Nils on an errand.

She waylaid Piet at the manor taking his lunch and said, "I urgently need to get into town, but Nils has left with the automobile. Could you please saddle my horse and bring him up here, while I go and change?"

"Certainly, Fräulein Annegret." Piet slightly bowed his head, before he called to one of the stable hands to get Pegasus ready for her.

While she went to her rooms to change into jodhpurs and a

thick jacket against the damp autumn air, she prayed that Stefan was available to take her over.

Mere ten minutes later she was downstairs again, ready and excruciatingly nervous. Not because of the subversive type of her request, but mostly because she would see Stefan again.

Piet was waiting for her with Pegasus, and once again she was grateful for the riding lessons she'd taken with Oliver. Without the horse she wouldn't be able to get into town, because while the villagers walked several miles through the forest on a daily basis, that didn't mean the lady of the manor could do so as well.

"Thank you, Piet. I'll leave the horse at the pub." They had an arrangement with the pub owner for these occasions, although usually the male employees residing at the manor were the ones to make use of it when they visited the town for business reasons.

Once she'd handed her horse over to the pub owner, she walked toward the wharf where the fishermen usually hung out. With every step she became more nervous and pondered how best to begin the conversation, since she couldn't very well ask him flat out, "Hello, Stefan, can you hide illegals for me or at least provide us with fake papers?"

She found him on his boat and stopped to watch his broad shoulders, while he did whatever maintenance work. Her courage waned, but after a few seconds she valiantly raised her voice. "Hello, Stefan."

He stopped what he was doing and turned around, a pleased grin appearing on his face. "Fräulein Annegret. To what do I owe the honor of this visit?"

"Ahem..." She struggled to get out the words, suddenly feeling like a teenager. "I... I mean... I need to go to Zislow. And Nils has taken the automobile... so someone suggested..."

"Suggested what?" He seemed amused at her hapless stuttering.

She really had to get a grip on herself. "I'm sorry, you must think me a complete idiot."

"Not at all. I believe you're a very smart woman." His smile broadened and two cute dimples appeared on his cheeks, sending her heart fluttering.

"Then let me try again: Nils is running errands with the automobile and an employee suggested that I ask around to see whether someone could take me over by boat."

"And, did you ask around?" His blue eyes held her captive.

"I'm asking you. I'll pay, of course."

He cocked his head to peruse her from top to toe, leaving a tingle in the wake of his gaze. "Do you need me to wait and return you here as well?"

She hadn't thought about that part in her haste to find an excuse to be alone with him. "I guess so. Probably. I mean, yes."

Again, his face broke into a huge smile. "Then hop in, we'll talk about the price on the way."

"Thank you so very much." She took his proffered hand, feeling its warmth and the roughness of his skin as he helped her into the boat.

"Sit over there." He motioned for her to sit on the bench behind the steering wheel and turned around to start the motor before he settled by her side. It gave her the opportunity to appreciate the boat. Between the steering wheel and the bow were several wooden planks on the ground covered with all kinds of nautical gear: ropes, fenders and a fishing net. But what she found most interesting was a small opening next to the column with the steering wheel.

Once he'd steered them out of the small channel onto the lake, she asked, "What's this?"

"Storage room. How'd you get here?"

"By horse."

"Oh right," he said with a pointed look at her jodhpurs and riding boots.

Now it was her turn to give him an amused gaze. "You have a keen perception."

He looked dumbfounded, but seconds later broke out into laughter. "I guess I deserved that."

"I guess you did." Once again their eyes locked and she felt a thrill go through her body, along with a strange sense of security. Emboldened by this feeling, she gathered up the courage to ask, "This may sound a bit strange, but there are sometimes people at Gut Plaun who need another place to stay for a while."

His face became serious. "Where nobody can find them?"

She nodded and relief flooded her system. At least he hadn't outright rejected her request.

"What do your Nazi friends think about that?"

She pursed her lips, giving him the most scathing look she was capable of. "I believe I already told you where I stand the last time we met."

Again, he laughed. "You did, but I didn't believe you. You must admit that in your position it's quite an unusual opinion."

"That's because you don't know me."

"Is this an offer to get to know you more intimately?" His soft voice engulfed her and she flushed furiously.

"Not at all. But if you don't want to help, I can understand."

He fell silent and for a while the only sound was the humming of the motor across the lake. Just when she thought, he'd decided to act as if she'd never mentioned subversive things, he spoke up. "I want to. Help, I mean. Although I'm not sure I can trust you. This could be a trap to hang me out to dry."

"I can only give you my word." She thought quickly. "If this were a trap, wouldn't I choose a more suitable place than your boat in the middle of the lake? Nobody can hear us or saw me step onto your boat. You might drown me right now and they'd never find out."

"You're right. You'd be more intelligent than that. I guess I believe you." His next question hit her without warning. "Does Oliver know?"

How on earth should she answer this? She couldn't implicate Oliver. Though it would give her story more credibility, because the two men had known each other since childhood. "He shares the same convictions I do."

"Whatever those convictions are."

"So can I count on you should the need arise?"

He nodded. "Not more than two people at any time, and for no longer than a week. Otherwise it gets too dangerous."

"A week? So short?"

His eyes rested on her for a while, before he said, "You're doing this for the first time, aren't you?"

Silently, she nodded, her gaze moving to the approaching shoreline to avoid having to look at him. Therefore she was completely taken aback, when she felt his hand on her arm.

"This isn't an exciting game, Annegret." She turned to look at him, wanting to protest, but changed her mind when she noticed the genuine worry in his face. "This is about real people whose lives are at stake. It is dangerous and fraught with failure."

"I know." She winced, remembering Lena. Naively she'd thought that once in hiding, Lena was safe. But that hadn't been the case.

"I'm just telling you this, so you won't do something stupid out of disappointment or anger. Not everyone we hide will survive. We don't know how long the war will last or what else will happen, but it's safe to assume that half of the submarines, as we call those going underground, won't make it for one reason or another."

Again, she was shocked to the core. Half of the people she protected so fiercely wouldn't make it? Her heart refused to listen to his words. That simply couldn't be true.

"I know it sounds disheartening, pointless even, but every

hour gained is a win. We cannot think in indefinite terms. We have to be content with a day survived, or a week. It is my firm belief that every day passed brings us closer to the downfall of Hitler's regime."

"That was a very philosophical speech I had never expected from a fisherman."

"Probably because I used to be a chemical engineer." His eyes wrinkled with a mixture of pride and sadness.

She bit her tongue to keep herself from asking the questions she was so curious about. *Did you really sabotage the factory you worked for? And if yes, can you perhaps give me tips how to do the same?*

They arrived at the Zislow jetty and he helped her out, agreeing to wait for her, since he had a friend in the village whom he'd visit for an hour or two.

16

Dora was busy placing provisions into a basket when Oliver came into the kitchen and pecked her on the cheek. "Ready, sweetheart?"

"Yes. Let me just take off my apron." Fräulein Annegret had given them the afternoon off, and allowed them to use the coach to spend the day in Schwerin. Since Dora had moved in with Oliver in the old gardener's house a few hundred yards from the manor, she had been complaining that it was so sparsely furnished. There wasn't much to be had, but she hoped they would at least be able to buy colorful fabrics to sew pillows from. Or perhaps a candleholder for the sideboard in the living room.

Even if she couldn't buy anything, she'd still delight in window shopping and having Oliver all to herself for the entire afternoon. He helped her into her coat and wrapped her into a thick blanket as she settled on the coachman's seat.

"I can't even move," she protested.

"You'll be grateful for the warmth once we get going."

It had become rather chilly during the past weeks and the warm days of late summer were but a memory. In the cold season they got up before sunrise and went to bed long after. But even throughout the day, Gut Plaun seemed to be trapped beneath a thick blanket of fog that wouldn't let the sunlight pass and cast shadows over the land in an eerie way.

Personally she liked this time of year, since it reminded her of home. Not that the Ukraine was eerie and dark, but she'd often felt the melancholic mood after the harvesting season. As if nature itself was sad about the empty fields. It never lasted long, because once winter arrived with snow and ice, everything changed again.

People from the city often complained about the darkness of the winter, but this wasn't true in the countryside. As soon as the earth was blanketed with white snow, it never got truly dark, in contrast to the dreary November days.

"So quiet today?" Oliver asked. Usually she kept the conversation between them going. But today, she had an important announcement to make and didn't know how.

"It's all been a bit much."

"Are you nervous?"

"About what?"

"The wedding." He reached out to put his arm around her shoulders and she leaned against him in her cocoon.

"Not about the wedding."

"What then?" Oliver might not talk much, but he had a keen perception and picked up on mood changes both in humans and horses with ease. She had often observed him with the horses and sometimes wondered whether he could actually communicate with them. They definitely understood every word he said, and he seemed to be able to read them from the movement of their ears.

"Do you think the war will be over soon?"

"Who knows. All signs are pointing toward Hitler's defeat, but nobody can say how long it'll take. It could be weeks or years."

"Years?" Her voice screeched. "Kiev has just been liberated, that has to count for something?" Like most Ukrainians she hated the Russians, but since the initially welcomed German occupiers had turned out to be even worse, she had secretly rallied for the Red Army to oust them from her home country, in spite of her worries about what might happen to her, married to a German.

"As I said, we may believe the end is near, but you know the fanatic Nazis, they will drag it out until the last soldier has died, and there are still many, many men left in Germany."

A frightening thought constricted her throat. "You?" If the Nazis were desperate enough, would they draft him again, despite his war injury?

"It's not very probable, but I wouldn't put it past this lunatic as a measure of last resort. Rumors have it that men serving on the frontlines are hastily patched up and sent right back into combat, only to die from their injuries a week later."

"Now I'm even more worried."

"Don't be." He pressed a short kiss on her cheek. "For now I'm safe. Not only because of my injury, but also because as manager of an estate deemed important for the war effort, I'm exempted."

It was a small consolation.

"Let's not think about the war on such a beautiful day." As if to prove him right, the sun peeked through the fog, painting circles of light onto the landscape.

Biting her lip, she was quiet for so long that he turned toward her, concern etched into his features. "What's wrong?"

"I need to tell you something," she whispered softly, sensing how he stiffened at her words, and quickly adding, "It's nothing bad, I hope?"

"You're not going to tell me you've changed your mind and want to call off the wedding?" His voice was filled with panic.

"No, no." Suddenly she felt stupid. Oliver loved her, so why was she afraid to tell him?

"Then what is it?"

Dora peeled one hand out of the blanket and put it on his leg. "I'm expecting."

"You're... with child?" His voice was rough, incredulous even, but at least not furious as she'd worried he might be.

"Are you mad?"

He shook his head. "I'm... stupefied. God, Dora... I'm going to be a father. That is... unexpected."

"We will manage." Dora had never considered becoming a mother without her own mother, aunts, sisters and cousins nearby to help her raise a child. It simply had never occurred to her, and she understood Oliver's apprehension. Who would teach her how to deal with a baby all on her own?

Squeezing her hand, he said, "It's both frightening, and wonderful. And one more reason to get married right away." Oliver knew how much she missed her family and had wished they could attend her wedding.

Although more important reasons than love and nostalgia had convinced her it was best to tie the knot as fast as possible. Despite her German naturalization papers, people viewed her as a foreigner and were naturally suspicious. This, she hoped, would change after she became Mrs. Oliver Gundelmann.

"When is the baby due?"

"I have only missed my monthlies for the first time."

"But how can you be sure then?"

"I just know. It feels different." She smiled. "It will be a summer baby, and who knows by then the war might be over and we can visit my parents."

"Let's hope so." He stayed quiet for a while and then asked, "Does anyone else know?"

"No, and we should keep it that way until after the wedding."

"That's probably a good idea."

17

As the temperatures dropped, Margarete worried about the wellbeing of her workers. Last year she'd sourced blankets for them, which had been a challenge in itself, since all warm materials were sent to the Eastern Front.

But she feared it wouldn't be enough and she wondered what else she could do to ensure their survival over the winter. It didn't help that rations had been cut once again, for the manor and the factory, which left her hands tied when it came to supplementing their diet.

In addition, during the cold season there wasn't much food to be scrounged in the forest surrounding the estate. She'd asked the head of the farm to plant winter vegetables like red beet, kale and parsnips, though that wasn't much more than a drop in the ocean.

Oliver had told her that a group of young and relatively strong women had "died" and been led to live in a cave in the woods, but he had refused to tell her details, claiming she'd go there herself to look after them and might thus threaten the safety of anyone involved.

He knew her well. She wouldn't have been able to resist the

temptation to check up on them, bringing more warm clothes and more food. But she also knew he was right, Fräulein Annegret traipsing deep into the woods all by herself loaded with bags was bound to raise suspicions.

The ringing of the telephone interrupted her correspondence with several Nazi charitable organizations asking, or better demanding, her to do her bit for the war effort and donate. They requested anything from pots and pans, coats and boots, to money, all things she'd much rather give to the prisoners.

Yet, she had to uphold her cover and answered the letters with enthusiastic phrases, awaiting the ultimate victory, offering as little as she could without appearing to be stingy.

She picked up the receiver of her extension and said, "Yes, Frau Mertens, what is it?"

"Fräulein Annegret, Herr Volkmer wishes to see you."

That was quite unusual, because the factory manager normally dealt with Oliver. "Why doesn't he see Oliver?"

"Because you gave him the day off."

"Oh, right. Well, if it can't wait, send him up."

"Yes, Fräulein Annegret."

A short while later a knock came on the door and she called out, "Come in, please."

"Excuse me, Fräulein Annegret, I wouldn't have disturbed you, but it is important."

"Please have a seat and tell me what has you so aggrieved." She beckoned him to take a place on the armchair in her parlor.

"I probably should have talked to Herr Gundelmann, but I wanted your opinion first. The Wehrmacht logistics division confirmed that they can't supply the steel ball bearings we need for one of the production lines anytime soon."

Margarete tried to make an intelligent face, although she had no idea what exactly he was talking about. "Can't you use something else?"

He rubbed a finger across his chin. "Fräulein Annegret, all our machines are set up for precision work and axle bearings are an integral part to output quality. We can't run the machines at the needed speed and accuracy without the steel balls."

"Can we manufacture these balls ourselves? Perhaps redesigning one of the machines?"

He rolled his eyes, even as he tried to look respectful. Obviously she'd said something very stupid.

"Fräulein Annegret, that is a very good idea, unfortunately there's an acute steel shortage. We've been using less and less of the steel balls, but for technical reasons I won't go into, this isn't ideal. Suffice to say if we don't get replacements, we'll ultimately have to shut down some of the production lines."

Well, if that wasn't good news, what was? No more bombs for Hitler. But the joy lasted less than a few seconds, because if the factory stopped manufacturing, the Jewish workers would immediately be deported and the others relocated to another bomb-producing factory. There really was no way to win this game. She sighed, wondering when her life had become so complicated.

"For how long can you keep up with what we have?"

"Difficult to say, since wear depends on many things. I'd say we have replacements for about four to six weeks. Two months at the most."

She inhaled deeply. Two months, that gave them time to address the problem, though she had no idea how. But Herr Volkmer certainly had, or he wouldn't have come to ask for her opinion before consulting Oliver. She wondered what exactly he had in mind.

"Do you have a suggestion of what I could do to help?" After all, that was why he'd come, presumably, to request her help. Maybe he needed her to make a few phone calls, pull the weight of her name, mention the rank of her father.

"Actually there is something you could do, but..." He

seemed hesitant to spell it out. "It's a lot to ask from a young lady like yourself."

Now he had her intrigued. "Please, speak frankly and let me decide for myself."

"Normally we would simply order them from the supply office but with the war and all, our best chance of procuring what we need is to send someone to talk to the manufacturer directly."

"So you want me to telephone the manufacturer? Who is it?"

"His name is Herr Lindström, and he's in Stockholm."

"Stockholm? But that's in Sweden?"

"Yes, Fräulein Annegret, and it's a lot to ask, but I believe if you went personally, we would get the shipment we need to continue production."

"You want me to negotiate with Herr Lindström?"

"I'd give you all the specifics and your task would be to convince him to sell his products to you and not to the English."

Her eyes went wide. "The English are competing with us?"

"The whole world is in need of steel to produce their armaments. Sweden is the country that produces most of it. On top, they are neutral and can chose with whom to do business. Herr Lindström is known to value personal connections to business partners. So if you would pay him a visit..."

"Me? I don't know." She hedged. The whole affair seemed so daunting. Going to Sweden and talking face to face with a man who presumably was a rich and important industrialist in his country. *Remember, you're rich yourself!*

She could see Volkmer's point. If not even the Wehrmacht could get the needed materials from Herr Lindström, he wouldn't negotiate with some random factory manager either. But perhaps a rich heiress who shared a similar social status might be able to appeal to him. "Wouldn't I need a special permit to travel to Stockholm?"

"You would. That, by the way, is another point in your favor. A young woman might get a visa easier than a man who's needed for the war effort like me or Herr Gundelmann."

She nodded. "If you think it'll help, I'll do it."

"Thank you, Fräulein Annegret. I'll tell Herr Gundelmann in the morning and then we can arrange the details." He inclined his head and left the room.

Margarete got up. Once he'd left, she stood at the window overlooking the front yard. "Sweden? My goodness."

It was a frightening thought to travel all on her own. If only she could take Oliver with her, or Herr Volkmer. Even a foreman from the factory to support her with the technical details. But traveling as an unmarried woman with a man would certainly raise eyebrows.

She could vividly see Frau Mertens' disapproving gaze, lecturing her about the need to maintain her reputation. Perhaps the older woman would offer herself as chaperone. It was a tempting idea to take an ally with her, even if it was only the strict housekeeper. But then she shook her head, Frau Mertens was indispensable at Gut Plaun. Without her, none of the dozens of workers would get their meals.

Next, Dora came to her mind. She'd be the perfect chaperone, acquainted with Margarete's needs and preferences. In addition, it would be fun to have her as travel companion. Far away from the social restrictions at home, they could simply be friends who enjoyed a girl's night out in Stockholm.

Yes, she'd take Dora with her. Already on the way to pick up the telephone, she slowed down her steps. It wouldn't work. The maid would never get a travel permit, worse, the authorities might get suspicious if a recently Germanized Ukrainian requested a visa to neutral Sweden.

No, she couldn't risk exposing her maid. She could twist and turn it however she wanted, she had to chin up and travel alone.

The trip to Stockholm was the answer to her prayers. Hadn't Oliver talked about escape lines running through northern Germany to smuggle people out of the country?

If she went to Stockholm, she might be able to contact someone who helped operate these activities.

18

"The blacksmith is coming next week, but in addition to his usual pay he wants the right to shoot a deer in our forest," Piet said.

Oliver furrowed his brows. "That's quite unusual."

"He made it clear he won't come otherwise."

Oliver thought for a moment. Annegret had pressed the men to hunt more animals than normal to enhance the diet of both farm and factory workers, since meat was so hard to come by.

On the other hand, they needed the blacksmith urgently. One deer more wouldn't do any harm. "Tell him it's a deal, but he has to come to my office and I'll assign him the piece of forest where he can hunt."

He had to steer him clear of the cave where some ex-prisoners were hiding. They had strict orders to keep out of sight, but it would be inviting disaster to have the blacksmith, a staunch Nazi, hunting in the vicinity of their hideout.

"Good. Anything else?" Piet asked.

"No. I'd better get on my way." Oliver loved being at the stables and always found reasons to linger more than was actually needed. But since other work was waiting for him, he reluctantly took his leave to walk up to the manor.

About halfway, Annegret approached him, dressed in jodhpurs. "Good morning, Oliver."

"Good morning, Annegret. Going for a ride?"

"Yes. I was hoping you could accompany me."

"I'm sorry, but I'm needed in my office."

She laughed. "Come on, I know you want it."

"I really can't."

"This is important."

"Well then, your wish is my command." That much was true, but he was too responsible to neglect his other duties. "Only half an hour."

"That'll be enough."

As soon as they'd left the stables behind and were out in the fields, she steadied her horse into a walk. "Has Volkmer talked to you?"

"Not yet, we're due to meet this afternoon."

"There seems to be a shortage of steel ball bearings at the factory."

Oliver gazed at her in surprise. It was very peculiar that Herr Volkmer should confide in her about the shortage of some commodity.

"He suggested I travel to Sweden and visit with the manufacturer."

He stopped his horse and looked at her dumbfounded. "He did what?"

"That's what I thought too, but it makes sense. If production lacks they'll re-allocate workers and you know which ones they'll take first. And," she glanced around to make sure nobody was in sight. "I might find contacts over there who can help with our other problem."

It took him a few seconds to realize that she meant the Jewish workers who had to disappear. "Now that's a game changer. If you really could... I mean, that would be fantastic."

"See? I was hesitant at first, too, but last night I brooded over the situation for many hours instead of sleeping and I believe this opportunity is the answer to my prayers."

"Don't get your hopes up too high, nothing might come out of it," he warned her.

"I know, but then at least I tried. If I don't travel to Sweden, most definitely nothing will come out of it."

He laughed. "Well spoken. So I guess it's decided. You'll need a visa, a travel permit and who knows what else."

"Yes, that might be a problem. Perhaps Horst Richter can help."

"That should only be your last resort. The man in charge is Thomas and I wouldn't go over his head. Knowing him, he won't take it well if you don't pay proper homage to his authority. Besides, he seems to be quite fond of you, and that'll certainly help."

"Uggh..." She rolled her eyes. "Too bad I'm not fond of him."

"We all have to make sacrifices for the Reich," he said it with a teasing tone, but saw how she recoiled at his words and added, "A harmless flirt, nothing else. I never suggested you should get married to him." Though that was exactly what the politicians, kings and queens had done for centuries to cement their power. Hadn't Empress Maria Theresa of Austria famously married off her many children to crowned heads all across Europe? Including the very unfortunate Marie Antoinette to the King of France.

"I don't like it, but I do see your point. He keeps asking for a visit, so I guess I'll telephone his office this afternoon."

"It's a delicate situation, to be sure. But we need Thomas' goodwill for most everything, especially where the factory is concerned. Keep this man happy if you want your workers to survive."

"I'm afraid you are right." She looked so miserable he wanted to hug her.

They passed the junction to where the former prisoners were hiding. He wasn't due to check in on them until the next morning, but decided to pass by and let them know about the blacksmith. As soon as they reached the stables, he said goodbye to Annegret, walked into the unused quarantine box and grabbed the bag with provisions Dora had left there.

Then he mounted Sabrina again and returned to the forest. The patch where the prisoners had fortified an existing cave under his tutelage, was empty and silent, no trace of the presence of human beings. He had chosen this place because it was remote enough from the paths crisscrossing the forest as to be safe from passers-by.

He passed the entrance to the cave, continuing until he came to a deer stand. There he jumped down, tying Sabrina to a post. In the unlikely case someone came by, they'd recognize the horse as belonging to Gut Plaun and would assume the rider was working in the woods.

Then he returned to the entrance of the cave that was visible only to the expert eye and gave the agreed code phrase.

From the inside, he heard shuffled steps, then a wooden board was moved to the side, opening up a small gap, through which he squeezed inside.

"Herr Gundelmann, has something happened?" a woman named Carola asked him, alarm visible on her face, because she hadn't expected him until the next day.

"No, nothing. How are you coping?"

She led him into the surprisingly warm cave. They had cleverly constructed several ventilation holes that let in some light. Not enough to actually see anything, but at least it wasn't pitch-dark inside. "We're fine. The watch post saw a horse rider and warned us. That was you, right?"

"Yes." Oliver smiled with satisfaction. The devised warning system worked. The women were supposed to stay inside as much as possible, but he appreciated that being trapped inside a dark cave day and night for an extended period of time was unbearable. Thus the watch posts. "I brought more food." He handed her the bag.

"Thank you so much. We caught a fox last night and cooked it."

Grateful that he didn't have to resort to such exotic food, he wondered how fox tasted. "Make sure not to produce smoke."

"We do." Carola smiled at him. "We're very grateful for everything you have done for us."

They both knew that it was hard to live in the woods, even with regular provisions from the manor. Was it worse than toiling in the factory? Maybe. Certainly better than being shipped off to the east.

"I actually came here to give you a heads-up. The blacksmith is going to shoot a deer in our forest. I'll assign him a patch as far away from here as possible, but you never know."

"We'll be careful."

"Don't get scared if you hear shooting over the next days."

"Not easy to do that." Her fine features reminded him of Lena, the escapee Annegret had found last year and he wondered what Carola's background was. Almost imperceptibly he shook his head to thwart the thought. It was best not to know, since he didn't want to get attached to these people. Helping them required a clear head, unclouded by emotions.

"Is there anything else you need?"

She shrugged. "Freedom would be nice."

"Unfortunately that'll have to wait until after the war," he answered.

"Any news on that front?"

He knew the escapees were desperate for information, so he explained. "The Englishman is bombing Berlin to shreds. The frontline in the east is going back and forth, with no end in sight. The Americans are moving up the Italian boot, but Northern Italy is still controlled by the Nazis."

"That means we can't hope for a fast end." Her voice was even, not betraying the disappointment she must feel.

"I wish I could say anything different. Rumors have it that Germany cannot win this war, but Hitler will drag it out to the last man. And who knows how long that'll be." He felt he needed to give the woman some hope. "A year at most."

She sighed. "Let's hope it's earlier than that."

19

Thomas strode into his office with purposeful steps. Today would be the day when he organized what was long overdue: the round up and deportation of the remaining Jews in his district.

Goebbels had declared Berlin free of Jews several months earlier, and if it could be done in a metropolis of several million citizens, there was no reason why a single Jew should roam freely in his district.

"Lothar, I need you in my office," he called into the telephone to his subaltern, whom he'd graciously offered to be on first name basis several days ago. Not because he liked the man, or even enjoyed his company, but because it was easier to speak off the record when one used first names instead of rank.

He stopped in front of his impressive desk, satisfaction spreading across his face. For a poor boy he'd come far, and the next promotion was already in sight. Obediently reporting that his district was *judenfrei* would be the nudge his bosses needed to speed up the process and transfer him to a more important district, where he could do the same.

Katze announced his approach with clomping steps that

betrayed his questionable style and elegance. Rarely had a man looked so frumpy in the black SS uniform. It was a puzzle to him how the burly man had ever made it into the SS, since he was neither tall, blond, good-looking nor intelligent.

His only good traits were exceptional brutality and the habit not to question given orders. Apart from that, Thomas expected the other man to be lacking in morals as evidenced in the infuriating grant of exemptions for hundreds if not thousands of Jews. Hence, his offer to be on first name basis, to make him slip up.

"Yes, Thomas, what's up?"

"How many Jews are still in the district?"

"I'm not sure."

"How can you not know such a vital statistic?"

Lothar stood there looking crestfallen, not offering any explanation, or even an apology.

Thomas groaned. One day he would work with professionals only. Snappy, alert, intelligent, dapper men raptly listening to his orders and implementing them swiftly. "I have decided we shall follow the example set before us in Berlin and make this district free of Jews."

"Most of the remaining subjects work in ammunition factories," Lothar objected.

"That is not a problem. We'll start with the others. I want you to organize a raid tomorrow night. Get as many reinforcements as you can from neighboring districts and go in with the due determination."

Lothar's face lit up. An *Aktion* that involved roughing up Jews was much to his taste. "Consider it done."

Thomas nodded. "From now on no more exemptions. Send out a communication to all industrialists giving them a heads-up that we'll deport every last Jew in the district by next spring. That'll give them enough time to train new employees."

"*Sieg Heil!*" Lothar shouted in an exaggerated attempt to show his loyalty, clicked his heels and left the room.

Contemplating his next steps in the quest to extirpate the eternal enemy once and for all, Thomas asked his secretary to make him a coffee and settled down at his desk. Several minutes later the telephone rang, interrupting his strategizing.

"Oberscharführer Kallfass," he barked into the phone.

"Thomas?" a gentle voice asked.

"Annegret! My dear, what a pleasant surprise. To what do I owe this unexpected delight?"

"I have a small problem with the factory and was hoping you could give me some guidance."

His chest swelled with pride. That sweet woman had already taken to him in such a way that she consulted him for advice. "I am at your full disposal to help in any way I can."

"That is so incredibly kind. I had barely dared to hope that you wouldn't be too busy since I know you have so many more important tasks to attend to."

Like exterminating the Jews. He refrained from saying it aloud, since he remembered how squeamish she'd reacted on their ride out. Admittedly, it needed a strong stomach to tackle some of the gorier tasks.

"Should we meet in person to discuss your problem?"

"May I give you a first account over the phone? It's nothing secret."

"Certainly." It wasn't what he'd hoped for.

"It seems we are having a supply problem in the factory. Steel ball bearings, I have been told. My manager has located the manufacturer in Sweden. After talking to them on the telephone he feels we could get a much more positive outcome if I visited them in person. Do you think that's a good idea?"

"Hmm." He hadn't expected that. "A beautiful Fräulein all on her own in a foreign country? That might be a bit dangerous, don't you think so?"

"That's what I was thinking, too. But both Oliver and Franz

are both so busy, they won't be able to travel. And I can't just send anyone, can I?"

His mind worked feverishly. Her factory was important for the war production, and the Axis powers were continually short of steel ball bearings, or simply steel for that matter. If she could charm some Swedish industrial into selling her vast amounts of steel, it could have a powerful impact toward winning this war. But she was so trusting and kind, they would steamroll over her during the negotiations. She needed a man to protect her not only business-wise but also personally.

"I'll do it," he said, already dreaming about a cozy trip with Annegret, working closely together day and night. It would be their first accomplishment as partners, with many more to follow. They'd be Germany's new power couple, just younger, better looking, and more intelligent than even the Goebbels or von Ribbentrops.

"You'll do what?"

"I'll accompany you."

"Oh... I couldn't possibly accept that offer."

She was being modest and he liked that streak in her, it contrasted so nicely with many of the haughty society girls he'd met. "It's my pleasure and also my obligation to assist you in such an important matter."

"Well... then... I shall thank you so very much."

"Come to my office and I'll take care of the travel arrangements, including permits and visas."

"That is so nice of you. I really hate to be a burden, but if you insist, I'll make the trip to your office. Shall I bring Oliver or Franz with me to discuss schedules and such?"

"No need." He was desperate to have her alone and never one to let a good opportunity pass, he said, "Since you will be coming to Parchim anyway, would you do me the great honor of accompanying me to a dinner party on Saturday? It's nothing too formal; the mayor invited me to celebrate the birthday of his wife and I'd love to present you to some people."

"Thomas, thank you so much for the invite, but I'm afraid I'm indispensable at the manor at such short notice."

"Please don't say you don't have time. The food and the company will be excellent. You work so hard for our Fatherland, you deserve to enjoy the beautiful things in life."

"Serving my country is my joy."

He had got to hand it to her, she was incredibly determined not to slight her duties in favor of more pleasurable things. Another character trait that made her the perfect wife. Still, he got the impression her work was an excuse and in reality she'd love to attend the party. And which woman wouldn't want to? She simply needed a little nudge to silence her conscience. "We'll meet men who can help speed up the visa for our trip to Sweden."

"You never give up, do you?" she asked.

"Not when my heart is set on going out with the most beautiful woman in Germany."

"Now you're exaggerating. But I surrender to your efforts. Is there a dress code?"

His heart leapt with joy. Just the thought of holding her in his arms while gliding across the dance floor filled him with yearning. "Full-length evening gown for the women, gala uniform for the men. Shall we meet at five p.m. in my office and take care of travel formalities first, before heading to the mayor's house? We're expected there at seven."

"I'll be on time. Thank you so much again." Before he could say anything, she hung up, leaving him feeling slightly irritated. He'd hoped to continue chatting with her, but perhaps she was too shy, or reluctant to exchange compliments over the telephone.

For the rest of the day he walked on clouds, dreaming about

a spectacular future together with her. Nobody and nothing would be able to stop them once they joined forces.

In Sweden they would secure an important steel shipment. If Annegret—under his tutelage—negotiated well, it would suffice to supply not only her factory, but possibly the entire district. Then, the higher-ups in Berlin would inevitably take notice of him and give him a more prestigious position, as foreign commercial attaché perhaps? He and Annegret would travel the world, representing the Third Reich, being on first name terms with all the world leaders, politicians and industrialists alike.

When home in Germany, they would reside on the celebrity island of Schwanenwerder in Berlin, in a splendid villa, rubbing shoulders with Nazi leaders. The Führer, known to admire beautiful women, would be enchanted by Annegret and would become a frequent guest in their house.

Returning to the present, he picked up the phone receiver to call his boss and explain that he needed to travel to Stockholm.

"But why do you need to go there?" his boss asked.

"She's just a woman and afraid to travel alone. I offered myself, because I believe a well negotiated contract could be beneficial not only for her factory, but for the entire industry in the area, including the dockyards up at the Baltic Sea."

There was a pregnant pause on the line, leaving Thomas fearing his boss would deny the request.

"It wouldn't be wise if you participated in the negotiations, because those Swedes are sticklers with their neutrality."

"Yes, Herr Sturmscharführer, you're absolutely right." Thomas thought fast. "I never intended to, I thought more of consulting her before and after the negotiations. And to give her a feeling of security that the SS has her back and is protecting her."

"That is a noble intention. Doesn't she have a family member to chaperone her?"

"Unfortunately not. The French Résistance heinously killed her brothers last year, and her father, SS-Standartenführer Wolfgang Huber..."

"Oh, she's Huber's daughter?"

"Yes."

"Then, we absolutely must accompany her. When exactly is the trip planned? I might be able to travel myself."

Thomas squeezed his free hand into a tight fist to keep himself from screaming with frustration. "That would be very much appreciated. Let me talk to her and come back to you with the exact dates. May I tell her that either you or I will ensure her safety on this trip?"

"Yes. We need more forward-thinking men like you, Kallfass."

Thomas preened beneath the compliment. "Thank you, sir."

"By the way, have you been able to put an end to the resistance activities in your district?"

"I have some promising leads," he lied. If his boss wanted to see results, he could always arrest some shady figure and beat him into confessing whatever sin was required.

"Good. Good. Let me know any findings."

"Certainly, sir." Thomas hung up, deflated. He couldn't risk his boss being the one to accompany Annegret to Stockholm, or his entire plan would go up in flames.

A smile appeared on his lips and he called his boss's number again. The young secretary who'd eyed him with plenty of interest during his last visit, asked, "Was there anything else you needed, Herr Oberscharführer?"

After a short, flirtatious conversation, he knew his boss's unpostponable appointments and mapped out the visit to Stockholm accordingly. Fate was smiling down on him, since

Annegret's ball bearing shortage was going to benefit him in so many ways.

Most of all, he'd arranged for the perfect conditions to make his move on her. He, Thomas Kallfass, her most devoted admirer, giving her the confidence she needed when being away from her familiar surroundings. She'd be so grateful for his support—and hence amenable to his advances. He already imagined them enjoying the extravagances that came with a luxury hotel in a city that wasn't under the constant threat of Allied bombings. A bit of dining and mostly wining, and she'd succumb to his charms. Of course he'd be respectful, yet insistent, until she allowed him into her bed.

Since she was a well-bred young woman, she wouldn't take her slip-up lightly and he'd offer to get engaged right away to keep her reputation untainted.

His hand felt in the drawer of his desk to check the content of the box of condoms, but then thought better of it. If he impregnated her, it would be the culmination of their love, in addition to making things so much easier. With a baby on the way, he could request for a speedy process to get a marriage license. By the time the new year arrived, she might already be Mrs. Thomas Kallfass.

He leaned back in his seat, pleased with himself and the world.

20

"This gown is lovely," Dora said as she helped Margarete put on the floor-length midnight-blue taffeta gown.

"You don't think it's too flamboyant?" Parchim wasn't Paris and Margarete had no idea how the other women would dress and she didn't want to outshine the birthday girl.

"Not at all. It is very subtle."

Margarete looked into the mirror, noticing the strategically placed folds and drapes. Walking a few tentative steps, the fabric rustled along the floor, making it seem as if she were floating.

"Don't worry, it will be perfect." Dora knelt by her side to fix a torn hem. "But you need higher heels, or you'll step on it."

"Bring me the matching blue ones from the other closet." It was one of the several outfits Wilhelm had bought for her in Paris, and slightly too elegant for the occasion, but she had no time to call the seamstress to alter one of the gowns Frau Huber had left in Gut Plaun.

"The Oberscharführer will be delighted, I can assure you of that."

Margarete pulled a face and shook her head. "I'm only doing this because I couldn't find a way out of it."

"He does look quite dashing and has impeccable manners."

Margarete rolled her eyes. "Sometimes I wish I could simply disappear."

Dora gasped. "Please, don't say that, Fräulein Annegret. So many people depend on you."

"Don't worry, I won't do anything stupid." Although she often felt like the situation was overwhelming her. No sooner had she come to terms with her role as Annegret Huber, the next problem had come along in the form of Thomas Kallfass, who was intent on courting her.

Her stomach tied into knots thinking about the party tonight and the plenty of occasions it would give him to get handsy, while she had to grin and bear it. It might be preferable to allow him into her bed, close her eyes and think of the people she protected. If he got what he was after, he might get bored soon enough and move on to other conquests.

"Which pieces did you want to wear?" Dora held out the open jewelry box for her to choose.

Margarete looked at the diamonds, worth a small fortune. She hadn't dared to sell them to buy extra food or fake identity papers, out of fear someone might recognize the family heirloom and ask unwelcome questions.

An idea crossed her mind. She smiled. If papers could be falsified, so could diamonds. She'd have to make careful inquiries.

"How about the cameo and the bracelet?" Margarete pointed to the pieces.

Dora nodded and helped her affix the brooch to the chain around her throat. "You look lovely."

"You did a great job with my hair," she complimented Dora, picking up a hand-held mirror to inspect the back of her head. Her brown hair was twisted up into large curls pinned in a basket pattern to the back of her head. Her skin glowed with health, unlike her factory workers who were always pale and gaunt. Margarete reminded herself that whatever awaited her later that night, it was nothing compared to what the prisoners had to put up with every single day.

"Thank you, Fräulein Annegret. May I ask you a question?" Dora said, looking at the coffee table, where Margarete had left a few biscuits on the plate.

"Go ahead."

"May I have your permission to take these biscuits?"

Margarete automatically nodded, before she considered the question to be strange. "Doesn't Frau Mertens feed you enough?"

"No. That's not it." Dora curtsied nervously.

"Then what do you need the biscuits for?"

Dora worried her lower lip.

"If you want my help, you need to tell me the truth."

"My friend Olga, she's a foreign worker like me and..."

"They don't feed her properly." Margarete felt the rage rushing over her.

"No, Fräulein Annegret." Another curtsy. "Remember you asked me to put out my feelers?"

Margarete nodded.

"Turns out Olga's employer is hiding a young girl, and they don't have a ration card for her."

That could mean only one thing. The girl didn't possess proper papers, possibly a Jew gone underground. "Isn't her employer the old Frau Gusen?"

"Yes. She and Olga might help us with other things, too," Dora said.

"I see. I'll make sure to always leave food on my plate from now on."

"Thank you so much, Fräulein Annegret." Dora prepared

to leave, but Margarete stopped her with a gesture. "Be careful, we don't want Frau Mertens to accuse you of stealing."

"I will."

Just as Dora closed the door, the phone rang and Margarete picked up the receiver. "Yes?"

"Nils is out front with the coach," Frau Mertens informed her.

"I'll be right down." Due to petrol rationing they rarely used the automobile these days. She could have applied for an additional allowance, but had decided to stay as inconspicuous as possible. In addition, using the coach instead of the motorized vehicle was one more way to show her dedication to the war effort.

Thomas, naturally, had offered to come and get her, but luckily she'd been able to talk him out of that endeavor. In no way did she want to depend upon him to return home after the party, since being alone with him in the confined space of a vehicle at night would only invite situations she didn't welcome. No, she'd much rather have Nils waiting for her, ready to drive her home whenever she desired to leave.

She descended the stairs, mindful of the full-length gown and high heels she was wearing. Frau Mertens was waiting for her, giving her a once over, before she handed her a hat and coat. "Wishing you a nice evening, Fräulein Annegret."

"Thank you." Margarete stepped through the front door and walked toward the coach, where Nils helped her up. Once seated, he put a thick blanket around her shoulders and another one across her legs.

"That should keep you warm, Fräulein Annegret."

"I'm fine."

He took the reins into his hands and clucked his tongue to put the horses into a trot. "Wouldn't you be more comfortable in the automobile?" he asked after a while.

"I'd rather save the petrol for an emergency."

He nodded, never one to talk much. Therefore she was quite surprised when he spoke up several minutes later. "This war has been going on much too long already." She jerked her head toward him in shock. What he said was nothing short of undermining military morale and punishable by death. "Don't look so disturbed, Fräulein Annegret. I may be old, but I'm not stupid. I know what you're doing and all this touting for the war effort doesn't fool me."

She swallowed, fearing he might be a mole, tasked with hearing her out. "I know nothing about military strategy, but I agree with you on one thing: there have been too many victims and we're all looking forward to the time when the war has been won." She purposefully didn't add *by Germany*, to leave it open where her allegiances lay rather than implicating herself.

Nils chuckled. "I could have denounced you plenty of times if I'd wanted to. You know, I supported Hitler back then when he planned to take back what they stole from us in the Versailles Treaty. But this? He's become greedy and deluded, if you ask me."

"If this is how you think, then why don't you do anything?" she finally said.

"I'm a simple old man. What could I do?" He shrugged. "Nothing but keep my feet still and wait."

She had a sharp retort on her tongue, but thought better of it. He, like everyone else, was afraid of the Gestapo and SS. As long as it didn't affect them personally, most people preferred to bury their heads in the sand and pretend not to notice what was going on.

At least she had discovered his true feelings toward Hitler and might use that knowledge at a later point. Nils might not actively resist, but she could count on him not to report anything peculiar he saw around the estate.

As they arrived in front of the SS headquarters, she gave him the evening off. "I don't know yet how long this party will last. Here are some Reichsmark, so you can wait in the pub over there."

"That won't be necessary," he said, despite looking eagerly at the offered notes.

"Don't be silly. It'll get cold waiting out here all night."

"Thank you, Fräulein Annegret."

Once he was gone, she wondered whether it had been a mistake to give him the money, since he might get drunk as a sailor and wouldn't be able to drive them back to the manor. She shrugged it off, since she'd come to know him as a responsible man.

Margarete squared her shoulders and forced a pleasant smile on her face as she entered the SS headquarters. It wasn't so much the institution that caused her to shiver, because she'd gotten used to dealing with Nazi authorities face to face, but the prospect of having to confront Thomas.

As unobtrusive as he was, he had designs on her—and she didn't know how much longer she could avoid his advances without offending him. For the sake of the prisoners under her care, she'd have to put a good face on the matter.

He must have been waiting for her because he strode down the stone tiled hallway the moment she stepped through the door.

"Good afternoon, Annegret," he greeted her effusively, reaching for her hand and blowing a kiss on its back. "You look absolutely glamorous."

"Thank you, Thomas." Her smile was frozen on her lips as she took his offered arm and followed him to his office. The rustling of the taffeta echoed from the empty walls, making her acutely aware of her overly elegant attire. She just hoped they wouldn't run into other clientele.

"Here we are." He opened the door to his office and beckoned for her to step inside.

It was the first time she'd come here since Thomas had

taken the position and she had to give him credit for the changes he'd made to the formerly drab office. It sported not only the obligatory Hitler portrait and Swastika flags hanging on both sides of it, but he'd filled the dark wooden walls with expensive paintings and a magnificent chandelier adorned the windowsill.

He must have noticed her gaze, because he asked, "You like it?"

"The chandelier is exquisite. I believe one of the most precious ones I've ever seen."

His face lit up with pride. "You wouldn't believe that a Jew could have such delicate taste. I acquired the chandelier alongside the paintings and other stuff a week ago when we deported another round of this scum."

"How nice." She almost gagged.

"That weasel had an entire attic full of hidden treasures rightfully belonging to the German nation."

Her self-control was reaching its limit and she couldn't suppress a sarcastic remark. "It's a wonder you didn't catch a nasty disease from touching it."

He looked crestfallen, involuntarily wiping his hands on his uniform. "You think so? I had it cleaned and polished, but perhaps I should call the pest controller to give it a thorough fumigation."

"Oh." She had to exert all her strength not to break out into laughter, or groan with despair. "I'm sure a good cleaning is enough."

Giving her a doubtful glance, he clicked his heels and said, "Shall we attend to business before changing over to pleasure?"

"Yes, please." Margarete wondered how much longer she could hold up the plastered smile. This turned out to be a lot more tedious than entertaining a room full of eager SS men in Paris. At least there, Wilhelm had watched over her, cutting short all unwelcome advances from his colleagues.

Here she was on her own—and she depended on Thomas'

goodwill to issue travel papers, exemptions for Jewish workers, needed supplies, and whatnot. Thomas of all men, was the one she couldn't give the cold shoulder to.

"I have taken the liberty to issue your travel permit and prepare your visa application. You just need to sign it and I'll send it off to Berlin with priority mail in the morning."

"That is so kind of you." She bent over the desk to pick up a pen and signed the forms he'd deposited there. Thomas stood by her side, looking at her with nauseatingly lovesick eyes. "Is that all?" she asked.

"Just another stamp and they can go into the mail." He opened the right drawer of his desk, taking out a wooden box with a key in the lock. Once open, the interior exposed several stamps lying on red velvet. With an assured movement he grabbed one of them, pressed it on the huge ink pad on his desk and then on the two documents she had just signed.

"That's it." He blew over the fresh ink, looking at her expectantly.

Unsure what she was supposed to say she resorted to thanking him. "Thank you so much again. I wouldn't know what to do without you."

His smile intensified and he stepped so near his aftershave seemed to caress her cheek. "You never have to. I'm fully at your disposal."

"That's nice to know." Her neck hair stood on end and she quickly stepped out of his reach.

"I have a surprise for you."

"For me?"

"Yes. I can't let a lady in distress fend for herself, now can I?"

She didn't feel distressed at all, except for him being much too insistent.

"I'm able to accompany you to Sweden. My boss gave his

permission and my visa request will be handled together with yours. Won't that be fantastic? We'll be an invincible team."

Her features derailed, but she caught herself within a second. "That is truly a surprise, Thomas." He'd told her the idea over the phone, but she'd pushed it away, hoping it wouldn't come to fruition.

"What better way to celebrate than heading over to the party. Shall we?" He held out his arm for her, and there was nothing she could do but take it.

21

Thomas couldn't keep his eyes off Annegret. She looked truly stunning in her midnight-blue gown and the ruffle of the taffeta when she walked sent little shivers of anticipation through his limbs.

It would be such a pleasure to slowly open the zipper of her dress, slipping the sleeves from her shoulders and watch the gown fall until it pooled around her feet like a beautiful pond.

His loins itched at the thought of her porcelain skin exposed to his view. He'd caress it softly with his fingers and press little kisses—

"Heil Hitler!" Lothar Katze saluted.

"Heil Hitler!" Thomas and Margarete followed suit. She had slipped from his arm to give the salute and he acutely felt the loss of her softness close to him.

"This is my subaltern Unterscharführer Katze," he introduced him, cursing Lothar's bad timing.

Annegret bowed her head in acknowledgement. "We already had the pleasure. The Unterscharführer was essential in exposing the crimes of my late father's estate manager."

Katze grinned like she'd offered him a candy. Thomas,

though, pursed his lips, how come he didn't know about that story? It was hardly believable that the below-average man had single-handedly solved a crime.

Trying to get rid of Lothar, he said, "We are due at the mayor's house."

"I know, I'm going there myself," the insufferable man responded.

"What a nice coincidence. Would you like to join us?" asked Annegret, much to Thomas' chagrin. How could she even entertain the idea to keep the company of this man?

Seeing how Lothar accepted the invitation eagerly, he forced himself to be polite. Annegret must feel pity for the man who'd had to attend the occasion without company. And the nice person she was, she'd offered to include him in their party. That might not be in Thomas' current interest, but it showed once more how perfect a wife and hostess she would make.

"It's only a three-minute walk across the market square," he said with a gaze downward to her feet.

"As long as it doesn't rain."

His love for her grew with every second and once again he held out his arm, but she didn't seem to notice, because she was conversing with Lothar.

Once they crossed the square, they stood in front of an elegant three-story structure. Men and women in formal dresses were arriving, both on foot and in vehicles, but none of the ladies looked as beautiful and pure as the one by his side. Annegret was truly the epitome of an Aryan woman, the only blemish one might point out being her brown hair. Perhaps after their wedding she could dye it blonde.

The mayor and his wife stood at the entrance, personally welcoming their guests.

"Oberscharführer Kallfass. The lovely Fräulein Annegret Huber. What a pleasure to have you with us."

"The pleasure is all mine, Mayor." She extended her hand

in its long glove with inimitable grace, revealing the difference between a well-bred German society girl and those who just pretended to belong.

Inside, the ushers showed them to a large round table with elegant dinnerware and fine crystal goblets, while Lothar was led to a second, smaller table. Thomas couldn't help but heave a sigh of relief. He surely didn't need his subaltern to occupy Annegret's attentions throughout the evening.

As soon as all the thirty-something guests had taken their seats, a waiter came and filled the glasses with champagne. The mayor toasted his wife, Thomas as the highest-ranking SS officer gave a speech in the name of the Reich, and then more waiters rushed in and filled the table with platters loaded with food.

"I almost forgot these things existed," Annegret said as she bit into a slice of orange.

He frowned. "Don't you have oranges at the manor?"

She looked at him slightly puzzled. "There are no rations for exotic fruits."

"You need to use ration cards?"

"We do."

"I'm sure if you put in a request, you'll be exempted. I'll put in a good word for you with my superiors." His chest inflated. Poor Annegret who had to put up with the nuisances of normal folk. She would be grateful for his help.

Much to his surprise, she shook her head. "That is incredibly thoughtful of you, but I would feel like we at Gut Plaun aren't doing our bit for the war effort if I accepted your offer."

His chest deflated. Had she just scolded him for being unpatriotic? Certainly not. "If this is your wish, my dearest Annegret."

After dinner, a man settled at the piano to play a Viennese waltz. The mayor and his wife did the honors and one by one the other couples joined them on the dance floor.

"Shall we?" he asked Annegret, who enthusiastically agreed.

She was light as a feather in his arms and danced the way she did everything: with poise and as if she'd done nothing else for all her life. Much later, when they both were short of breath from exertion, he led her back to their table.

After some more speeches in honor of the Führer, the Reich and the imminent victory, the waiters brought a selection of desserts. He indulged in the sweetness of a cream cake, the full aroma of chocolate mousse, savoring it to the fullest, because even for a man in his position these sweets were a rare treat, since sugar was exceptionally hard to come by.

When he invited Annegret for another dance, she politely declined. "I'm so sorry, but my feet are hurting." After glancing at the delicate watch on her wrist, she added, "I probably should call it a night. It's a long way back to the manor and we get up very early on the estate."

Disappointment fought with pride at her determination to make herself useful. It was heart-warming to see how she fully supported the war effort, even to the extent of denying herself the pleasure of dancing the night away.

"Let me escort you out."

"Thank you. Nils is waiting for me at the local inn."

"That's much too far to walk with your sore feet." He turned around and instructed one of the waiters to rush over and tell Annegret's driver to pick her up at the mayor's house.

Much too soon, her servant pulled up with the coach and got out. Thomas helped her climb onto the box seat, inwardly cringing. That means of transport was not befitting her social status. He should have insisted on driving her in his black office automobile.

Distracted by his thoughts, he'd waited a second too long, and her lovely face was already out of reach for the kiss he'd intended to press on her cheek.

He contented himself with kissing her knuckles and said, "I had a lovely evening. Thanks for accepting my invitation."

"It was my pleasure. Goodnight."

"Goodnight." Then he stood and watched the coach disappear into the night, his heart yearning to meet her again.

22

Oliver tossed the delivery slip onto his desk and picked up his schedule for the remainder of the day. More deliveries were scheduled, both for the factory and the estate. A shipment of ammunition was to be sent by train the next day and he needed to double check with Franz that everything was in order.

A knock on the door interrupted him. "Come in."

"Morning, boss." Piet stood in the doorway, filling it with his sturdy frame. His visit meant trouble, because it was most unusual for the stable master to come up to the manor to seek him out.

"What's the problem?"

"About half of the lads have just been drafted."

"How's this possible? We requested exemptions for all of them."

Piet shook his head. "We didn't for the young lads. They sent notice to everyone turning seventeen within half a year."

"But they're not supposed to be drafted until their birthday." Oliver beckoned for Piet to sit in front of the desk. "I suppose now that they've got their papers, it's too late to ask for exemptions."

"Yes. They'll tell us to get new stable hands."

"New ones from where? Most of the younger boys are with the Hitler Youth operating anti-aircraft guns or whatever other stuff. Are we supposed to employ eleven-year-olds who don't know the mane from the tail of a horse?"

"The Wehrmacht told me to make do with who we have," Piet said.

Oliver jumped up. "God, kill me now! Do these desk jockeys even know what utter bollocks they're spouting?"

Piet smirked. "Fact is, we need more hands, boss. There's a delivery coming up in spring and the horses aren't ready, not by a long shot."

"I'll see what I can come up with. Meanwhile, use the farmhands if you must." Harvest was done and they were about to release the seasonal workers, mostly foreign civil workers.

"Will do, boss." Piet left the room, leaving Oliver to think.

Maybe he could solve two problems with one strike. The stables weren't monitored by the SS, but by the Wehrmacht. The two institutions didn't see eye to eye on many issues and often worked uncoordinated. If there were knowledgeable horsemen among the Jewish prisoners in the factory, he could move them to the stables to replace the drafted boys.

That would increase the 'churn' Thomas wanted so much, since any cursory observer would naturally assume the Jews had died. Nobody would invest time to verify their actual fate. Out of sight, out of mind.

He jumped up to fetch his coat and hat, rushing into the small dining room where Annegret was taking her breakfast.

"Oliver, why in such a hurry?" she greeted him, sipping from her coffee.

"I think I have a solution to our problem."

Her head jerked up. "You have?"

"Can we go for a walk?"

She nodded. Both of them knew better than to risk being

overheard. "Give me a minute." She rang a bell and Dora came inside, stopping in her tracks with the brightest smile, when she saw him. Giving him a wink, she turned toward her mistress. "Fräulein Annegret, would you like some more to eat?"

"No. Please get me my boots and the heavy coat. We're going to take a look at the paddock."

"Yes, Fräulein Annegret." As fast as she had arrived, she disappeared and returned minutes later with the requested garments.

She exchanged her elegant house slippers for the sturdy boots, put on her coat, hat and gloves. "Ready."

As soon as they were out of earshot, Oliver explained. "Piet told me half of his lads have been drafted this week. And I thought we could replace them with Jewish workers from the factory."

"But they'd still be at risk of deportation, maybe even more so, because the stable hands aren't essential workers."

"We would have to let them die at the factory, so they don't show up on any lists."

"But how can we legally employ dead people?" Annegret asked, as they walked along the paddock, checking the fence poles to keep up appearances.

"We can't. But if we got them false identification papers—"

"We ruled that out already. Or have you found a source?"

"Hear me out first. For the men—and the stable hands must be men—we can't give them German papers or they risk being drafted."

"Right, I hadn't thought of that."

"But what if we somehow arrange for foreign papers? We could use Dora's ID as a sample. They don't even have to be perfect, because police here won't know the difference to a genuine one."

She wrinkled her nose. "That might work... And then we bribe someone at the labor office to give them a work permit."

"Or we steal blank permits."

She stopped and shook her head. "That's too dangerous. At least around here where everyone knows each other. It would only be a matter of time until the man in charge of the labor office gets the scent of it and then we're done for."

His shoulders slumped, because she was right. They had to get the man in charge onto their side. There were simply too many people working at Gut Plaun to keep this a secret, and they couldn't feign ignorance either, since they always went through the labor office for civil workers. His idea wasn't as foolproof as he'd thought.

Annegret gave him an encouraging nod. "Don't be sad. Who's in charge of the labor office?"

"There's the local one, but he's a staunch Nazi and will first take the bribe and then rat us out."

"What about Parchim?"

"Not sure that's a good idea with Thomas intent on making this a model district."

She shuddered. "And I really don't want to spend any more time than necessary with him. The thought of him accompanying me to Stockholm already has my stomach tied in knots."

"You don't have to go, you know that?"

"But I must. Lives depend on me." She put out her chin in a show of inner strength that was the complete opposite to her sweet looks and kind demeanor. "Back to our other problem. What about the labor office in Schwerin?"

"That's a long way from here."

"You went there when I fired you, remember?"

He remembered all too well the dark days when his entire life had been upended by Gustav's intrigue.

"Here's an idea," she continued. "You ask in town if they can provide you with a few legal foreign workers, but it won't be enough. Then you ask in Schwerin. In such a big town there must be someone open to bribes."

"That might work. We don't even need fake papers for them, because they can pretend they were destroyed in a bombing. We should pay Stefan a visit."

Her cheeks took on a rosy hue. "What does he have to do with this?"

"First, he hates the Nazis and second he worked at the dockyards in Schwerin and might know who we can ask for help."

"Good. You go to the local labor office and I'll talk to Stefan," she suggested.

"Alright." Oliver grinned. He hadn't failed to notice how interested she was in the fisherman.

"There's one more thing I'd like to suggest," she said.

"Go ahead."

"There's an older man in the factory kitchen. His name is Ernst Rosenbaum. Can you see that he gets moved to the stables once we have the permits? He doesn't have experience with horses, but he is a fast learner."

"And you want him safe?" Oliver looked at her as she bowed her head to signal affirmation. He wondered what her interest in him was, since a kitchen worker already had it comparatively easy. A few seconds later it clicked in his head. Her real name was Margarete Rosenbaum. The old man must be a relative of some sort.

The epiphany took his breath away. How awful it had to be to find your own family in such deplorable conditions and not being able to get them out.

"I'll keep him in mind," he said, swearing to himself that he'd make sure her relative survived.

23

The next morning, Margarete had an unexpected, but welcome visitor. She looked up from her work, as Dora came into her rooms.

"He's here to see you, Fräulein Annegret," Dora said with excitement.

"Who is he?"

"The fisherman."

"Oh my God! How do I look? Give me five minutes, before you bring him into the parlor, will you?"

"You look very nice."

Margarete shooed her away, and rushed into her private bathroom to refresh herself and brush her hair. After a last glance into the mirror, she took a deep breath and stepped into the parlor.

Less than a minute later, a knock on the door announced her visitor and she put on a neutral expression, hoping to conceal her nerves. "Good morning, Stefan, what a wonderful surprise."

"The pleasure is all mine." He waited until Dora had left

the room and closed the door, before he continued. "I'm here because of our last conversation."

It was a thrill and a disappointment at the same time, since she'd secretly hoped he had come to see her.

"I remember it well. Is there anything I can help you with?"

His intense blue eyes scanned the room, before he answered. "Is it safe to talk?"

"It is. But if you prefer, we can take a walk?"

"That won't be necessary, it's raining." His gaze rested on her for much too long to be appropriate.

"I'm not the spoilt girl you believe I am... and I have a raincoat," she protested.

He broke out into a huge grin. "You truly aren't who you pretend to be."

Panic surged through her veins, but she shrugged it off. He hadn't meant his words literally—and even if he knew the truth, wasn't he helping her kind? She had nothing to fear from him.

"Don't look so scared. We can stay inside, no problem. It'll be more suspicious if the two of us traipse around in that drenching rain. It would give the town gossips plenty of fodder."

"Right. Can I offer you something to drink? A hot cup of coffee, maybe?"

"A coffee would be nice."

She beckoned him to take a seat and picked up the telephone to order coffee and biscuits from the kitchen. Then she sat opposite him. "So why are you here?"

"There has been a problem, and we need to move a person fast."

"And you are asking me to hide them here?"

"It would only be for a few days, until another transport can be arranged."

"What kind of transport?"

He pressed his lips into a thin line.

She sighed. "You're not going to tell me anything, are you?"

"No."

"Can I at least know the name of the person?"

"No." He furrowed his brows. "She's a youth and goes by the name of Maria."

"Maria, how original." Half of the German girls must be called Maria either as a first or second name.

"Originality is not always advisable."

"Ach, Stefan, if you want me to help you, you need to trust me!" In that moment, a knock came on the door. "Come in!"

Dora opened the door and entered with a tray. She set the table for two and disappeared with a wink at her mistress, who felt herself flush.

"If I didn't trust you I wouldn't be here." Stefan bit into the deliciously smelling sweet bread rolls fresh from the oven. Thanks to their beehives, Gut Plaun produced some honey. "But the less you know, the safer for everyone involved."

She grumbled her acceptance. How often had she stated the same phrase? "When shall this happen?"

"Today."

"You aren't a man of many words, are you?" she said in an attempt to break through his reserve.

"No." He softened his gruff answer with a charming smile that warmed her insides. For him, she would hide all the fugitives in the world.

Deciding, if he trusted her with the life of a girl in hiding, she would trust him with her secrets, too, she said, "I'll take her in and others if the need arises, but I need something from you in exchange."

His eyebrow shot up, his expression becoming wary. "What?"

"We have people in need ourselves. Oliver mentioned you might have contacts at the labor office in Schwerin."

If he was surprised by her request, he didn't show it. His voice was as calm as before when he asked, "To do what?"

"Give us permits for foreign civil workers who lost their identification in a bombing."

"Well played, Fräulein Annegret. You certainly are a lot more than you appear to be."

"I take that as a compliment." She didn't care whether he'd meant it that way, although the warm glimmer in his eyes gave her reason to believe that he shared the feelings she had for him.

"His name is Hubert Falke. Don't mention me. He's not on our side, but he urgently needs money to pay gambling debts."

"Thank you. Is there anything else?" she asked, taking the last bite of her bread roll.

He took a deep breath, before he asked, "There's a dance two weeks from now. Would you go with me?"

"Me?" she replied, looking over her shoulder just in case he might be talking to someone else.

"Unless you don't want to..."

"No. I mean, yes. I'd love to."

"Really?"

"Really. But aren't dances forbidden?"

A smile lit up his weather-beaten face. "Don't we all do forbidden things once in a while?"

"I guess." She couldn't well argue with him. After discussing traitorous activities, going to a clandestine meeting where young people danced was one of her least severe crimes.

"Shall I pick you up with my bicycle to get into town? From there we take the train."

She hesitated for a moment. "I'd rather meet you in town than perch on the handlebars."

Again he laughed infectiously. "It does have a rack, but if you prefer to meet in town, shall we say, six o'clock at the train station? Saturday in two weeks?"

"That would be perfect." Her mind was already going through her wardrobe to think of the perfect outfit to wear.

"Whom shall I contact about Maria?"

She thought quickly. Since the request had come as a surprise, she had nothing prepared. Nevertheless, it was best if she wasn't directly involved. "Bring her to the main gate after dark. Dora, my maid who you just met, will be waiting there. Make sure you aren't seen."

"This war won't go on forever." He said it with such assurance that she wondered whether he had information that wasn't readily available. Although he'd probably never tell her even if she asked.

"I should hope not."

24

Finally, the deportations were gathering steam and Thomas was well on his way to ridding the district of Jews.

A knock came on the door. "Come in."

A man in his sixties with a full head of white hair entered. He was using a cane, but walked surprisingly fast for an old man. His chest flaunted the Golden Party Badge, an honor awarded to party members from before 1933 or those with special merits.

"Herr Naumann, how can I help?" Thomas jumped up to show the rich industrialist the appreciation he deserved.

"May I sit?" Herr Naumann asked.

"Of course. Can I offer you something? Coffee, maybe?"

"My wife insists it's not good for my health, but if you happen to have real coffee, I'd certainly drink one."

"I'm so sorry." Thomas blushed. He hadn't been able to get real coffee anywhere. It seemed the few pounds still available in the country were reserved exclusively for the highest brass. "A schnapps, perhaps?"

Herr Naumann nodded, settled awkwardly into the offered

chair and came straight to the point. "I've come here because of the deportations."

Thomas had given all the businessmen a heads-up to replace the Jews working for them with more suitable people. "If you're worried about replacing the Jews, we can get you as many foreign workers as you need."

"That's exactly what I'm worried about, son."

Thomas hated the condescending tone, but didn't dare to disrespect the bearer of a Golden Party Badge with a sharp retort.

"You don't seem to understand why these Jews are essential for my factory. They work better and more efficiently than the foreigners, because they know it's their only chance to survive. Desperation does wonders for morale." Herr Naumann smirked.

"We can assign two foreigners for every Jew you have to let go." Thomas tried to keep the frustration out of his voice. Why couldn't the businessmen be more reasonable?

"Apart from the obvious problems this creates, have you ever thought how much more prone foreign workers are to sabotage? I'll have to employ trustworthy supervisors to keep an eye on them, and as you know German men are mostly needed as soldiers these days."

Did he hear a hint of criticism in the old man's voice? In any case, he was turning into a nuisance and Thomas decided to cut the conversation short. "I do agree with all the ifs and buts you bring up, but never forget that it's the Führer's dearest wish to rid his beloved Germany of the Jewish plague. My intention is to deliver him a district free of Jews for his birthday in April, and I'm sure whatever sacrifice is needed, it will be well worth it to make our Führer happy."

"It is settled then," Herr Naumann stated, obviously knowing when further resistance was futile. "How much time do I have to make the necessary changes at my factory?"

"Calculate on a month or two at the most. We'll have a concerted action arresting every last Jew on the same day."

"What about those from the camps?"

"I didn't know you used prisoners in your factories."

Herr Naumann shook his head. "Not me. My workers are there on their own account. But some of my fellow industrialists do."

"It was Himmler himself who ordered to make all camps on German ground free of Jews. Why should the criminals being held in camps have a better fate than the rest of the pack? No, every single Jew, whether already a prisoner or not will be deported."

"I understand." Herr Naumann leaned forward. "You are clearly an honest man, dedicated to racial purity. This has become a rare combination, considering everything we know."

Thomas bristled. "The Führer's wish is my command, and it should be yours, too."

"It is." The old man leaned on his cane to stand up and walked toward the door, where he turned around and said, "Although... Aren't you sometimes afraid that this will come back to haunt us?"

Thomas was not. Instead he made a mental note that Herr Naumann was old and getting soft. More SS presence in his factories might be needed to keep things running smoothly.

25

"Dora, we need to go," Oliver called out, wondering what was taking her so long. They were late getting into town to the registry office.

Suddenly she appeared in the main entrance to the manor, where she, Frau Mertens and Annegret had put the last touches to her outfit. Due to tradition, and superstitions, as he often remarked, the groom hadn't been allowed to see the bride in her dress before the big day.

His jaw dropped. She looked absolutely stunning in her lightweight off-white gown with little roses appliquéd on it. She'd mentioned that Annegret had offered to alter one of Frau Huber's dresses for her, but he'd never imagined such an amazing outcome.

Looking down at his worn and aged black Sunday suit, he suddenly felt inadequate. The next moment he shrugged the sensation aside and pride mixed with love rushed through his veins as he took in Dora's appearance. Her hair was braided and pinned up in an elaborate hairdo. The high-waisted dress had a wide-swinging skirt enhancing her lithe figure. Only a person who knew the treasure she carried under her heart would make out the slight bump forming beneath the material.

This instant, she was merely a blushing bride but in another five months she would become the mother of his child. A fact that made him proud and terrified at the same time. There didn't seem a fast end to the awful war and every day both of them got sucked deeper into the traitorous activities that would cost them their lives if they were found out.

He took her elbow and directed her out to the waiting coach, where he helped her up on the box seat together with Annegret, who looked elegant, yet modest in her dark-green two-piece suit with matching gloves and hat, a warm woolen stole around her shoulders. He wrapped his bride in a thick blanket, careful not to damage the fine dress, and couldn't resist stealing a kiss from her lips, although he was supposed to wait until after the ceremony.

The rest of the employees lined up beside the coach. A few dear friends would walk or cycle into town to meet them after the civil ceremony in front of St. Mary's Church.

He took the driver's seat and clucked his tongue to set the horses into a trot. Despite having looked forward to this day for months, a queasy feeling entered his stomach. Within the hour he'd be responsible not only for himself, but for his wife and future child.

"I'm so nervous, I'm afraid I'll mess up," Dora said, echoing his sentiments.

"There's nothing to mess up. You only have to say 'yes' when the registrar asks you."

"Won't he make me repeat the vows?" Her voice sounded so small, he wanted to wrap her into his arms, which unfortunately wasn't possible due to her dress and the thick blanket around her shoulders.

"No. That comes later in church."

She sighed.

"Do you miss your family?" he asked.

"A lot. I so wish they could be here."

"We'll visit them once the war is over." At least he hoped they would, because who knew how the world would look then.

"At least our friends will be with us."

About half of the remaining stable lads and the permanent farm hands lived at the manor and had become like family to them.

"You two are so happy with each other and that's the most important thing," Annegret entered their conversation.

"Thank you for organizing everything for us," Oliver said.

"And helping with my naturalization papers," Dora added.

"No need to thank me. It was the least I could do."

Oliver side-glanced at the woman he'd hated for such a long time, still not comprehending how he hadn't noticed it was an impostor who'd returned to Gut Plaun the previous year.

They arrived in front of the town hall, where Oliver helped down the two women and tethered the horses to a tree. His parents were waiting on the steps and together they walked into the "wedding room", which was nothing more than an office with several rows of seats for the guests.

"No more guests coming?" the registrar asked.

"No."

"Who are the happy couple?"

Oliver and Dora stepped forward, thinking it was pretty clear from Dora's dress that she was the bride, and he obviously had to be the groom, since his father, the only other male present, was a long-time acquaintance of the registrar.

"Now the witnesses, please."

Annegret and Oliver's father served as the two required witnesses for the ceremony. The registrar held a speech, reminding them of their duty to be loyal servants of the Führer and Fatherland, bearing many sons to become warriors for Germany.

Then he said, "Herewith I declare you husband and wife. If you will sign the wedding certificate now." After the witnesses had signed as well, the registrar handed them the certificate together with Adolf Hitler's *Mein Kampf*.

"This is a gift from our beloved Führer. May it enrich and inspire you."

"I'm sure it will," Oliver answered, even though he wished to tear the book into shreds. The registrar then turned to Dora. "Never forget your two most important duties are to obey your husband and bear many children for our Führer."

Poor Dora nodded her agreement.

"Congratulations!" Annegret hugged first Dora and then Oliver.

After the ceremony they walked the short distance to the church, where several friends waited for them, along with many villagers who'd come out of sheer curiosity.

———

Dora gazed wide-eyed as they approached the church and whispered, "The entire village has gathered."

"Just a few dozen." Oliver squeezed her hand. "Don't be afraid. The more people who are here, the better for us."

She knew he was worried about her status, since the hostility toward foreigners reached another all-time high after every devastating loss the Wehrmacht sustained.

Seeing her here with Fräulein Annegret's support would silence even the most vicious critics. She needed every ounce of goodwill possible among the townsfolk, since she was elbow deep in subversive activities. Maria had been the first "submarine" to hide at the estate, but certainly not the last.

After the Mass she shook the hands of dozens of people until she longed to get home, put up her feet and cozy up to her new husband. But this wasn't to be. Fräulein Annegret had used the wedding as an excuse to invite every important person in the district to a reception later in the day.

Fräulein Annegret wasn't one for formal parties, so the biggest event prior to today had been a dinner in honor of the Gestapo officers residing in her house for several days the previous year. Therefore she had framed this event, to show her approval of the alliance between her estate manager and the Ukrainian girl, while at the same time giving a long-awaited social reception for the party nobility.

Dora hissed in a breath when she saw the long line of cars and coaches parked on the driveway leading up to the manor.

"What am I supposed to say to all these important people?" she asked Oliver.

"Just say 'Thank you for coming' and smile. They'll soon talk about their oh-so-important work and we can slink away and celebrate, just the two of us."

Dora took the place beside him at the main door to the manor, shaking ever more hands and repeating the same words over and over again. Like Oliver had promised, none of the guests expected to make conversation with her, since they all seemed more interested in greeting the mistress of the house and telling her how much they appreciated the invitation and how they hoped for fruitful business relations.

As much as she'd opposed the idea of a big ceremony, she had to admit it was the perfect occasion to show the Nazi hierarchy where Gut Plaun's allegiances lay.

The guests took their seats in the large dining room that had been decked out more splendidly than Dora had ever seen since working at the manor. Usually it was her task to serve the visitors, so she enjoyed being on the other side.

It was a scene akin to something from *Cinderella*. Dora the humble maid found herself sitting in a room full of glitter and glamour. Frau Mertens and her helpers had unwrapped the fine Meissen china and the silver cutlery. Crystal wine and champagne glasses completed tables that were adorned with dried flowers, fir twigs and silver-colored bows.

Oliver and she sat at a smaller table in the corner, along with his parents and some close friends, while Fräulein Annegret presided at the large table with all the important guests who'd come to show the local world how much they supported the Nazi regime. Next to her sat the Mayor of Plau am See, on the other side Oberscharführer Kallfass, who was in his element talking about the importance of the war.

Dora's friend Olga had gotten the day off and took a seat at the bridal table, after giving Dora a bear hug. Having a fellow Ukrainian was as close as it got to having family attend.

"Are you happy?" Oliver asked after the toasts had been said.

"Very."

During dessert she talked with Oliver's parents and Olga. Then she and Oliver danced, although he was both reluctant and clumsy and all-too-happy when the music stopped. As he led her back to their table, he whispered into her ear, "I say we make a run for it."

She giggled, nodding her acceptance. Serendipitously his parents excused themselves, because it was getting late and it was a long walk back into town, and Olga decided to join them.

It was the perfect occasion to slip away. Which they did. Under the pretense of accompanying his parents to the gate, she and Oliver left the party and never returned.

Instead he stopped in front of their small house, swept her up in his arms and carried her across the threshold. "Welcome home, Frau Gundelmann."

26

Thomas had noticed the bridal couple leaving the party, no doubt to beget their first child for the Führer, and decided it was time to change the emphasis of the event. He took a spoon and clinked it several times against his glass. As the noise died down, he raised his voice.

"I want to thank our hostess Fräulein Annegret for hosting this illustrious event, celebrating not only the union of a young couple, but also to show her undying loyalty to our marvelous Führer."

Heil Hitler salutes interrupted his speech and he benevolently stared down at the other guests, the way he had practiced countless times in front of the mirror. This was the perfect opportunity to assert himself in front of the gathered industrial and political elite and let them know that he'd made a claim on the beautiful hostess along with her estate. He gave a short nod, before he turned toward Annegret and put a hand on hers.

"It is no exaggeration when I say that Fräulein Annegret has outdone herself with this splendid party. The events organized by her late mother were legendary for their style and class, and

I'm sure everyone will agree that the daughter has stepped up to the task and filled very big shoes with undeniable grace.

"After the death of her family, this young woman has taken on the daunting task of not only running the manor, but the entire estate, including the nitropenta factory. She's the perfect German woman, and while her foremost goal is to found a family and bear children, she hasn't once complained about the hardships she has confronted. Always with a smile on her lips, Fräulein Annegret has buckled down and hasn't spared herself from exhaustion to serve our country.

"Some of you might know she was crucial in solving heinous crimes against the Reich, committed by her father's estate manager. For that, and her untiring activities furthering the war effort, I, in my position as SS district leader in Parchim, want to thank her in the name of everyone gathered here." He made a pause so people could applaud.

Annegret made to rise, but he squeezed her hand and whispered, "Not yet, my dear."

He waited until the applause died down and raised his voice again. "Thank you so much for joining us today, celebrating our love for the Fatherland. I have yet another announcement to make."

He felt how Annegret stiffened beside him, needlessly, because he'd never announce their relationship before consulting with her.

"Most of you will know about the constant struggle to procure enough steel for production and it is my greatest pleasure to announce that Annegret and I will soon travel to Sweden to negotiate directly with the steel manufacturers."

Lothar Katze, his stupid subaltern, interrupted the speech with applause, before he could say his last, and possibly most important sentence, making it clear that he and Annegret were soon to be more than business partners. Unfortunately more guests joined the applause, and the Mayor of Plau am See clinked his glass to issue a toast himself.

There was nothing Thomas could do, if he didn't want to rudely interrupt him. In any case, if the businessmen and functionaries around the table had only half their wits about them, they'd come to the right conclusions. Still, it would have been so much more rewarding if he'd been able to speak it out loud.

Then the mayor, the priest, and Herr Naumann, representing the industry leaders, held speeches. Finally some stupid parvenu from a neighboring district took the floor, claiming that after Goebbels had declared Berlin free of Jews several months ago, his district had followed suit immediately, unlike Parchim.

Thomas pressed his lips into a thin line. His predecessor had been much too lenient, issuing exemptions left and right. Judging by the amount, one might think Jews were indeed necessary to run the industry around here. But that would soon change. On Hitler's birthday he'd announce that the district was completely free of Jews. What better present to give to a man who already owned everything?

"Will you excuse me, please? I need to attend to my guests," Annegret's sweet voice interrupted his musings.

"Of course, my dear. Shall I help you?"

"No need, really. I'd rather you enjoy yourself."

"Duty first, and pleasure second."

"You are always so eager to serve your country." She smiled at him and rushed off, a little bit too fast for his liking.

"Great speech." Lothar came up to compliment him.

It would have been even greater if that stupid man hadn't interrupted it. Thomas sometimes wondered how Lothar had passed the qualifying examination for the SS, given his low intellect. "We have our work cut out for us, you heard the man boasting that his district is free of Jews."

"We can't let them get all the praise, now can we?" Lothar said.

"It would be a great birthday gift for the Führer."

"But... what about all the exemptions?"

"We'll revoke them."

"That will be a cause for discontent." A sheen of sweat appeared on Lothar's forehead and Thomas wondered what his problem was. His subaltern had many flaws, but being a friend of Jews wasn't one. He'd heard many tales of Lothar executing one of the vermin with his own hands, back in the golden days, when apparently public whippings had been a regular happening at Annegret's factory.

"Hm... Who exactly filed those requests in the past?"

"Mostly factory owners. Farmers, anyone who needs labor."

"Can't they just use prisoners of war?" Thomas remembered the conversation with Herr Naumann. He'd chalked it up to the old man getting soft, when indeed he realized now that there must be a more widespread problem. Couldn't these people understand that while eradicating the Jews might seem cruel, it was absolutely necessary to ensure the survival of the Aryan master race?

By now, Lothar stepped uneasily from foot to foot. "They claim the Jews have a unique talent or skill that can't be easily acquired elsewhere."

"Nonsense. We have given every businessman a heads-up and they have enough time to train replacements before we strike with our final action to the Jewish problem. Let the filth train their own replacements. Although, the irony will unfortunately be lost on the simple-minded subhumans." He looked at Lothar, prompting him to applaud.

"Yes, Thomas. That is a brilliant idea." But he said it with little enthusiasm, which left Thomas suspecting not all was what it seemed with his subaltern.

27

Margarete could barely keep her fingers still. Today was the big day, when she'd go out with Stefan—to a clandestine dance no less. He'd told her that it was nothing formal, just a few friends getting together for music and fun.

Though to her it sounded like the biggest adventure. After attending the mayor's party and hosting the event on Oliver and Dora's wedding day, she was curious how normal people diverted themselves.

Officially all dance events were forbidden. The propaganda ministry had explicitly defended the ban on dancing as an expression of the youth's solidarity with the frontline soldiers. Strangely enough this solidarity didn't extend to the high society, who were legendary for their opulent parties, all in the name of Führer and Fatherland.

"Dora, how do I look?"

"You look perfect, Fräulein Annegret." They'd opted for a simple, yet elegant light purple dress with a slim waistline, elbow-length sleeves and a—war-ration approved—straight skirt. Over the dress she wore a cloak in the same color, two shades darker, made from a heavy wool that would keep her warm.

"Don't you think I'm overdoing it?"

"Not at all. It's chic, but modest."

"I don't want to draw attention." She had decided to ask Stefan not to introduce her to his friends as Annegret Huber, owner of Gut Plaun, but simply as Gretchen, the nickname her family used to call her when she was younger. Uncle Ernst still used it these days. Thinking of him brought worry into her heart and she pushed the thought away. She'd done everything in her power to alleviate his hardships and keep him safe.

Dora shook her head, and giggled. "I could loan you one of my dresses?"

"You would do that?"

"It was a joke." Dora opened her eyes in shock. "But if you wish... I'll give you my Sunday dress."

Margarete pondered for a moment, wishing to look beautiful for Stefan, but also wanting to blend in with his friends. Although she didn't know them, she was pretty sure none would be able to afford a dress like the one she was wearing. "I'll take it."

"Are you sure Fräulein Annegret? It's not... it's quite old and has been patched up."

"Please, can you get it for me?"

Dora nodded and rushed off. Seconds later, Margarete observed her crossing the yard and running toward Oliver's house.

Several minutes later, she returned, heaving like a locomotive, carrying not only her Sunday dress, but also her only coat. "Here you go, Fräulein Annegret."

After putting it on, Margarete looked in the mirror, barely recognizing herself. It wasn't the sophisticated heiress looking back at her, but a simple village girl, wearing a clean, yet worn gray dress with white and rosé flowers printed all over. It was buttoned in the front and a small belt accentuated the waistline.

Since she was taller than Dora, the hem ended above the

knee, making her feel audacious. Just imagining Stefan appreciating the shape of her knees made her entire body tingle.

"You look nice, Fräulein Annegret," Dora said hesitantly.

"Just nice?"

"Well, your own dress is so much prettier..."

"I know. But I want to look like everyone else."

Dora nodded, her face expressing incomprehension.

When Margarete arrived at the train station, Stefan was already waiting for her, his flaxen hair gleaming beneath the fedora. Her heart jumped a little when she saw him. He didn't wear a shiny uniform or an elegant suit, but he still made her weak at the knees.

"Good evening, Annegret." He gazed at Dora's shabby coat. "You're traveling incognito?"

She felt herself flush furiously, grateful for the blackout. "I... I thought, maybe if you couldn't tell your friends who I am?"

He stepped nearer, until she could see his features in the moonlight. "And who do you want to be tonight, if I may ask?"

Perhaps myself would be nice. But telling him that, of course, was out of the question. "Just a village girl like everyone else. Can you tell them my name is Gretchen?"

"Gretchen..." Her nickname dropped like honey from his lips, sending tingles through her body. "I like that name. It fits your personality."

A distant hissing announced the arrival of the train and he took her hand. "Come. I've got our tickets." She followed him onto the platform dimly lit with blue emergency lights that supposedly couldn't be seen from a passing airplane.

Not that there had been bombings around here. Although further up north near the Baltic Sea, where the important harbors were situated, it seemed that every month the range of the British and American bombers increased.

It didn't take long until they disembarked the train. Stefan took her arm and led her at a brisk pace toward a house at the edge of town, completely ignoring the darkness. He knocked three times and a short time later, the door opened and a petite blonde hugged Stefan. "This is your friend?"

"Yes. She's Gretchen and can be trusted."

"Good. I'm Sandra. Welcome." She ushered them inside, closing the door behind them.

"Thank you for having me." Margarete shook the proffered hand, reached into her handbag and fished out a bag of sweet bread rolls.

"God Almighty! Where did you get these beauties?"

"My grandmother makes them."

Stefan cast her a conspiratorial glance at the effortless lie. Sandra led them into the basement void of windows, so neither light nor sound of their illegal music would get outside.

Soon enough everyone was talking at the same time, until Sandra said, "Enough talking. We're here to dance," and put a record on the gramophone.

Popular schlager music alternated with forbidden jazz and swing. Margarete danced for hours until her feet hurt and her heart was beating violently.

"I need a break," she shouted into Stefan's ear, who nodded, put a hand on the small of her back and led her upstairs into the deserted kitchen.

"A glass of water?"

"Yes, please." He took out two glasses from the cupboard, pouring first one for her and then one for himself from the tap.

His familiarity with this house and his friends, especially Sandra, gave her a twinge of jealousy. She brushed it away, since she had no right to believe Stefan was anything but friendly to her.

"You are completely different than I had you pegged as," he said after emptying his glass.

That would be because I'm not really Annegret. "People often say that. They have a certain picture of me, but it turns out the reality is different." It was her standard excuse.

"I like the reality a lot more." He moved closer and she waited half-anxious, half-joyful for him to kiss her, but after a moment he slightly shook his head and stepped back. "Tell me something about yourself, Gretchen."

"Why?" She instinctively recoiled at his question.

"Isn't that obvious? I want to get to know the real you, not the image you present to the world." His eyes shone with honesty, and curiosity. She knew she could implicitly trust him and yearned to tell him her secret, but it wasn't prudent to do so. Yet, she wanted to connect with him in a more genuine way, giving him something about her nobody else knew.

"I don't know how to swim."

"You must be kidding me."

"No, it's true. I never learned to swim properly. I know, I should have, but there was simply never the opportunity." She remembered that Annegret, frequently vacationing near the lake, would most certainly have learned to swim, while a Jew like her wasn't allowed to go to the public pools or beaches. "When I was a child I refused to leave the shallow waters, because of all the stories I've heard about people being caught in underwater weeds and drowning."

He raised his hand and stroked her cheek with his thumb. "Next summer I'm going to teach you how to swim, if you would like."

"That would be nice." Her heart flowed over with sweet emotions.

"We probably should get on our way back," he said.

"What time is it?" she asked him, surprised.

"It's past three a.m. and I need to get to work before dawn."

She couldn't believe she had danced through the night. It was the first time in forever that she'd completely forgotten all her sorrows and had simply been herself, enjoying a night out like any other girl her age. "I had a wonderful time with your friends."

"And with me?" he asked with a cheeky grin.

"With you most of all." Again she felt the blood rushing to her cheeks and hoped he wouldn't notice.

"Would you like to go out with me again, perhaps next week?"

"I'd love to... but I can't." His face fell with disappointment, therefore she quickly added, "I'll be traveling to Sweden."

He seemed to relax. "Now that is a valid reason. I feared you were brushing me off."

"I wasn't!" A gaze into his face told her he was joking. "You're... awful!"

"Am I, really?" He took her hand and squeezed it softly.

How much she wished she could sink into his arms and soak up the comfort he provided. But things were... complicated. She was Annegret Huber and he was just a fisherman. People would gossip, which was the last thing she needed. And Thomas... he'd hate having a rival and might stir up trouble, should he find out.

"You're not. But for many reasons, this can't flourish."

He looked crestfallen, but seemed to understand, because he nodded with sad eyes. "About Sweden. Where are you traveling to?"

"Stockholm."

"That's such serendipity. Wait here, will you?" Without further explanation he rushed into the basement and a short time later returned with a triumphant look on his face. "This is a game changer. I know someone in Stockholm who works for the Swedish foreign ministry. If you meet with him, I'm sure he can help with some things."

She stared at him, uncomprehending what an employee in the foreign ministry would be able to do for her steel shortage that the industrialist Lindström couldn't? But then it dawned on her: Stefan was talking about their other business, hiding fugitives. "Will he trust me?"

"Tell him I sent you. He'll hear you out. And I'm sure he can help."

She cocked her head, anguish sweeping over her. Meeting with a Swedish diplomat might be the answer to her prayers, but on the other hand it seemed horribly dangerous, since Thomas was accompanying her to Sweden. What should she tell him? What if he suspected something? "How do you know him?"

"We used to study at the same university and became fast friends. He fell from grace and was expelled from Germany after a concert where he coughed during the national anthem."

"Now that is a grave offense and I'm surprised they didn't send him to prison for it."

"Are you serious?" Stefan's mouth hung agape, before he noticed her smirk. "Well, that point goes to you. But really, go and visit him. He'll help."

"What should I ask him for?"

"Anything. He's been doing this for a long time and will know what help he can provide."

"Why don't you ask him yourself, since he's your friend?"

"Oh, Gretchen," he said her name with such softness it reverberated through her body. "You'll need to learn a lot about subversive work. I wonder how you made it until now without being discovered?"

"Because I'm one of them," she remarked. "Nobody suspects me."

"See, that's the exact reason why I can't contact Lars myself. As Oliver surely told you, I was accused of sabotage and although they could never prove anything, they fired me from my job as an engineer and even deemed me unworthy to fight for the Reich as a soldier."

She wanted to ask him whether the accusations were true, but didn't want to interrupt him.

"I'm pretty sure I'm still under surveillance and traveling to Sweden or even Berlin to visit the Swedish consulate would raise more than one red flag."

"That makes sense. So I simply visit the foreign ministry in Stockholm and ask to speak with him?" He made it seem so easy, but she already felt shivers of fear running down her spine.

"No. I'll give you his home address. You could go out for dinner or something. Two young people having fun."

"You want me to have fun with him?"

His eyes turned dark as he shook his head. "Only to pretend you do. You should know that I care very much about you."

"I do." She quickly averted her eyes, before something unseemly might happen. Something she craved and feared at the same time.

"What are you afraid of?" he asked, his voice velvety, warming, reassuring.

"My situation is dangerous. If something happens to me, I don't want to implicate you."

He laughed a hearty laugh. "Honestly, I think they have a lot more evidence against me than they could ever have against you."

That's because you don't know who I really am. She inhaled deeply. "Is it true? That you sabotaged the production?"

"What do you think?" His hands had found their way onto her elbows, sending warmth, comfort, and fear though her veins.

"I think it's true and if it is I'd like you to teach me how to do the same." There, she'd said it.

He stepped nearer, scrutinizing her face. "What exactly do you want to sabotage?"

"Production in my nitropenta factory."

"Good God, woman, you really are serious about this!" His hands moved up to rest on her shoulders. "What you're suggesting is incredibly dangerous."

"I know. Therefore I need someone with the expertise to make it seem like a coincidence. A bomb or grenade that doesn't explode. Something they won't be able to trace back to the factory."

He stared into her eyes for the longest time, a multitude of emotions running between them, until he said, "I'll help you." And then he finally pressed a soft kiss on her lips. It lasted maybe a second or two, but Margarete felt as if the world exploded around her into light and colors, heat racing through her veins and jolting her heart awake.

28

"Are you sure you have everything you need?" Dora asked.

"I'll be in Sweden for less than a week and you already packed four suitcases for me, what could possibly be missing?" Annegret replied.

"It's just... Sweden seems so far away." Dora was probably more anxious about the upcoming trip than her mistress.

"I'm sure I will manage. Can you please ring Nils to carry the suitcases downstairs?" Annegret put on her gloves and hat, before she beckoned for Dora to help her into her fur coat.

Winter had taken over the country with force, and Gut Plaun lay beneath a blanket of snow. It wasn't as cold as it used to be in the Ukraine, although the humidity of the lake made it harder to tolerate.

Dora used the telephone to ring downstairs and advise Frau Mertens to send up Nils, then she arranged the pillows on the sofa to keep her hands busy. She'd have plenty of time on her hands when Fräulein Annegret was away and didn't require her services, and that prospect frightened her.

Despite being Frau Oliver Gundelmann, she still felt she had to justify her presence in Germany by constantly working.

"Dora," Fräulein Annegret suddenly said in a very earnest tone.

"Yes, Fräulein Annegret." She was so disturbed that she resorted to curtsying despite knowing how much her mistress despised this old-fashioned gesture.

"While I'm gone, perhaps you could use the extra time and go into town... you know... ask around for our cause."

"Oh... yes, of course. I had already planned to do this. Although Oliver is dead set against it. Ever since he found out about the baby, he has become overly protective and doesn't want me to do anything remotely dangerous."

Fräulein Annegret smiled. "I can understand his point of view, but where would the world be if we all hid in our houses and didn't help those in need?"

"You are so brave," she said with honest admiration.

"Not at all. I'm full of fear at all times, but I would feel evil not doing my bit."

A knock on the door caused them to fall silent.

Fräulein Annegret called out, "Come in."

Nils appeared in the doorway, took the first two of the suit-cases and left to stash them in the automobile.

"Take care," Fräulein Annegret said and walked out into the hallway, leaving Dora feeling strangely abandoned. She finished dusting the rooms, before she walked downstairs into the kitchen to see whether Frau Mertens had work for her.

But the housekeeper waved her off. "You go and attend to your husband. I'll see you in the morning."

"Thank you, Frau Mertens."

Dora decided to visit Olga in town. The other girl worked with an elderly lady who treated her almost like a daughter. If she hurried up, she could get there before dark, hoping Oliver could pick her up in the evening, since she hated walking alone through the forest at night. Nothing had ever happened in this remote area, but she irrationally worried she might stumble and freeze to death in the snow before someone found her in the morning.

On her way, she stopped by their house and left a note for him. She put on the thick coat Fräulein Annegret had given her, a hat and gloves, and marched the four miles into town.

When she knocked at Olga's door, it took quite a while until she opened with an anguished expression on her face.

"Oh, it's you. Come in."

The elderly lady was sitting in her rocking chair next to the range in the kitchen. "Who is it, Olga?"

"A friend of mine, Dora from the manor. We can trust her."

"Good evening, Frau Gusen," Dora said, musing at the strange introduction. But her confusion didn't last long, because the woman called out, "You can come out, Lili."

Seconds later, a girl of maybe ten years crawled from beneath the sofa and rushed into the kitchen to settle next to the range at the old lady's feet. Lili stared with wide eyes at Dora, who felt compelled to say something. "Hello, I'm Dora. I'm a friend of Olga's."

Lili nodded, but no words left her mouth.

"She's quite shy," Olga said as if it were the most normal thing in the world to hide someone beneath the furniture. "Can I offer you tea?"

"Yes, please."

Olga walked to the range, where a Thermos stood next to a pot with simmering potatoes, took it, poured tea into a mug and motioned Dora to follow her into the living room. "Here you go."

"Thank you." Dora took off her gloves and pressed her cold fingers around the mug, sniffing the hot yellow liquid. "Sage."

"No coffee, no black tea. I imagine it's different at the manor," Olga said.

"Not really. We have *Ersatzkaffee*."

"Eek. I have no idea how anyone can drink that stuff. I prefer infusions, what's more sage is good against coughing."

"So, she's the one you're hiding?"

Olga nodded. "But it's getting more and more difficult. The neighbors are getting suspicious, just yesterday the block leader came for an unannounced visit, presumably because we hadn't obeyed the blackout. I swear, the real reason was to sniff around."

"That hiding place under the sofa won't be any good if someone actually does a search."

"Lili is supposed to be in the attic, but it's too cold up there. The kitchen is the only place we can heat. So for now she's downstairs with us."

"How can I help?" The words tumbled out of her mouth, before she even realized it.

"We need warm clothes her size."

Dora bit on her lower lip, thinking. "I'm sure I can find some woolen dress or something. But it has to be done in secrecy."

Olga was beaming with delight and wrapped her arms around her. "Oh, Dora, I knew I could count on you. We can arrange to meet elsewhere. At the grocer's and then walk a while together, exchanging bags in the process?"

"I guess that would work." Olga's mistress lived in a tiny house on the fringe of town. It would be an easy task to hand over the bag without anyone noticing. Emboldened by the situation, she forged ahead and asked her most pressing question. "Once in a while someone else has to hide for a day or two. Would you be able to help?"

It took several long seconds, before Olga nodded her head. "We would. But as I said, the attic is very cold, and it could be only for two nights at most. We have to make sure the block leader doesn't notice."

"That won't be a problem. I guess someone could divert her.

Go to her house, indulge her in some trivial gossip about who was wearing what to church."

"Great idea."

"Don't you have to ask your mistress first?"

"No." Olga shook her head. "She's been complaining that she wants to do more, despite not being able to leave the house."

"I'll let you know as soon as we need you." Dora emptied the mug. "Thank you so much."

"We Ukrainians have to stick together, don't we? The Nazis have shown their true colors, so we don't play nice anymore."

Dora gave her friend a hug, put on her gloves again and left the house, running straight into the block leader, a burly woman with a wicked tongue.

"Good evening, Frau Harmsen," she greeted her.

"Aren't you Fräulein Annegret's maid? What was your name again?"

"Frau Gundelmann"

"So, what are you doing in town at this hour?"

"My mistress sent me to run some errands for her." Dora had an idea. "The old Frau Gusen is in such frail health, she can't even leave her house. Fräulein Annegret was kind enough to have me bring her wood for the stove. You know how cold it can get in these old houses."

Frau Harmsen made a scoffing sound. "Tell your mistress my thanks. But next time you come during daylight. It's not safe for a girl to sneak around after dark."

"I will." Dora rushed off, making a mental note to inform Fräulein Annegret about her supposed involvement as soon as she returned. She'd be onboard with the ruse, especially when she told her the good news of having found two more helpers. In any case, she had a valid excuse to visit Olga and hide food and clothing beneath the wood she supposedly provided for the old woman.

As she walked over to the local pub, she saw the coach from the manor coming down the other street.

"Dora. Are you finished with your errands?" Oliver called out.

"Yes."

"Hop on."

He wrapped them tightly into the thick blanket and she snuggled up to him beneath. As soon as they'd left the town behind, he said, "I worried when I read your note. Has something happened?"

"Nothing. You remember Olga?"

"Your Ukrainian friend?"

"Yes. She and her mistress are hiding a girl in their home. Today, I visited them and the person they're hiding is a girl, maybe ten years of age."

"Goddamn. These Nazis have no shame."

After a long silence, she asked him, "How was your day?"

"Good. I hope. I asked Franz to make a list of all the prisoners and what kind of skills they have, including experience with horses, mechanical or electrical skills etc."

"Does Franz know what this is for?"

"No. He's a decent enough chap, although a true patriot and in favor of the war. I doubt he would support our subversive activities."

Dora nodded pensively. "Fräulein Annegret once mentioned that he thinks the Jews should have emigrated years ago. Those who stayed have no one to blame but themselves. He also thinks forcing them to work is fine, but he doesn't condone the unnecessary brutality."

"That's what I suspected. We can't make him privy, or he'd surely run to the Gestapo and turn us in, out of a misguided sense of duty."

"What if he finds out?"

"Finds out what?" Oliver asked, as he swung the whip and lightly tipped the back of the lead horse to make it go faster.

"Why you need the list. It's to transfer men to the stables, right?"

"You're too clever for your own good." He squeezed her hand beneath the blanket. "We'll have to wait until we have work permits before doing the transfer."

"When will this ever end?" She sighed.

"I don't know, my darling. Hopefully soon. News from the front isn't all that positive anymore. A strategic regrouping here, a straightening of the frontline there. It all means the same: retreat."

"I hope you're right." She fell into silence, soaking up the warmth and comfort his presence provided her.

29

Thomas had canceled his trip at short notice, claiming his boss had decided it didn't look good for an SS officer to visit a neutral country. It had been a relief, but now she felt utterly alone.

Nils drove her all the way to the airport, which took almost three hours due to the bad state of the roads. Once they arrived, he carried her suitcases inside, where a Lufthansa stewardess approached her. "Can I help you?"

Glad for the offer, Margarete smiled. "I am booked on the flight to Stockholm."

"Come with me." The stewardess waved at a porter to help Nils with the suitcases and led her to a counter, where another woman stood.

"Your name, please."

"Annegret Huber, I'm booked on the flight to Stockholm."

The woman took a list, searched for her name and said, "There you are. May I have your identification, travel permit and visa, please."

Margarete handed over her documents, anxiety growing inside her. After the explosion in Paris, Horst Richter had helped her to apply for new papers, this time with her picture instead of Annegret's.

The document was real for all intents and purposes, and the stewardess couldn't know that the woman claiming to be Annegret Huber wasn't actually her. Nobody could know.

"I'll take you to the airplane," the first stewardess said, turning around to Nils. "Your driver may leave now, since he's not allowed onto the airfield."

Nils took his cap into his hands, "Good luck, Fräulein Annegret!"

"Safe travels home. I'll telephone the manor upon my return."

When he left, Margarete felt utterly alone. For a split-second she thought that being with someone, anyone, even Thomas, would be preferable to traveling alone. But then she straightened her shoulders and scolded herself for being such a chicken.

It wasn't the first time she'd traveled alone either. In fact, the trip to Paris had been much more fraught with danger.

"Follow me." The stewardess led the way to the airfield where an impressive JU 52 with huge rectangular windows stood, gleaming in the sunlight.

It was Margarete's first time boarding a flight and her stomach squeezed at the thought of precariously hanging above the clouds in a machine that must weigh many tons, certainly more than the air it wanted to float upon.

"It's not dangerous, is it?" Her voice was small as she asked the stewardess.

"Not at all." The other woman smiled. "We're taking the shortest route across the Baltic Sea and since Sweden is a neutral country, the Allies won't attack us over their territory."

What was meant as reassurance caused a completely different fear to shoot up, since Margarete hadn't considered the possibility of being shot down. "They shoot at civilian planes?"

"This is your first flight, isn't it?"

She nodded.

"There's absolutely no reason to worry at all. I know of only one passenger flight on this route to crash, and that wasn't due to enemy action."

"I see." Margarete swallowed hard, bravely putting one foot in front of the other as she climbed up the staircase to board the plane.

"Would you like something to drink?" the stewardess asked her after showing her to her seat and helping her with the seat belt, while the porter heaved her suitcases into the luggage area.

"Can I have red wine, please?" The wine would hopefully calm her nerves. Within minutes all seats had been occupied, exclusively by men in suits, presumably industrialists or diplomats. Being the only woman on board made her feel even more anxious, and she cursed herself for agreeing to this trip. What could she, a young, albeit rich, woman achieve when dealing with old, worldly-wise, and equally rich men?

She shouldn't be here. It was a waste of time and money. But it was too late, the door had been closed and the motor roared up, bringing the aircraft to full speed until it raised itself into the air. Beneath, the people, vehicles and buildings became small as ants and finally disappeared beneath a blanket of clouds. Above them, the sun shone with a brilliance Margarete had never experienced before, and she looked in awe at the fluffy, white material beneath that looked like freshly fallen snow.

The beautiful sight instilled newfound courage into her. She'd take it one step after another, working hard for the best possible outcome of this journey—for both her official business and the clandestine one.

The aircraft landed in Stockholm and she disembarked, unsure how to find her way to the hotel. But Herr Lindström had made provisions and sent someone to pick her up.

At the hotel, the receptionist told her in flawless German that the driver would be waiting for her to change and would then drive her to the concert hall.

"I hope you don't mind me taking the liberty of arranging tickets," Herr Lindström said after greeting her.

"Not at all," she lied, despite wishing she could just drop onto her bed, exhausted from the journey.

He led her into the box and she silently thanked Dora for insisting on packing two long evening gowns, or she would have looked rather out of place compared with the other women present.

The conductor, a German living in exile, pushed the orchestra to peak performance. The concert hall filled with the sounds of instruments, stunning the audience into silence. Margarete, by no means a connoisseur of classical music, was captivated and closed her eyes, letting the music wash over her.

Forceful, loud pieces alternated with soft, caressing ones and she felt as if her body became lighter until she floated on a cloud of musical notes. Violins soothed her sorrows, a clarinet refreshed her courage, the timbals reminded her of freedom. At the end of the performance, she felt refreshed and liberated, with the certainty that life would go on. Always.

She clapped until her hands were sore. It was the most fantastic concert she'd ever witnessed. In fact it had been her first concert, because as a Jew she hadn't been allowed to attend cultural performances and in Paris Wilhelm had preferred to take her out to the opera or cabaret.

"Thank you for inviting me. This was absolutely marvelous," she told her host and his wife.

"We do value culture and it's always a pleasure to have like-minded business partners," he said in a pleasant tone, although something told her this had been a test.

"I love classical music, but unfortunately in the countryside we never have the opportunity to attend such high-class performances."

He nodded. "I took the liberty to check your exact location and it seemed rather remote. Wouldn't you prefer to live in the capital?"

Unsure how honest she should be with him, she carefully chose her words. "I used to live in Berlin, but duty requires me to stay near the factory."

His lips seemed to smirk, as he answered, "Perhaps the destruction of your parental home helped with your decision to flee Berlin?"

This man was shrewd and she wished she had asked Horst Richter, the experienced Gestapo interrogator, to accompany her. He would know how to counter such a bold statement. She smiled noncommittally. "It is no secret that our country is at war."

Frau Lindström joined the conversation by giving her husband a warning glance and saying, "Let's have a glass of champagne in the foyer."

Margarete's feet were hurting in her high heels, in addition to being tired to the bone after her travels, but she couldn't think of a polite way to decline. Therefore, she followed her hosts downstairs, where they introduced her to a multitude of concert-goers. Some greeted her cordially, others uninterested and the rest seemed to look at her with disdain. Apparently the people here were as conflicted as their government on how to best cope with Hitler's regime. They all walked a fine line between too little and too much cooperation in their quest to remain neutral.

After some conversation she finally found the opportunity to politely decline the invitation to go for another drink elsewhere, citing that she had to get some sleep before the meeting in the morning.

Two days passed in a whirlwind of activities. She met with

Herr Lindström and several of his managers, feeling absolutely inadequate for this kind of negotiation, and wishing a thousand times per day that Oliver, Herr Volkmer or even Thomas were by her side, helping her to navigate through the maze of clauses.

In the end, they agreed with a handshake that Herr Lindström's factory would provide the steel ball bearings she needed.

On the morning of her third day she finally found the time to visit the address Stefan had given her. She went early so as to catch Lars before he went to work.

When she rang the bell to his residence, an apartment in a well-off area of Stockholm, a man in his early thirties with the blondest hair she'd ever seen, opened the door. His hair, eyebrows and lashes as well as his skin were almost white, giving him quite the peculiar appearance.

"*Godmorgon, hur kan jag hjälpa dig?*" he greeted her.

"Excuse me, I don't speak Swedish," she said and he immediately squinted his eyes and switched to perfect German.

"Good morning, how can I help you?"

"My name is Annegret Huber and I'm a friend of Stefan Stober. He sent me here—"

"Come in," he interrupted her sentence and stepped back to let her inside.

Just then she realized that despite wearing a business suit, he was barefoot. Stepping into the hallway, she wondered whether she should take off her coat or not, but he rescued her by saying, "I was just having breakfast. Would you like a coffee?"

Smelling the scent of real coffee, she eagerly nodded. "Yes, please."

He helped her out of her coat and led her into the kitchen that was equipped with several modern electrical devices on the counter and a table with two chairs on the opposite wall. It was small, but cozy, and it was warm.

"Sugar or milk?" he asked, putting a steaming cup of coffee in front of her.

"Black, please." Thanks to the cultivation of sugar beet, there was no sugar shortage in Sweden, but she wanted to taste the real coffee without additives.

"How's Stefan?" Lars sat down opposite her, a huge cup in his hand.

"He's fine. Working as a fisherman in Plau am See." Stefan had told her she could trust Lars, so she didn't think anything about telling him details.

"With his old man?"

"His grandfather."

"So that's where he disappeared to after they sacked him." He gave her another once-over and came straight to the point. "What brings you here?"

"We need your help." Since Lars didn't utter a word, she felt compelled to explain. "You'll find out anyway. I own an ammunition factory that employs prisoners from the camps." He raised an eyebrow, but stayed silent, which was slightly unnerving. "I was hoping you could help to smuggle the Jews at risk of deportation out of Germany."

Finally, Lars opened his mouth. "Well, that's an ambitious undertaking. But why on earth should I help a Nazi who uses Jews to produce weapons that kill people?"

She leaned back, locking eyes with him. "I'm not a Nazi."

"You sure look like one to me."

"That just proves how good I am at subterfuge."

He gave her a full-belly laugh, but immediately stopped and crossed his arms in front of his chest. "I'm not convinced."

"Stefan trusts me."

"You sleep with him?"

"Of course not!" she protested, even as a treacherous heat crept into her cheeks at the memory of their kiss.

"You're not good at lying."

If only he knew how adept she'd become at living a fake life. Perhaps the key to success was that she often forgot who she actually was and didn't have to pretend anymore. Over the past years she had actually become Annegret.

"I've done all I can to make the lives of my workers more bearable—more food, fewer hours, no physical punishments, and I've gotten rid of the cruel foremen who used to work there. They have proper clothing, shoes when we can manage, bedding and plenty of clean water to drink and wash. I even provide access to medical care when it's needed."

Lars suddenly listened intently. "You're serious."

"Very. But there's a problem. Our new district leader wants to deport all Jews, even those used for forced labor, and those with exemptions."

"They need to disappear before he does," he summarized her predicament.

"Yes, but I can't do so without proper papers and a place for them to go."

"You are playing a very dangerous game, young lady."

"I know. But how can I do anything less? I'm in a unique position to help people who would otherwise end up dead. But I can't do it alone."

"No, you certainly can't," he agreed. "How many workers are currently under your care?"

"Almost a thousand."

Lars' eyebrows disappeared beneath the strands of hair that hung over his brow. "A thousand Jews? Good lord."

"Only about half of them, the rest are prisoners of war and foreign workers, who are safe working in the factory." A long silence ensued, until she couldn't withstand it any longer and said, "Stefan said you would help me."

He looked up, his light blue eyes shimmering with determination. "I will. Meet me at the Molins fountain in the

Kungsträdgården." He smirked. "But don't tell Stefan, he's quite jealous."

She wanted to protest, telling him she and Stefan weren't a couple. Instead she asked, "What time?"

"Five p.m."

"I'll be there. Thank you."

"See you tonight, my dear." He got up, helped her into her coat and took her to the door.

She used the rest of the day to do some sightseeing in the city that was so refreshingly devoid of any traces of war and the Nazi party that dominated all the other places she'd been to.

It was her first time out in the city on her own. Despite the language barrier, she felt without a care in the world. Walking through Gamla Stan, the old town, she admired the colorful buildings dating back to the thirteenth century. Strolling through the labyrinth of tiny, winding streets she felt transported back to the Middle Ages, which she had read about in books she'd found in the library at Gut Plaun.

The smell of saltwater and fish wafted through the air, even as she arrived in front of the Royal Palace and looked in awe at the façade of the huge building with more than 600 rooms. According to her travel guide it was the biggest palace in Europe, bigger than Buckingham Palace in London.

The grayish sky gave the structure a dark and brooding appearance, nothing like the light and playful Versailles Palace in Paris.

In the afternoon, she returned to the hotel to have a meal and refresh herself before going out again to meet Lars.

30

At exactly five p.m. Margarete walked toward the fountain where she was supposed to meet Lars. Despite the relaxed atmosphere she'd experienced in the city throughout the day that was so different to Germany, she felt anxiety creeping into every cell.

She was so used to always glancing over her shoulder, that she noticed a couple walking a short distance from her. Immediately she assumed the worst, fearing Gestapo informers were shadowing her.

Several steps later, another glance. The couple had taken a different path and she sighed in relief. It was an entirely irrational fear. Then she saw a white-blond head coming toward the fountain from the other side.

"Hello, Annegret. Let's take a walk," Lars greeted her and took her arm. He led her deep into the snowed-in park and she couldn't help but compare Stockholm to Plau am See.

The two towns were like day and night: Stockholm the Swedish capital, a thriving metropolis with a lively cultural life, seemingly happy, smiling people and a surprisingly laid-back attitude. On the other hand there was Plau am See, a quaint little town next to the lake, but despite the picturesque landscape, the atmosphere reeked of oppression and apprehension.

Everyone always did what she'd done earlier, the "German glance" across one's shoulder to make sure nobody was within earshot. Not only people who worked against the regime were wary of the surveillance state, since anyone could receive a friendly, or not-so-friendly, invitation by the Gestapo after being denounced for saying a wrong word.

The only people who never looked over their shoulder were the two-hundred-percenters like Olga's block leader, a woman who spewed nothing but Nazi propaganda and wouldn't know how to utter a critical word if her life depended on it.

"Did you spend a nice day?" Lars asked.

"Yes. My business concluded yesterday and I used the time to visit the tourist attractions in your beautiful city."

"Open your handbag."

She followed the request without comment. He removed an envelope from his briefcase and dropped it inside. "On such a short notice there wasn't much I could do. In the envelope are fifty blank protective passports, identifying the bearer as Swedish subjects awaiting repatriation. They aren't legal documents, but with the seal of the Swedish Embassy they should look official enough to be accepted by the authorities. Use them wisely."

"Thank you." She would have to think how to best put the forms to use, but owning such a document would at least exempt the Jews from having to wear the yellow star.

"Can I take you anywhere? I have a car at the entrance to the park."

"To my hotel would be nice. I'll be leaving first thing in the morning."

"Take care, and give my best regards to Stefan. Tell him I hope to meet him again after the war."

"I will certainly relay your message, and once again, thanks so much for your help."

"You're welcome."

The next day, Margarete arrived at Gut Plaun after a strenuous trip. She was bursting with energy and couldn't wait to share her exciting news.

"You're back, Fräulein Annegret. Why didn't you telephone ahead? We would have sent Nils to pick you up," Dora asked.

"No need, I was lucky enough to be offered a ride by some acquaintance."

"How was your trip?"

"Exhausting but successful. I was promised a six-months supply of steel ball bearings." Margarete pondered whether to tell Dora about the protective passes as well, but decided not to. It wasn't that she mistrusted her maid, but more that she wanted to protect her. Too much knowledge would put a person in danger.

"That is such good news. Oliver will be so pleased."

"Is he in his office?"

"No. He had to leave the estate for some important meeting with the Wehrmacht supply department and won't be back until morning. Shall I alert Frau Mertens right away to prepare dinner for you?"

"Yes, please tell her I'll eat in my rooms." She needed to flop down in her favorite armchair overlooking the yard and put up her hurting feet. After freshening up from her long journey and eating her meal, she itched to visit Stefan and tell him about the meeting with Lars.

But since it was already late afternoon, she decided to postpone this endeavor until morning. Instead, she walked downstairs to find a book in the library. When she arrived at the ground floor, she saw a man in a striped uniform entering the servants' quarters.

It wasn't unusual that prisoners came to the manor, usually to fetch provisions from the basement, or to help Frau Mertens with the heavy work. She was about to turn away, when she recognized Uncle Ernst.

Looking left and right to make sure nobody was observing her, she motioned for him to wait. The better provisions hadn't helped him gain fat and he looked frightfully skinny. "Are you alone?" she whispered.

"No. The guard went for coffee and a cigarette to the kitchen."

"What do you have to do?"

"Carry the potato sacks from the storage to the handcart."

"I'll help you." Before he could protest, she preceded him down into the basement, where she looked over her shoulder once more and then wrapped her arms around his bony shoulders. "Uncle Ernst. Are you well?"

"As well as can be expected. Thank you for transferring me to kitchen duties, I don't think I would have lasted much longer pulling the heavy carts."

"And this?" she said with a glance at the bulky sacks he was tasked to carry upstairs.

"Usually a colleague does it. But he sprained his ankle and I'm covering for him."

"You're much too frail!"

"It's only this one time, and he would never be able to do it."

Margarete sighed. Having a sprained ankle wasn't reason enough to exempt a prisoner from work and send him to the sick bay.

She itched to tell her uncle about her plans to rescue the Jews in her factory by letting them "die" and giving them fake permits, but once again couldn't risk doing it. Being so secretive, even with the people she implicitly trusted, was the hardest part of her current life.

"I'll watch over you, you know that."

"I do, Gretchen." He smiled at her, exposing a missing tooth, a keepsake from one of the previous camps he'd been to. "It's a strange feeling, really, when I should be the one to watch over you."

"You have done so much for me. Do you remember when I was a child? How you taught me to ride a bicycle?"

He took her hand. "We had good times. Have you heard from my Heidi?"

"Not since I wrote her a postcard in coded words that I found you. I'm sure she's fine. I would have heard if something had happened to her."

"I pray for her every day. She tried to protect me, you know. Normally Jews married to a German are safe from deportation, but they came up with some hilarious accusation, arrested and convicted me in a sham process and then deported me as a criminal."

"Heidi never mentioned this."

"She didn't want you to know that your uncle is a convicted criminal."

"Oh, Uncle Ernst." She squeezed him again, carefully so as not to break his frail bones. "Everyone convicted by the Nazis is in reality a hero. You're my hero."

From upstairs she heard steps and whispered, "Be quick or you'll get into hot water." Then she shouldered one of the potato sacks, almost going down on her knees at the weight, promising herself she'd do everything to keep her uncle safe.

As she arrived on the first floor, she ran into Frau Mertens.

"Fräulein Annegret, I've been looking for you everywhere. The Reichskriminaldirektor is on the telephone for you."

"Thank you, I'll take it in the library." Margarete strode to the other room, glad that Frau Mertens didn't have time to ask why she had been in the basement, a location the housekeeper considered her realm.

"*Guten Tag*, Horst. How are you?"

"Too much work like always, but getting along well. My wife sends her regards."

"Give her my thanks, will you. I was about to call you later tonight to report back on my trip to Sweden."

"Judging by your voice, I gather it was successful?" The man had an uncanny ability to read his counterpart, whether it was in person or even over the phone.

"You're right, it was. I got all the steel I needed and more..." She recounted the official part of her trip, leaving out the subversive meeting with Lars.

After listening without interrupting her, he finally said, "I'm so very proud of you, Annegret. You're a true asset to the German nation. My main reason for this call was to give you a heads-up that I'll be in your area within the next weeks."

"When?" she asked.

"I'm not sure yet, and I might not be able to give you advance notice due to the matter of my work there."

She shivered, hoping it wouldn't involve anyone she knew. "You're always welcome at Gut Plaun. Whenever you manage, simply come to the manor and we'll arrange something."

"I'm looking forward to seeing you again."

"Me, too."

31

Thomas signed the last papers awaiting his signature, with a neat and tidy, yet strong and determined hand. He had practiced for a long time to perfect his signature.

After blowing on the ink to dry it faster, he mustered his array of official stamps and took the one with the Imperial Eagle and his position as district leader. Then he stamped the seal exactly onto the white space beside his signature, making sure the eagle's head was up, because there was nothing imperial about a bird hanging upside down. He hated the carelessness with which some of his colleagues put their seals all over the place, never taking care which direction the eagle looked.

When he finished, he cleaned his desk to leave it spick and span for the weekend. As much as the Latin phrase *Mens sana in corpore sano*, a healthy mind lives in a healthy body, was valid, he believed another saying to be just as true: a messy desk represents a messy mind.

Looking at the calendar on his desk, he realized that Annegret should have returned from Stockholm the day before and wondered why she hadn't telephoned. It was understandable that she might have been too tired from the trip to phone him last night, but today as well?

She might be ashamed to tell him that she hadn't been able to secure a success in the negotiations. Yes, that must be the case. The shrewd businessman Lindström had pulled her over the barrel and she didn't know how to face Thomas to admit her defeat. She might even be angry at him for not accompanying her as he'd initially promised.

His bosses in Berlin simply possessed no foresight when it came to business dealings. At times he felt as if he was the only intelligent man in the SS. If the Führer knew how many bad decisions were made in his name, he'd immediately stop this nonsense. Unfortunately even the omnipotent Hitler couldn't hear and see everything and all these sycophants around him didn't dare to tell the truth.

He shrugged off the thought. For now he served the Reich as best as he could and when the opportunity presented itself, he would alert the Führer to some of the less advantageous things going on in his beloved country.

If Annegret didn't get in touch with him by the end of the next day, he'd arrange to pass by St. Mary's Church on Sunday. Normally he steered clear of Mass, since the Führer didn't appreciate religion. In this instance, though, he'd make an exception, as his goal wasn't to listen to some priest spew ludicrous superstitions, but to *accidentally* meet Annegret and offer her a gracious way to tell him about her unsuccessful trip to Stockholm.

Two days passed and she neither telephoned nor visited, so on Sunday morning he climbed behind the wheel of the black office Mercedes and drove to Plau am See. Christmas was just around the corner and despite the efforts of the government to convince the people that this old-fashioned festivity wasn't something to preserve into modern times, most Germans—religious or non-religious alike—still clung to it.

On his way he passed through several villages with decorated trees and nativity scenes on the main squares. It was a shame actually, and he hoped with time the people would see that they didn't need to worship a non-existent god, when they had the Führer to look out for them.

Whereas in the forest lay pristine snow, in town it had turned into a grayish slush. He parked in front of the rather impressive St. Mary's Church and stepped straight into a muddy puddle.

Muttering a curse, he started the motor again and drove a few yards on. This time he made sure there was no puddle, before he stepped out. But first, he wiped his boot clean with a rag he used exclusively for that purpose. A member of the SS never showed up with dirty boots. First lesson they'd learned at the Napola elite school.

Mass was about to finish in a few minutes and he pondered where best to wait until Annegret came out, so he could accidentally bump into her.

His musings were cut short by the whinny of a horse and he looked around, recognizing the coach from Gut Plaun parked on the other side of the square. He'd combine duty with pleasure, admire the fine horses and wait for her there.

Minutes later, he heard steps behind his back and turned around to see Annegret standing in front of him. As always she was impeccably dressed, with a long fur coat, a matching hat, leather gloves and shining black boots.

"Thomas? What are you doing here?" she asked in surprise.

"I had business around the district and since it's almost noon I decided to stop for lunch." He took her hand and breathed a kiss on the back of it. "How was your trip to Stockholm?"

"Perfect. I'm sorry, I should have telephoned you right away, but things are so busy at the manor. We signed a contract for all the steel ball bearings we need."

"That is such a relief to know." He vacillated between admiration for her shrewdness and disappointment that she'd been able to secure the deal without his help. Since she didn't offer additional details, or even an invitation to join her for lunch at the manor, he took things into his own hands. "I'd love to hear more. Perhaps you'd like to join me for lunch?"

Her face fell, but only for a moment, before she had the same pleasant expression again. "I'd love to. Although I'm afraid the restaurants in town will be a culinary disappointment for someone like you."

"I'm not picky," he lied.

"That's good to know. Do you have a place in mind already?"

In reality, he'd expected her to invite him to the manor. In addition, she could have offered him to stay for a horse ride. So he shrugged and answered, "You're the local. Which place do you recommend?"

She seemed to think for a while. "There's really just one place and it's nothing special."

"It'll have to suffice," he said with a slightly dour expression. Why couldn't she simply invite him to the manor if all the restaurants in town were so bad?

"Let me advise Nils."

"I'll drive you back, so he doesn't have to wait." This would give him another chance to angle for an invitation. It wasn't at all like her to behave so rudely.

"Thank you." She walked over to her handyman, who nodded and then climbed on the coach seat, waiting for several of the live-in employees to jump into the back.

Thomas took her arm and led her toward his vehicle. "Where are we going?"

"We can walk. It's just a few minutes down the street."

"Nonsense. We're driving. I already soaked my shoes in a puddle. You wouldn't want to experience the same."

"Of course not. How thoughtful of you."

She directed him to the restaurant and as she'd promised it took less than a minute to drive there. Due to the petrol shortage there were no other motorized vehicles around and he parked directly in front of the restaurant, running around to the other side to open the door for her.

Her judgment about the restaurant, unfortunately, was true as well and he already regretted inviting her for lunch. They had only one meal on the menu and that left much to be desired. Still, he tried his best to make pleasant conversation.

"I'm so pleased to hear that you could solve your supply problem. I hope your trip wasn't too strenuous."

"It was indeed a marathon of meetings, both business and social, but we must all make sacrifices for the war effort. It was a small price to pay for securing the steel ball bearings." She cast him a bright smile that warmed his heart. Not many women in her position would have been so uncomplaining.

"Hopefully you had some time to enjoy yourself, too."

"Oh yes, I did. On the first evening, Herr Lindström invited me to a concert. It was fantastic."

He could only imagine how stupendous she must have looked in a ballgown similar to the one she'd been wearing to the mayor's party. A stab of jealousy hit him, since he'd wanted to be the one to sit by her side.

"I love classical music, who was the conductor?"

She scrunched up her nose, as if in deep thought. "Wait... Alfred Westrich. Yes, that was his name."

"What? How could you? He's a traitor!"

"I'm sorry, I had no idea. What did he do?"

"He protested, quite violently, against the book burnings and then evaded his rightful punishment by fleeing the country."

"If that isn't more than enough reason to label him as a vicious traitor," Annegret agreed.

Mollified, he said in a much softer tone, "You shouldn't have attended his concert."

"I'm disconsolate. How could I not have known this?"

He patted her arm. "It's not your fault. You were still a child when it happened." He wasn't much older than her, but at the Napola one of the lessons had consisted in learning the names of famous artists who'd betrayed their nation by criticizing one thing or another.

32

After receiving the announcement that all Jews would be deported in the near future, Oliver had rushed to Parchim to deal with the issue. But Lothar Katze had declined to help this time, quoting his hands were tied.

Time was running out, and Oliver started one last attempt to convince Thomas, but he was unfortunately neither corrupt nor empathetic.

"You again?" Thomas asked, slightly annoyed.

"I'm so sorry. But if we're going to lose all our essential workers at once, the factory simply won't meet the quota—possibly for months."

"Look, I understand your conundrum and if it's any comfort to you, we agreed to wait several weeks to give you the time for training new labor."

"Well, that is a relief indeed." Oliver calculated in his head. They'd been putting the Swedish protective passes to use, moving people into bigger cities, where they had a better chance to stay unrecognized. Unfortunately they could only do so one by one, as not to raise suspicions. Throughout the past three weeks they had spirited away ten prisoners giving them a chance to live as "Swedish subjects awaiting repatriation."

Yet, close to five hundred still remained in the most precarious situation, the hatchet of deportation looming over their heads. He could never get all of them to safety in such a short time, especially since the work permits for supposed civil workers still hadn't manifested.

He needed to buy more time. "Can we at least get temporary exemptions? Until we have found and trained the replacements?"

"No more exemptions." Thomas tipped forward with his fingers on the tidy desk to emphasize his words. Then he locked eyes with Oliver. "But I can see that you're doing your best to support our Führer, and therefore I'm willing to help."

Oliver's heart jumped. "That is so generous of you."

"Here's my offer: give me a list of one hundred non-essential Jews by the end of the week, and I'll postpone deportation of the rest for another month. This will ensure you can keep up production, while at the same time allowing me to stay on schedule."

"That is... I don't know what to say." Oliver inhaled deeply to control the shock washing over him. A horrible devil's deal if it was a deal at all. Annegret would be heartbroken.

"No need to thank me. We're both on the same side." Thomas bowed his head. "I'll be awaiting your list."

Oliver got up, offered a consummate Hitler salute and turned to leave, feeling like he'd been run over by a stampede of panicked horses. Once outside the SS headquarters he walked with slumped shoulders to Sabrina, who was waiting for him tied to a fence.

She rubbed her nose against his shoulder, except today he wasn't in the mood. Too big was his tribulation. "How am I going to tell Annegret?" he asked the horse.

"Tell her what?"

Oliver jerked around to see Lothar Katze standing behind him. "I'm sorry, Herr Unterstumführer, I didn't hear you coming."

"Is it about the exemptions?"

"It's hard to keep up production without skilled workers." He hedged, not trusting the other man.

"You know that I always understood the needs of the business people."

"And for that, we're very grateful." Oliver wondered whether Katze was going to extend some kind of offer.

He didn't.

Upon his return to Gut Plaun he told Annegret about Thomas' offer and they agreed not to do anything for the moment, since neither one of them wanted to play God and choose the one hundred people being sent to their deaths.

He knew the decision was coming from weakness but still couldn't force himself to take action.

Three days later he was about to leave for his morning visit to the stables, which he enjoyed too much to forego, even on such a dark and cold winter morning, when a man pedaled toward Gut Plaun at full speed.

Men arriving for work at the last minute wasn't unusual, but this person came from the opposite direction of town. As soon as the rider spotted Oliver, he waved one hand and shouted, "Herr Gundelmann!" without reducing his breakneck speed.

That reeked of trouble. Stepping toward the man, Oliver sighed inwardly and said goodbye to a morning cuddle with his favorite horses.

"What's up?"

The man's face was crimson red and it took him several seconds of heaving before he was able to utter, "There's SS at the factory, selecting workers for deportation."

"What! That bastard..." Thomas had promised the final

action wouldn't start until next month. Thinking quickly he opted to use the truck, both for speed and impression. "Come with me. You can tell me everything during the drive."

As soon as he'd settled behind the wheel, he sped out of the premises and down the road toward the factory. Meanwhile, the foreman had caught his breath and recounted, "Sorry to bother you, but Herr Volkmer won't be in before eight. I was preparing the change of shifts when a military truck stopped outside and a dozen SS men jumped out. They showed me some papers, claiming they had come to select one hundred Jews for deportation. Since nobody advised me of anything, I told them to wait until the factory manager arrives, but they said they had better things to do than to wait. So I told my colleague to keep an eye on them and raced to the manor to fetch you."

"I'll talk to them," Oliver said, although he knew well enough that there was little he could do if the SS had shown up with the goal of selecting Jews for deportation—and brought the proper papers to do so.

The wheels screeched as he veered through the gate, almost ramming the sentry who saved himself with a quick jump sidewards. Oliver rushed out of the vehicle, stomping directly to the gathered crowd, and approaching the first SS man he saw.

"Good morning, sir, I'm Oliver Gundelmann, the estate manager. May I know what you need from us?" He knew it was no use to appear haughty or in the slightest hostile, since the SS held all the cards, and he held none.

The man turned around. "We're here to arrest Jews."

The irony of arresting people who were already prisoners wasn't lost on Oliver. "Herr Unterscharführer," he said after a glance at the insignia. "SS-Oberscharführer Thomas Kallfass explicitly assured us that deportations won't start until February, to give us enough time to train replacements."

"You'll have to talk to him personally. He's over there."

That two-faced snake! Oliver wanted to scream with frustration. He approached Thomas, choosing to use the official address. "Herr Oberscharführer Kallfass."

"Oh, Oliver, good to see you." Thomas beamed with delight.

"What is this all about?"

Thomas raised an eyebrow. "You haven't forgotten our conversation, have you? I assumed you were too busy to make the list, so I took the liberty to do it myself." He waved a bunch of papers in his hand. "But now that you're here, even better. Follow me."

Whether he liked it or not, Oliver had to follow Thomas, as he strode across the assembly yard, list in hand, heading for the sick station.

"You'll agree that subjects who can't work, have lost their indispensability. Therefore we'll select them first." Inside the barracks, Thomas walked from bed to bed, picking out every patient with a yellow star on their prisoner garb. His men forced them to get up from their bunks to gather in the yard. Those who couldn't walk had to be carried by their comrades.

The look in their eyes broke Oliver's heart, knowing that they knew the end was near. Some would not even survive the transport to occupied Poland.

After combing the sick station, the laundry, the tailor shop, where prison uniforms, protective gear and shoes were made and mended, plus other supporting workshops, ninety-two quivering men and women stood in the yard.

"Who else should I select?"

Oliver tried to intervene, "Can't you take fewer? What's the difference?"

"Who do you think I am!" Thomas said scandalized. "I'm an honest man. I offered to deport one hundred, therefore I will deliver one hundred."

"It would never cross my mind to question your integrity, I

merely wanted to shorten the process since you must be awfully busy."

Thomas seemed to be enjoying the spectacle, since he clicked his heels and puffed out his chest. "There's no task more important than ensuring the race's purity. The Jewish poison has to be eradicated from our nation."

"I see." Oliver shrugged, careful not to antagonize him.

Thomas went through his list once more and finally gave a sly smile. "How could I forget the kitchen? Food given to this scum is wasted anyway."

A horrific realization hit Oliver right between the eyes. He barely suppressed recoiling from the impact. "We need them to feed Germans, too. Only about half of our workers are Jews, and about a quarter are civilians from nearby towns."

Thomas gave him a deadpan stare. "I need eight more, and I will select eight more." He then walked into the kitchen, where the first man he picked out was Ernst Rosenbaum.

Oliver didn't have the courage to look into the eyes of Annegret's relative, when the SS men shoved him into the yard toward the rest of the waiting prisoners.

"Where do you take them?" Oliver asked.

"Where do you think?"

"I do know quite well, where they end up." Oliver feigned a conspiratorial smirk. "Deservedly, if you ask me, but does it make sense to send a single cattle car all that way?"

"Of course not. We put them into the transit camp and wait until we have arrested a full thousand before we arrange for a train going east."

33

Margarete was having breakfast when she heard a motorized vehicle and walked over to the window, curious as to who might visit this early in the morning. She was about to turn around as soon as she recognized the estate vehicle, but then Oliver jumped out and rushed toward the manor.

Panic surged in her veins. He rarely, if ever, took the automobile because he much preferred to ride a horse. The next thing she heard were stomping steps racing up the stairs and a loud knock on her door.

"Come in!"

"We have a problem," Oliver called even before he'd crossed the threshold.

Looking at his disheveled state, she beckoned for him to sit down. "Take a breath and tell me."

"Thomas came to the factory and took one hundred Jews with him," he hissed, between heavy breathing.

"This early in the morning?" She realized the triviality of her question the moment the words had left her mouth.

"I assume they don't want to arouse undue attention. You know how much Hitler values public opinion."

She swallowed down the sharp retort on her tongue. "Is there anything we can do?"

"No." He looked excruciatingly uncomfortable.

An uneasy feeling spread in her stomach. "What aren't you telling me?"

"I'm sorry, Annegret, but your relative..."

"I don't have relatives," she protested before it dawned on her. "You mean, my real uncle? How do you even know?" She'd thought that she had kept her secret. Another shockwave hit her. If Oliver had made the connection, anyone else could, too.

"The last name."

"Oh." At least that was a small relief, because apart from him, nobody, not even Dora, knew her real name. Except that it didn't solve the main problem: Uncle Ernst was among those to be deported. In his frail condition she didn't doubt for a single second which line he would be directed to at the infamous selection ramp. "I have to save him."

"You can't."

"You don't understand. His wife saved my life and I owe it to her."

He put a calming hand on her shoulder. "I did everything I could, but Thomas was adamant."

"That spiteful scumbag! I knew all along his charming façade couldn't be trusted!" Margarete had learned the hard way not to trust people. Unfortunately her assessment of Thomas had turned out to be right. "Do you know where they're taking him?"

"To a transit camp."

"I'll go there."

"You can't. You'll blow your cover."

"I don't care. I have to try and save him, even if it's the last thing I do." Margarete got up and reached for her coat. "What are you waiting for? Drive me to the transit camp."

"Annegret, please. Be reasonable! They'll arrest you, too. That won't help anyone."

"What do you suggest?" She lingered with her coat in her arms, unsure what to do.

"Let's make a plan. We can pull a few strings, grease some palms, but it shouldn't be you who gets involved. You have to think of your other protégées. Do you want to endanger all of them for the sake of your uncle?"

From a rational point of view, he was right. But emotionally...? She pressed her lips into a thin line. "Alright."

"You're not going to do anything stupid?"

"No."

"Promise?"

She sighed. "If you insist. Will you let me know once you find something out?"

He nodded and left.

She waited two seconds, before she changed into jodhpurs in a hurry and used the outer staircase attached to her rooms. Oliver might not be willing to help, since he needed to keep the wellbeing of all Jewish prisoners in mind, but she knew who she would ask.

Making sure Oliver was in his office, she walked down to the stables, asked a stable hand to saddle Pegasus for her and set out toward town in search of Stefan.

As she rode through the forest, she realized that she didn't know where he lived. Fortunately the winter had been rather mild so far and the lake hadn't frozen over, except in a few shallow spots. There was a good chance he was still fishing and she'd find him at the wharf.

She left her horse at the local inn and walked down along the channel, admiring the mechanics of the lift bridge connecting the Elde River with the lake. When she saw his boat tied to its usual place, her heart jumped with joy.

It was empty. Her heart fell. She walked a few steps

onward, until she saw another fisherman, just coming in from the water. "Hello, do you know where I can find Stefan Stober?"

He cast her a suspicious gaze. "What'ya need 'im for?"

Stefan had told her that in the winter months he earned extra money by repairing ropes, so she answered, "We need some ropes for Gut Plaun."

If he'd recognized her or not, she didn't know. "Must be up at the fish market, having his catch weighed." All fish had to be sold to the central fishing authority, which then distributed it to the village shops in the district.

"Thank you." Since it was only a five-minute walk, she decided to seek him out at the fish market. Halfway there she saw Stefan walking toward her, breaking into a huge smile when he recognized her.

"Gretchen. What a lovely surprise. What brings you here?"

"Actually," she said, lowering her voice. "I was looking for you."

"For me?"

"I need your help."

"People to hide?"

"Maybe."

Instead of an answer he said, "Care to take a tour on the boat? I have a delivery of ropes to make on the other side of the lake."

"I'd love to." It was cold, humid and layers of fog wafted across the water, making it look like a mythical place from an ancient Greek legend. There were definitely better days for a boat tour, but as long as she was by his side, she didn't mind.

He jumped into his boat, then stretched out his hand to help her. "Hop in."

Silence settled over them as he steered them into open water. Suddenly she felt nervous. What if he thought it was too dangerous, reckless even, to try and save her uncle? She fidgeted with her hands until she finally broke the silence. "Does your grandfather know you're involved with the resistance?"

"As much as grandfather remembers things these days."

"I'm sorry."

"Don't be sorry. He had a good life and maybe it's for the better." Stefan ran a hand through his hair. "He'd be shocked to know what has become of this country."

She lapsed into silence again.

"You're quite the most extraordinary woman," he suddenly said, looking at her with a warm glimmer in his eyes. "Incredibly brave."

"I don't feel brave, most days."

"Being brave doesn't mean you aren't afraid. It means you step up to do what's needed despite your fear."

Once again, he surprised her. Such wisdom she expected from Uncle Ernst, the philosophy professor, not from a simple fisherman. *A chemical engineer*, she corrected herself.

Not that she cared. Being an outcast in a world that wanted her entire race dead had changed her perception about the value of a person. Stefan was definitely worth more than a hundred men of Thomas' sort.

His arm sneaked around her shoulder, pressing her against him. "Are you cold?"

"A bit."

"Take this." He pulled out an oversized raincoat and wrapped it around her. Despite being sheltered from the chilly wind, she missed the warmth of his body beside hers. "Now what did you need my help with?"

She sighed and told him the entire sad story, ending with the words, "One of them is the husband of a dear friend. I simply must get him out." It was her fault. They had been spiriting Jews away. Some into hiding places, others equipped with protective passes replacing their "burnt in a bombing" papers. Yet, she'd insisted on keeping Uncle Ernst close by, supposedly safe under her wing, working an easy job in the factory kitchen.

And now he was gone!

"It's not your fault. You've been doing all you can."

"It wasn't enough." Her entire family had been either arrested and sent to a concentration camp or "evacuated", as the Gestapo liked to call it, to free up housing space in Berlin for Germans. She was pretty sure none of them were still alive and she'd sworn to protect the one remaining Jewish relative she had.

"Sometimes not even our best efforts will suffice." He put a hand over hers, the heat emanating from him giving her solace.

"He's held in the transit camp."

"And now you want to go there to check up on him?"

"How did you know?"

His adorable dimples appeared on his cheeks. "It was an easy guess."

"Are you going to talk me out of it?" She pushed out her lower lip, inwardly steeling herself for the slew of rational arguments inevitably coming her way.

Instead, she heard a low chuckle and then, "Would you listen?"

"Probably not."

"Then, I guess I'll have to help you, if only to keep you out of trouble."

"You would do that?"

"I would do anything for you."

At a loss for words at his unexpected admission, she stuttered. "Th...thank you."

"Are you free this afternoon?"

"Yes, why?" she said, confused at the turn of the conversation.

"We can leave the boat at the wharf, hop on a train and pass by the transit camp to find out if your friend is still there."

"You would do that? Really?"

"How many times do I have to repeat myself?" His face hovered close to hers, his eyes shining with genuine sentiments. It made her all too aware of her own deception. He was willing to risk his life to help her, whereas she hadn't even told him her real name.

Appalled by herself, she shrunk back a moment before his lips landed on hers, the following hurt in his eyes crushing her soul.

34

Stefan delivered the ropes and walked to the bakery where Annegret was waiting for him. He couldn't make head nor tail of her. One moment she seemed to return his affections and the next she shied back from him, as if some invisible wall stood between them.

He scolded himself for being delusional, since he knew all too well what the reason for her reaction was: she was a rich heiress, he was a poor fisherman. She'd seemed to be different when he first met her, completely unaware of the class distinction between them and that had given him unreasonable hope.

Normally he didn't grouse about being demoted from a chemical engineer to a fisherman. It was physically hard work, yes, but compared to the stress and anxiety he'd been subjected to when working for a tank manufacturer, it was a delight. Most days he enjoyed the tranquil life, although it had stopped being peaceful when he'd decided to join an underground organization.

"I bought the train tickets while waiting for you," she greeted him with a heartwarming smile that melted his doubts away. In moments like this one he believed there was a future for the two of them.

"Great. Let's go to the train station." It was only a short walk and they were lucky to find a train waiting on the platform.

As they arrived at their destination, Stefan directed them to the transit camp, a former Jewish school that had been requisitioned by the Gestapo.

"What's your plan?" he asked.

"Go there and tell the sentry I need to talk to Ernst Rosenbaum."

He coughed out a laugh. "Now that's a plan."

"Do you have a better one?"

Since he didn't, she shrugged. "I'll go then."

Before he could protest, she strode off toward the main gate, head held high, exuding an air of authority only the rich and important knew how to pull off. He admired that woman. So petite, yet a force to be reckoned with.

He wished that somehow, by some miracle, they could cross the social divide and become a couple. Ready to spring into action the moment she was in danger, he observed as she approached the guard, waved a paper and disappeared into the building. Half-hidden behind a tree he waited for her return, his heart hammering against his ribs.

———

Margarete wouldn't let being scared to death deter her. She'd used the train journey to come up with a plan—flimsy and reckless—but a plan nonetheless. Taking a deep breath, she stepped in front of the policeman guarding the entrance.

"Good afternoon. I'm here to retrieve a man who's been deported by accident." She showed him the exemption letter, signed and sealed by the district headquarter.

"You can put this paper away. The only way these wretched people go is into a train east."

"Can I at least speak to him to make sure he's alright? His name is Ernst Rosenbaum."

"Sorry, Fräulein, but that's against the rules."

She put on her haughtiest expression, reached for a letter Horst Richter had sent her a while ago with his official letter-head, and waved it under his nose. "Do I really have to find a telephone and trouble Reichskriminaldirektor Richter from the Gestapo about this?"

The policeman wavered. After a while he nodded. "Ten minutes. And it wasn't me who allowed you in."

"Thank you so much." She stuffed the letter into her hand-bag, glad that her bluff had worked. "Where can I find him?"

"Probably on the second floor."

As she turned around to step inside, she saw another truck parking out front. SS men jumped from the driver's cab, no doubt about to unload a cargo of miserable Jews destined for deportation.

Ignoring her heartache, she stepped into the building. Her mission was to save her uncle. As soon as she reached the second floor, she saw him crouching against the wall on the cold concrete floor.

She forgot all caution and called out, "Uncle Ernst!"

He stumbled to his feet, his eyes shining with moisture. "My sweet child." They hugged for a long time, before he stepped out of her embrace. "You shouldn't have come. It's too dangerous."

"I had to. I'll do everything to get you out of here."

"Please, don't do anything that might endanger yourself. Your work is much more important than saving just one person. You have the power to keep so many alive, you can't waste it for this old man." His voice was firm, as his eyes showed the love, hope, anguish and anger he was feeling.

Margarete furtively wiped a tear from her eye, before she answered. "You always make it sound so easy. What do I care about the rest of humanity, if I can't rescue the people I love most?"

"That, my dear, is a very good question. It is indeed the fundamental principle on which the Nazis rely: people will only protest when it directly affects them or their families—but by then it will be much too late. If nobody stands up for strangers, in the end, there'll be nobody left to stand up for you."

"But..." She thought about how devastated Aunt Heidi would be, and another tear rolled down her cheek.

"You go and do good. Once in a while you think of your old uncle, will you? Tell my Heidi that I love her with every fiber of my soul."

She hugged him once more. "I'm not done yet trying to get you out of here. Just in case..." She took off her earrings, expensive pearl studs, and pressed them into his hand. "These will help."

"I can't possibly..." Uncle Ernst protested.

"You can and you will. Where you go from here, they could make the difference between life and death." Then she turned on her heel, fleeing from the room, because she sensed that she couldn't hold back her tears much longer.

She hastened downstairs, past the sentry, outside and onto the street with the intention to run and never stop again. Around the corner, she barreled into a broad-shouldered man, who had stepped directly into her path.

"Thank God, you're back. I was scared to death."

She didn't have a prayer to prevent launching herself at him. When she did, he wrapped his arms around her, holding her tight, while her entire body shivered. "I showed them the exemption, but they only laughed. Said they don't care. Only a dead Jew is a good Jew. It's awful in there. But he's fine. My un

— friend's husband. He's scared but composed. He's such a brave man. Always was."

"Shush. It'll all be fine." He rubbed his hands across her back in a soothing gesture.

An exasperated sigh escaped her throat. "How can you say that? Nothing will be fine. As soon as they have gathered enough Jews, they'll put them on a train to the east. And you know what happens there!"

It wasn't a secret anymore. Anyone who wanted to knew about the atrocities being committed. Too many Wehrmacht soldiers serving on the Eastern Front had told their relatives under the pledge of secrecy. Too many SS men had boasted of their foul deeds. Too many civilians had smelled the sickly-sweet scent of burning human flesh, had witnessed the dark clouds coming from high chimneys in the camps.

"There must be survivors. I'm sure of it."

She champed with rage. "The young and strong maybe, but not him. He's old and frail." She freed herself from his embrace and picked imaginary dust from her sleeve, before she tapped a finger to her ear. "I gave him my pearl studs. I hope they help."

"You're a very resourceful woman."

"I guess I am." She looked at him, yearning to tell him the truth about herself. "We should go home. It'll be dark soon and people at the manor will worry if I'm too late."

35

The next day Margarete visited the only person who had the power to help: the two-faced snake Thomas Kallfass. If she pretended to be deeply in love with him, he might find it in himself to show mercy. If not, she'd still bribe him with the kiss he desired so much.

To save Uncle Ernst, she'd do anything, even offer Thomas the opportunity to share her bed. She valiantly swallowed down the dread creeping up her throat. It might not go that far. Even if it did... she'd survive. At the hands of Reiner Huber, when working as his father's maid, she had experienced worse.

Despite not trusting Thomas, she knew without the shadow of a doubt that he'd never harm the woman he had his designs on. Like Horst Richter, his cruelty was directed toward those he considered beneath him.

"Dora, can you help me dress?"

"Yes, Fräulein Annegret. Where will you be going?"

"I need to run a few errands in Parchim and will meet with the Oberscharführer for lunch."

"Something modest?" Dora assumed.

"On the contrary. I want his jaw to drop when he sees me."

Dora blinked with confusion. "I thought you didn't like him."

"I don't. This is not about me, it's about the prisoners he took."

"Well then..." Dora opened the wardrobe, her nimble fingers gliding across the dresses, until they stopped at one. "What about this one?"

It was Margarete's jaw that dropped when Dora held out an absolutely stunning burgundy-red taffeta dress that reached almost down to her ankles. It featured a sailor-like triangle-shaped collar and a row of tiny fake buttons all the way down to the hips. The narrow skirt featured a slit in the middle, making it look like tulip leaves, opening to a billowing longer skirt in the same color and material.

"Don't you think that's too extravagant?"

"Not at all. You're going to the district capital. Plenty of women will be dressed like this."

"In Berlin maybe, but in Parchim?" Margarete had her doubts.

"You said you're on a mission to drop jaws and this is the perfect dress for it," Dora reminded her. "Especially with the matching hat, shoes and gloves, the Oberscharführer has no chance to resist your wishes."

"I hope you are right." Margarete inspected herself in the mirror. She entered the bathroom to apply lipstick, before she thought better of it. Hitler hated lipstick, since he thought it to be unworthy of a German woman. Thomas, with his absurd adulation for the Führer, would think the same.

She took the coat from Dora's hands and walked down the stairs to find Nils to drive her to the city. Giving herself a pep talk, she murmured, "Go convince the man he's completely in love with you and make him eager to fulfill your every wish."

Once she arrived in Parchim, she told Nils to wait for her, took a deep breath and walked into the SS headquarters, heading straight for Thomas' office on the first floor. Before she knocked on the door, she opened her coat and forced a smile to her face.

"Annegret, what a lovely surprise." His eyes darkened with desire as soon as he noticed her dress beneath the coat. "You look amazing."

"Thank you so much. I happened to be in town and was wondering whether you'd be free to have lunch with me?"

His eyes lit up. "I am swamped with work, but for you I'll make time."

"I won't keep you from your work for too long," she said, adding a coquettish flutter of her eyelashes. She'd colored them black with mascara, taking great care to make it look natural.

"Where shall we go?"

"I'll defer to your local knowledge." She smiled sweetly, doing her best not to choke on her disdain for him.

"Perfect. There's a wonderful restaurant around the corner."

She held perfectly still as he put his hand on the small of her back, ignoring the urge to scratch out his eyes and fling every known curse word at him for his heinous *Aktion* in the factory.

Throughout the meal he babbled on about his great achievements and how he was being considered for another promotion. One that might take him away from Parchim, possibly to Berlin, where all the important things happened.

"That's wonderful news," she fluted. It was terrific news indeed, if it meant she'd never have to see him again. Horst Richter had hinted that even the SS felt the shortage of eligible men and often couldn't replace a vacant position.

As much as she disliked Katze, he was preferable to Thomas, because with him greed preceded ideology.

"Won't you miss me then?"

Thomas' question caught her completely off guard. She

needed a few seconds to formulate an answer. "Of course I'll miss you, Thomas. But duty always comes first and it would never cross my mind to keep you from serving our country the best you can."

His expression softened. "That is one of the reasons why I love you so much. We think alike. We have the same goals, the same dedication to serve our country. You in your small women's world and me in the big world of the men." Horror seeped into her bones, since this was the first time he'd used the love-word.

"How well said." She really needed to tell him her request, because she couldn't stand his absurdities much longer.

The next moment, he took her hand and before she even realized what happened, pressed a kiss on her lips. It was demanding and insistent. Her intuitive reaction was to push him away, yet somehow she forced herself to open her lips. His tongue slipped inside, exploring her mouth. She counted to ten before she extricated herself from his embrace. "Thomas, we're in a public place."

"I'm sorry, Annegret. I was overwhelmed by my feelings for you and the fear of never seeing you again." He cleared his throat, took both of her hands into his, and said, "I didn't plan on this happening so fast, but sometimes in life circumstances demand action. My imminent promotion has shown me how much our lives are interwoven and how much I would miss you."

"But—" she tried to interject.

"Don't." He put a finger over her mouth. "Hear me out first. I know you feel the same way, and I couldn't be happier about that."

She barely controlled the urge to shrink back in horror.

"You and I, we have a wonderful future ahead of us. Each of us is destined for great things. Together we can achieve so much more. A strategic union will be the culmination of our love and would mean you can follow me wherever I'm going."

She had no intention of leaving Gut Plaun, since she had to care for her workers and all the other people who came for help... and Stefan. She certainly didn't want to leave him.

"My beloved Annegret, will you marry me?"

Her mouth fell open before she could prevent it. "Marry you?"

"Yes. You have so much on your plate. As your husband I will take over all your burdens. You wouldn't have to worry about the business side of Gut Plaun any longer. I will oversee everything, while you can fully concentrate on entertaining our guests and raising our children. With my authority and your social status, we'll rise to the top and will soon be named in the same breath with the Goebbels, Himmlers and van Ribbentrops."

She was near to fainting. He was serious about proposing marriage, although he made it sound more like a business partnership. *God help me!* "Thomas, I have to confess your proposal has completely taken me aback. We've known each other for such a short time."

He seemed disappointed at her lack of enthusiasm. "I know, it's a bit pressured, but that doesn't mean my feelings for you aren't genuine. The war gives an urgency to life and many loving couples forego long engagement periods under the threat of being torn from each other forever."

Except that I don't love you. "I... this is all new to me," she told him shyly. "I need time to process your words and your kiss." To emphasize her words, she touched her lips with her finger. "I'm bedazzled."

"It was marvelous, wasn't it?" He smiled.

She nodded.

"As your husband I will attend to your every need and do everything to make you happy. Always."

This was her one and only chance to free her uncle. If she had to marry Thomas for it to happen, so be it. "I appreciate your kindness and generosity."

"I'd do anything for you, my love."

"Indeed there's one little thing you could help me with."

"Name it and it shall be done."

She took a deep breath. "I know this is rather unusual, but a dear German friend of my mother married a Jew. Before my mother died I overheard her promising to help if anything should happen to her husband." She made a disgusted face. "I just happened to find out that he's among the ones you took from the factory yesterday. So I was wondering, if he could be released? I'm doing this solely to honor my mother's promise, since I respected her so much."

Thomas pressed his lips into a thin line. "What's his name?"

"Ernst Rosenbaum."

"I'll see what I can do."

"That's so kind of you." She forced herself to press a chaste kiss on his lips. "Thank you so much."

A church bell chimed. He looked at his watch. "I'm so sorry, my love, duty is calling. I'll drive to the transit camp this afternoon to inquire about your mother's friend." He cocked his head and stared at her. "I've never seen you without earrings. What happened to your pearl studs?"

She put a hand to her ear and lied. "I must have forgotten to put them on this morning."

"I'll see you tomorrow evening? We have a lot of planning to do for our wedding."

She didn't remember saying yes, except that little detail didn't seem to matter to him. "I'm looking forward to it."

He escorted her to where Nils was waiting, giving her another kiss to say goodbye. Up on the coach she broke out into violent shivers.

36

Thomas made a few urgent calls, before he left his office, letting his secretary know he wouldn't be back until the next day.

He climbed behind the wheel of the black office Mercedes and drove the forty minutes to the transit camp. It was a puzzle to him why some German women, like Annegret's mother's friend, stayed loyal to their Jewish husbands, when a divorce would be so much better for everyone involved.

What he was about to do ran contrary to his innermost conviction. He despised himself for having promised his future wife in a weak moment to release that man. Now he was confronted with a troubling dilemma: Being an honorable man, he always kept his promise. At the same time, releasing a Jew meant he had to betray his own convictions and cause damage to his beloved Fatherland.

An anguished sigh escaped his throat. What to do? Annegret would be so disappointed in him if he reneged on his promise and told her a Jew was a Jew and had to die.

He pressed down the gas pedal completely. The velocity went to his head, accelerating his thinking alongside the vehicle. A faint memory came up. An *Aktion* in Berlin a year ago. The ensuing protest at the Rosenstrasse. German wives with Jewish husbands had protested against their arrest.

The results had never been announced publicly. After a week, the Jewish subjects had been released in a cloak-and-dagger action, returned to their families with the request never to talk about the happenings with anyone.

If it had been his decision, he'd have taken and not only deported the blasted Jews but also their traitorous German partners. Alas, the Führer had once again shown his innate kindness and granted mercy to those who had defied him. A truly great statesman.

Thomas released the gas and smiled. He would follow the Führer's example and release one undeserving man to put those to shame who accused the Nazis of being cruel.

Upon his arrival at the transit camp, he approached the gate and showed his identification.

"Herr Oberscharführer," the policeman greeted him, inspecting the papers thoroughly. "Is there a special reason for your visit?"

"There's one prisoner I need to interrogate. His name is Ernst Rosenbaum. Where can I find him?"

The policeman shrugged. "When was he admitted?"

"Yesterday."

"He's probably on the second floor, downstairs are the newcomers. There's such chaos inside, you wouldn't believe it. I could go and find him for you, but I'm alone and need to guard the entrance."

"I'll go myself." Thomas sighed. If the Führer knew how badly staffed the transit camp was he'd haul the responsible men over hot coals.

Inside, the first thing he noticed was the bestial stink. He shrugged. Had he needed more proof that Jews were untidy swine?

The policeman hadn't promised too much. The chaos was

appalling: everywhere were people, crouching, sitting, standing in complete disarray. Some in prisoner garb, others in civilian clothing, their yellow stars muddied, their coats torn. He noticed several Jews in short sleeves. These subhumans didn't even know how to dress appropriately for the season.

A small boy cried for his mother, while an old man tried to soothe him. Jewish mothers apparently couldn't care less about their babies, abandoning them in this chaos. It was disgusting! Annegret would never leave their children alone.

At least the vermin had the good grace to make room for him, so he was able to cross the room to reach the staircase without having to tread on them, dirtying his boots. The appalling stink of human excrement intensified the further he got from the entrance. He held his breath until he reached the second floor.

Up there it was slightly better, but not by much. He positioned himself at the landing and bellowed, "Is Ernst Rosenbaum here?"

Nothing happened. He bellowed once more and, holding up an apple, added, "Who brings him here will receive this."

It didn't take long until a crone scurried toward him, her eyes cast to the floor as she murmured, "Herr Obersturmführer. The man you're seeking is in the last room to the right. His niece came here yesterday and gave him her pearl studs before she left."

What in the holy hell? More proof of the corruptness and disgustable ways of the Jews. He strode off to look for Rosenbaum, but that filthy bitch tugged at his sleeve, whimpering, "My apple, sir?"

What a brazen woman! "You didn't bring him here, so no reward for you, ugly crone, though," he looked directly into her fearful eyes, a giddiness fueled by absolute power overcoming his senses. "You tried to incriminate this man with a crime and you dirtied my sleeve. There's no place for scum like you in this country." He pulled out his pistol and aimed at her forehead.

It was a clean shot. Perfect even. A single drop of blood on her forehead. She dropped like a felled tree. The shot echoed from wall to wall, reverberating through the floors of the building. It didn't take more than thirty seconds until the second floor swarmed with SS, Gestapo and police, generously doling out whip lashes at anyone who moved, as well as those who didn't.

Thomas didn't bother joining in, since he had a job to do. He strode to the room where Ernst Rosenbaum was supposedly hiding. At the threshold he yelled again, "Ernst Rosenbaum. Come here!"

An elderly man got up with some difficulty and shuffled forward, his eyes cast downward, his shoulders slumped.

"Give me the earrings!" Thomas demanded.

"I don't have earrings."

"I know you have them." Fury was taking hold of him. If he needed more proof that all Jews were liars and crooks, there it was. "You were seen."

"A friend gave them to me to keep safe for her." Rosenbaum produced a precious pair of pearl studs from his pocket.

Thomas recognized them immediately. They were Annegret's favorites. The ones she hadn't worn this morning. Something sinister was going on here. No doubt, he was going to get to the bottom of it. The passionate kiss she'd give him as thank you for recovering her precious earrings tingled on his lips.

"What's the name of your friend?"

"I... I can't say," Rosenbaum stammered.

"She's a thief. These earrings belong to Annegret Huber." Thomas observed the other man closely, noticing a flash of horror in his eyes at the mention of Annegret's name. He swore, that no matter how much effort it took, he'd get the truth out of the Jewish swine. "You're coming with me." He grabbed Rosenbaum's arm and dragged him behind.

"I'll take this prisoner for interrogation," he told the policeman who'd let him inside earlier. Upon their arrival at the automobile he shoved the Jew into the back. The secretary would have to give it a thorough cleaning.

The next morning Ernst Rosenbaum confessed a crime so horrible Thomas swayed in shock. And it wasn't the theft of precious earrings.

37

Margarete paced her room, stopping every minute to look out the window, waiting for Thomas' black car to arrive.

When she finally heard the motor noise, she dashed to the window with her heart beating hard against her ribs. It was his black office car. She held her breath, observing what happened.

A man got out of the car, it was Thomas. But he didn't have a passenger with him. Releasing her breath, she scolded herself. He wouldn't bring a released prisoner to the manor. There were protocols for this. Right?

There were protocols for everything. Especially for releasing prisoners. Uncle Ernst would have to go to some office, sign documents, before he was returned to the factory. Not to the manor.

She moved away from the window, into the parlor next to her bedroom, anxiously waiting to hear footsteps indicating Thomas' arrival.

They came, much faster and heavier than she'd anticipated. Thomas must be angry, or perhaps he was in a hurry. Yes, he must be in a hurry. She composed herself, plastered a smile on her face and walked toward the door to greet him.

The door was thrown open and smashed against the wall before she reached the middle of the room. A fuming madman stood in front of her, his blue eyes narrowed into furious slits. "You... you... you traitorous bitch! You'll pay for this!"

Something had gone terribly wrong. Margarete quivered with fear, yet somehow managed to keep her voice steady. "Please, Thomas. Calm down. What's wrong?"

"You... you... you know exactly what is wrong! You dirty Jew!"

She reeled from the impact of his words as if he'd physically hit her. "What are you talking about? This is nonsense. You're agitated, let me get you some coffee." She grabbed for the telephone, but he caught her arm, before she reached it. "Ouch. You're hurting me."

Eyes blazing with unabated hate he hurled his next words at her. "Ernst Rosenbaum is your uncle, you filthy Jew."

The blood drained from her head, making her sway. This was the moment she'd feared all these months, and yet, when it finally had arrived, she was utterly unprepared. She asked in a whisper, "Who told you this lie?"

"Your uncle told me himself."

She wiped her palms on her woolen skirt and tried to reason with him. "Whoever told you this certainly wasn't my uncle."

"Cunning bitch. Accusing your own flesh and blood of falsehood."

"If I had an uncle, why would he accuse me of such a ridiculous thing? In any case, you have no proof."

"I do." He held out the pearl studs she'd given Uncle Ernst. This was bad, albeit not hopeless. She reached out a hand to take them, but he quickly closed his palm and stuffed the earrings back into his pocket.

She tried a different angle. "I'm so glad you found them. Remember yesterday, I told you I'd lost them. This person who claims to be my uncle must have stolen the earrings. If you would let me see him, I'm sure we can get to the bottom of this outrageous accusation."

He smirked. "Not much to see anymore. It took us all night until he finally confessed."

Again, she staggered as the blood sagged to her feet. Poor Uncle Ernst! She refused to imagine what they had done to him until he succumbed and told them the truth.

In the end, everyone talks, Armand, the leader of a French Résistance group had insisted. According to him it was merely a matter of time, the goal being to hold out long enough to give your colleagues a chance to disappear before the Gestapo came for them as well.

"He's a Jew. He'd say anything to save his life. But who will believe his word over mine?" Slowly, she gained back some confidence. What would Annegret do in her stead?

Margarete had been playing this game for such a long time, it wasn't difficult to channel the other woman. Stomping her foot, she yelled, "How dare you come to my house and launch this outrageous accusation at me! I'll call the Gestapo and have you arrested!"

He broke out into laughter. "Do that, my dear Annegret, or should I say Margarete?"

She shook her head, biting on her lip to prevent herself from launching into a tirade of curse words.

"I also received this." He held up a *Kennkarte* with her photo, the name of Margarete Rosenbaum and a fat yellow J stamped across the left side. It was the one she'd snuck into dead Annegret's pocket. How on earth had he gotten this? Although, it didn't matter. Despite being several years old, the woman in the photo was clearly her. Even if she continued to deny it, they could get dental records and proof she wasn't Annegret Huber, but some impostor. That alone was crime enough to disappear into a concentration camp for all eternity.

"Haven't you got a tongue in your head?" Thomas mocked her.

"How did you get the *Kennkarte*?" she whispered.

"Once I knew your real name, it was a piece of cake. Being a Jew you won't understand, but we Germans keep meticulous records. All I had to do was telephone the registry office in the borough of Berlin where you lived, and given the gravity of your crime, they sent it over with a courier right away."

Being backed into a corner, she played her last trump. "Thomas, please. We can talk about this."

"There's nothing to talk about."

"We can still get married. The entire estate will belong to you. My money and my social status are your ticket into the high society. Nobody would ever have to find out. What about your dreams? Do you want to give up everything now?" she begged him. She could see he hesitated for a moment, before his face contorted into an ugly grimace once more.

"Who do you think I am? I'm an honorable man, serving my Fatherland, not a greedy social climber ready to sell out all that is good for fame and glory," he jeered. "A marriage to a Jew is not only against the law, it's a threat to the public health. Having intercourse with someone like you contaminates the pure German blood and defiles racial purity."

She gave a sad smile. Thomas was seriously deluded. Unfortunately, within his twisted mind he stayed true to his ideologies and refused to be bribed. Although in her situation it would have been preferable to deal with a man like Lothar Katze, she had to give Thomas credit for standing up for what he believed to be right.

"What are you going to do now?" she asked, still somehow hoping he'd spare her.

"I'm going to take you to the transit camp, to be sent to Auschwitz at the first opportunity. Given your healthy condition, I'm sure you'll be chosen for hard labor, instead of instant death, if that is a consolation to you."

"I thought you loved me."

He spat at her. "I thought you were German."

38

Thomas stared at the woman standing in front of him. After being ousted as a traitor, she still kept her poise, kindling his fury. It would have been so much more rewarding if she had cowered at his feet, begging for her life.

Not that it would have mattered, since he had no intention of showing mercy to someone who'd viciously deceived the world for over two years. She'd lodged herself in the Huber estate the way a cuckoo lays its eggs into the nests of other birds, profiting off their good nature.

Incessant fury raged through his veins. That crone was so much worse than the average Jew. Neither precedence nor comparison existed for her crimes. What Margarete had done was the epitome of depravity.

A knock came on the door. "Come in!" he barked.

That little maid Dora stood in the door, giving a frightful look as she picked up on the tense atmosphere. "Fräulein A—"

"What do you want?" he interrupted her.

"Herr Oberscharführer, I'm so sorry, but Reichskriminaldirektor Richter has arrived." She curtsied not once, but twice, shooting nervous looks at her mistress, who at least had the grace to keep her mouth shut.

"What does he want?" What a nuisance that Richter had to show up at this of all moments.

Although having a witness, from the Gestapo no less, to Margarete's heinous deceit and Thomas' role in revealing it would be an asset. Richter, who'd been duped himself, would applaud Thomas for his brilliant mind.

Out of sheer admiration, and gratefulness, the older man would become the stirrup holder for Thomas' future career. "Please, have him come up. He can help with a slight dispute we're having."

The maid seemed unsure and gazed at Margarete. "Is everything all right, Fräulein Annegret?"

"I'll be fine. Please go ahead and tell the Reichskriminaldirektor to join us up here."

Thomas could be mistaken, but he sensed a silent understanding between the two women. He made a mental note to interrogate the maid later on. As soon as Dora was gone, he took a step toward Margarete and hissed, "He won't save you, you know."

She cocked her head. "I don't need saving, because my conscience is clear. You're the criminal here. You're the one who kills innocent people for nothing but the crime of being of Jewish descent. You're the one who tortures and maims. You find joy in shooting prisoners like rabbits. You deprive them of their most basic needs, starving, freezing or working them to death. You are the lowlife of humanity. Not me!"

He was so shocked, he had no retort. Wrath bubbling up in his veins at the insolence of a member of the most despicable race, he lunged out and slapped her in the face.

Her bewildered expression was worth a million. He observed with satisfaction how the mark of his hand burned bright red on her porcelain white skin.

The door opened and Richter stepped inside. Good Gestapo agent that he was, he immediately recognized the loaded atmosphere. "I'm sorry, have I interrupted a lovers' quarrel?"

"Not at all, Herr Reichskriminaldirektor, in fact I couldn't be happier for you to be present." Thomas stood straighter, towering over the older man by half a head. "This woman is a Jew."

Richter didn't as much as blink an eye. "Now, you must be aware that this is a very grave accusation. I gather you have proof?"

Margarete didn't even try to defend herself, she simply stared ahead, her arms crossed in front of her chest.

Thomas handed Richter the identification paper and explained. "She has fooled us all pretending to be Annegret Huber, when in fact she was their Jewish maid."

Richter pursed his lips, scrutinizing the document, and slowly nodding his head. Thomas already saw himself in Hitler's headquarters receiving a War Merit Cross for exceptional service not in direct connection with combat. It would be a splendid ceremony with distinguished guests, delicious food, and—most importantly—he'd get to shake the Führer's hand.

A fluffy feeling spread in his stomach. He didn't need the riches of some stupid heiress. After this outstanding achievement he'd be promoted with lightning speed. Senior members of the government would consult with him on tricky issues, ask for his advice and make him privy to the most important government decisions. He might even become a confidante of Hitler's, having personal access to the Führer, helping him shape the future of a great Germany.

"This seems a bit flimsy to base such a serious accusation on," Richter's voice broke through his fantasies. "Do you have anything else?"

He looked at Richter with disbelief. What was the man

talking about? An original *Kennkarte* that clearly proved the woman in front of them wasn't who she pretended to be. What more proof did he need? "In fact, I do. I have the testimony of her uncle, Ernst Rosenbaum, whom she tried to save from deportation and visited in the transit camp." Thank God, he'd left the man alive—just barely.

"A Jew? You know as well as I do that his testimony is worth less than the dirt beneath your fingernails."

Thomas couldn't figure out what Richter wanted. Shouldn't he be interested to expose such a heinous deceit? Instead he was... playing devil's advocate. Of course, that was the reason. The seasoned Gestapo agent wanted the case to be one hundred percent watertight, since the entire Huber estate was at stake.

He relaxed his jaw muscles and said, "Herr Reichskriminaldirektor, I applaud your thoroughness. You will see that this case is absolutely watertight. Apart from the original *Kennkarte*, which you hold in your hands, I have the testimony of her uncle, a Jew, and these." He removed the earrings from his pocket and showed them to Richter, while keeping half an eye on Margarete to make sure she didn't intend to make a run for it.

Richter nodded with a grave face. "I don't recognize them. They are just a pair of pearl studs that could belong to anyone."

Something didn't add up, but before Thomas could decipher the meaning of the queasy feeling in his stomach, Richter took out a silver cigarette lighter, lit the *Kennkarte* and watched it burn.

Unable to move, or speak, Thomas stood frozen in place, his eyes riveted to the licking yellow flame voraciously devouring the paper until black ashes fluttered onto the thick Persian carpet.

"Oberscharführer Thomas Kallfass, you are arrested for stealing valuable pearl earrings from the rightful owner

Annegret Huber, and accusing her of a heinous crime she never committed. This falls under the offences of defamation, slander, theft, and, most important of all, subversion of the war effort."

"What? You can't do that!" Thomas stammered. By the time he finally thought of defending himself with his weapon, Richter had handcuffed his hands behind his back and shoved him into the plush armchair.

Keeping his revolver trained on Thomas, Richter stepped to the telephone. Moments later he spoke. "This is Reichskriminalrdirektor Richter from the Gestapo headquarters in Leipzig. I have arrested a traitor and thief. Would you please send your men to Gut Plaun."

Thomas' chin fell to his chest. The game was over. His career was over. His life was as good as over, and he still didn't understand how or why.

He had done nothing but his duty to defend the Reich from evil.

39

Oliver was at his office, sifting through orders for food, raw materials, seeds, cloth, and whatever else the estate needed to function, when Dora dashed through the door.

"Oliver..." she panted, her face hot and flushed.

"What's wrong?" He immediately assumed the worst for their baby and jumped up, hitting his knee painfully against the leg of his desk.

"Fräu...lein Anne...gret." Dora pressed out between huffed breaths.

"What's wrong with her?" Despite the apparent graveness of the situation, relief washed over him. At least Dora and the baby were fine. Later, he'd impress upon her once again that she had to take it easy, but for now he let it go.

"She's upstairs with Oberscharführer Kallfass and... it was so strange. She seemed horrified, but said she'll be fine. I'm worried about her."

He glanced at his wife, whom he loved with all his heart, and who had a tendency to worry too much about her mistress.

"I'm sure everything is alright."

"No. I know it isn't. She couldn't tell me, but you should

have seen her face. She was terrified. Please, can you go upstairs and make sure this man doesn't do anything awful to her?"

He sighed. "I'll check up on her. But only if you sit down for a minute and catch your breath. It's not good for the baby if you get so worked up." Walking to the door, he kissed Dora.

"Reichskriminaldirektor Richter is up there, too," she said.

He nodded and rolled his eyes once he was sure she couldn't see it. If Richter was with Annegret, she was safe. Since Dora would never forgive him if he didn't check up on her mistress, he climbed to the second floor anyway and knocked on her door.

"Come in," Richter's sonorous voice called.

Oliver opened the door and froze mid-step.

"Oh. It's you, Herr Gundelmann. I was expecting my colleagues."

Oliver was speechless, taking in the peculiar situation: Annegret stood pale as a bedsheet next to the window, while Thomas slouched in the armchair, his hands behind his back in what seemed to be a rather uncomfortable position. Acrid smoke hung in the air, covering up a more primal smell: mortal fear.

Finally, regaining his voice, Oliver asked, "I'm sorry to interrupt. Is everything alright?"

"Indeed it is." Again it was Richter who spoke, while Annegret stood like she'd turned into a pillar of salt. "This man," he said, pointing at Thomas, "has stolen precious pearl earrings and has tried to blackmail Fräulein Annegret by threatening to accuse her of being a Jew if she doesn't comply."

Oliver flinched, wondering how Thomas had found out the truth. "What beastly behavior!"

"It was sheer luck I was here to put a stop to such a horrendous crime."

"Indeed. As estate manager of Gut Plaun I have to thank you for your decisive intervention." He thought quickly. "I have suspected this man to be after Fräulein Annegret's money for a while now. Though it never occurred to me he would resort to stealing and blackmail."

"Ahh... we never really know the people close to us, now do we?" Richter stared directly at Annegret.

"I guess not," she said, her voice thinner than usual.

"Will you need me for anything?" Oliver asked.

"I might... could you stay here and watch this criminal until my colleagues arrive?" Richter said.

"Of course."

"This is a lie! She's a Jew. I can prove it!" Thomas shouted from the armchair, half rising in a clumsy movement. Only now Oliver realized that his hands were handcuffed behind his back. Before Thomas managed to fully stand up, Richter was by his side and knocked him on the head with the butt of his revolver.

Thomas fell back into the armchair.

"I should have him executed for spreading these ugly lies. My friend, the SS-Standartenführer and his lovely wife would turn in their graves if they knew what this lowlife is insinuating." Richter looked pointedly at Oliver. "I'm sure you agree with me."

"I certainly do." Oliver wasn't sure whether Richter was testing him. Did he know the truth and wanted to know on which side Oliver stood? Or was it a trap? He'd feign ignorance. "I would never in my life work for a Jew. No decent German person would. I can assure you, Herr Reichskriminaldirektor, at Gut Plaun we're striving every day to serve the Reich better than the day before. Lies and deceits have no place here. Once again, I must thank you for your decisive action."

It didn't take long until the Gestapo arrived and dragged Thomas behind them down the stairs, after generously doling out punches to his ribs and head for speaking out of turn.

"He'll be sent to the camp in Mauthausen for his crimes," commented Richter, before he addressed Oliver. "Could you ask the maid to clean up? Annegret and I will take a walk meanwhile. The poor thing is shaken by what has happened and some fresh air will help her get over the shock."

"I'll send Dora right up. Thank you for taking care of Fräulein Annegret."

"It is the least I can do."

40

Still shaking, Margarete followed Horst Richter downstairs, giving Dora an encouraging smile when she passed her.

She didn't quite understand what had happened, since she'd been convinced Horst would gladly deport her if he ever found out the truth. Had she misjudged him and the Gestapo officer owned a kind heart, even for Jews?

His framing of Thomas had been brilliant. She had to give him credit for coming up with such an elaborate ruse in the blink of an eye. His colleagues had asked few questions, and she hadn't even had to lie, because the topic of her genealogy never came up.

Instead, she'd truthfully answered that the earrings were hers and Thomas had been quite incessant in his pursuit of her, even though she'd—very subtly—tried to let him know that she wasn't romantically interested in him.

Horst led her to his automobile, motioning for her to get into the passenger seat.

"I thought we were going to take a walk?"

"We are. But not here. I don't want one of your employees to overhear us."

She got inside and he started the motor, driving in the direction of the lake.

"Why did you do this?"

His fingers drummed on the steering wheel. "It was necessary."

"Thank you." What else was she supposed to say to the man who'd unexpectedly saved her life?

"Don't thank me. I didn't do it for you. In fact, I despise you! You should be on a train to Auschwitz along with the rest of your horrible breed!"

She hadn't misjudged him after all. It was an assurance of her discernment, albeit extremely perturbing. If he hated her so much, why hadn't he just let Thomas have his way?

"Let's take a walk and I'll explain."

She hadn't noticed that he'd stopped the vehicle nearby a popular bathing spot. In summer the town youth came here to swim, sunbathe and dive from a rock into the water. This time of year though, the place was completely deserted.

They walked the short distance through the dark forest, lying in peaceful silence. The only noise was the soft lapping of ripples against the pebble beach.

"What Kallfass found out must be the boldest, meanest, most subversive deceit I've come across in my entire career with the Gestapo. And believe me I've seen everything. But this? How could you! Defiling the memory of Annegret's parents by posing as their daughter. Staining the German race by pretending to be one of us. You're a disgrace!"

"Why didn't you—"

"I'll tell you why. If I had backed up Kallfass' story, some upstart would soon have asked questions. I'm a powerful man with equally powerful enemies. They would have a field day with my mistake. Can you imagine the vicious gossip about how I got taken for a ride by a Jewish sow?" He shook his head. "No you can't. It wouldn't have taken long until I would have been shunted aside, ending my days in some inconsequential desk job. Or worse, demoted. An overzealous man on the make might think it beneficial to initiate an investigation against me, claiming I derived a personal profit from installing you as heiress of the Huber estate."

They had reached the beach. He took the path to the right, leading up and around the bay. The breeze brought a soft buzz to her ears.

"Goddammit! Me? I'm honest to the bone. Would never steal a single penny from the Reich. No, I had to prevent any of this from happening. With your word and mine against his, there was no doubt whom to believe. The theft of the earrings was just the icing on the cake. A beautiful touch to seal the case."

The moon was shining strong enough for her to see his satisfied expression. "So you did all this because you were afraid to ruin your career?"

"Yes."

The buzzing became louder and she wondered what it could be. "Now what? We'll just pretend that nothing happened?"

"Not at all." They had reached the top of the mound. She'd never been at the lake at night and gazed in awe at the reflection of silver moonlight on the black water surface. It was such a peaceful atmosphere, the quiet forest behind them, the beach with the sound of lapping ripples beneath and the two of them up on the rock overlooking the majestic lake.

Under different circumstances she would have enjoyed the view. At this moment she wondered why Horst had brought her here of all places.

He grabbed her arm. "I'm going to kill you."

"No, please!" she screamed at the top of her lungs, struggling against his grip.

"You must understand that it is the best solution." Despite her struggling, he dragged her to the ledge.

"Help, please help!" Her screams echoed across the empty water.

"Nobody will hear you. It's just the two of us."

"Please. Don't kill me! Help! Someone come and help me!" Her squealing got louder with every inch he dragged her toward the ledge. She was losing the struggle, could already see the end of the rock.

She intensified her efforts, mobilizing every ounce of strength, fighting him back inch by inch. Encouraged by her success, she pushed, shoved, whacked and kicked against the big, sturdy man who was so much stronger than her. Until he released her.

Surprised by the sudden lack of resistance, she stumbled and fell face first onto the frozen earth. It took a few seconds for the impact to subside. She caught her breath and crawled forward, away from the water.

"Not so fast," Horst said, his black boots appearing directly in front of her face. "Get up. Slow."

The telltale click of a revolver made her realize the hopelessness of her situation. Too scared to try anything, or even to scream, she did as he demanded and came first to her knees, then rose up to her full height, her hands in the air.

"This doesn't have to be difficult. You'll behave, walk to the ledge and jump down. It will be a fast and painless death, I promise. Once in the water you'll freeze to death within minutes. Nice and easy. You'll be unconscious long before you drown." He motioned for her to walk toward the ledge. "You should thank me, Jew. Your ilk rarely gets such an easy way out."

"Thanking you for killing me? You must be crazy!" she howled, even as she followed his orders, feverishly thinking of a way out. There was none. Horst was much stronger than she was, and he had a weapon.

"No, dear. Just think how much worse it would have been if I hadn't rescued you. Going to Auschwitz, being worked to death. Toiling under the most horrid conditions day after day, with barely any food. Would you rather experience that?"

"No! Let me go! Help! Someone help me! He wants to kill me!" She changed her approach and begged him, "Please, Horst. I'll disappear forever. Nobody will ever be the wiser. Please... just let me live."

"You know I can't do that." He shook his head, almost as if he were sad. "I grew quite fond of you. You were the daughter I never had. But you deceived me. A Jew! The worst of the worst. Scum that's not worthy to lick the dirt from my boots. If I let you live, you'll procreate and have many Jewish brats intent on destroying our great nation. No, I have to get to the root of the trouble, eradicate it once and for all. Every last Jew on this earth must be extirpated."

"How can you say this?" She realized he would never give in. Her time on earth was running out.

"Now, let's get it over with, my feet are getting cold." He motioned for her to turn around. "Walk. The less you fight, the sooner it'll be over."

Fear numbing her limbs, she struggled to follow his command, until she finally managed to take a step. And another one. And one more... she stopped at the ledge, unable to do what he wanted.

She didn't have to, because mere seconds later a shove against her shoulder propelled her forward, forward... and she fell... fell... fell... into the void. "Aaaahhhhh!"

Filling her lungs with air in a desperate attempt to fight for her life, she splashed into the water, the cold immediately sucking the oxygen from her lungs, attacking her nerves.

Yet, she fought, struggled against the heavy woolen coat

dragging her down, until she somehow came up again, breathed in much needed air. If only she had learned how to swim! Her desperation grew, as the cold numbed her limbs, made them heavier and heavier, until they wouldn't move anymore, and she sank into the darkness.

41

Stefan was on his way to the secret fishing grounds for eel, that his grandfather had taught him about. The fatty fish was a staple on the menu of the villagers and he could be sure to get a good price for his catch. Usually he wouldn't fish eel during winter season, but the hardships of war had suspended traditional rules.

Catching eel needed patience and skill. He prided himself on having both—and the knowledge of their preferred hunting grounds. When he arrived, he moored his boat up on a tree and placed fresh bait into the eel basket before he submerged it.

Working in absolute silence, he was all but finished when he heard a blood-curdling scream. He thought it was a wounded animal, but seconds later there followed another scream that was definitely human.

He couldn't quite make out the words, surmising to decipher *help* and *please*. Whatever it was, he had to find out. At this time of the year, and especially after dark, nobody visited this part of the lake, except maybe some teenager playing in the forest had tripped and couldn't get up on his own.

Untying his boat, he started the motor and drove in the

direction where the scream had come from. He turned his head to listen with his good ear. It didn't take long until he heard more screams and then he saw them: two dark silhouettes up on the rock the village youth used as a diving platform during the summer.

The smaller person, a woman, judging by her high-pitched screams was taking tentative steps toward the ledge, while the bigger person stood behind. "What's the stupid bloke waiting for?" Stefan muttered under his breath.

The man moved slightly and Stefan's blood froze in his veins when the moonlight reflected on something metallic and he recognized the form of a revolver.

Dear God! He's going to kill her. Stefan put the motor in full gear and had almost reached the rock when the woman fell into the water, causing a huge splash. The ripples from the impact caused his boat to roll. In the moonlight it was hard to see, so he steered toward the middle of the circle of waves, waiting for her head to bob up again.

It did.

"Come here!" he yelled. She struggled wildly, showing no intention to swim toward him. It was a good twenty yards. Considering the impact, the cold water, the heavy clothing... she would have to be an excellent swimmer to have a chance at all. But why didn't she at least try?

Because she can't swim, the realization flashed through his mind. As he throttled the motor to approach her with care, her movements became slower and slower, until she turned on her back.

In the moonlight, her face gleamed white. His heart stopped beating as he recognized Annegret. Her body lay completely still, slowly sinking deeper into the icy water. Within two seconds he'd reached her and bent across the railing, grasping first one shoulder and then the other one, to heave her into the boat.

"Annegret!" He slapped her cheeks several times, hoping she would open her eyes. Nothing happened.

Except for the rain shield he had nothing to warm her up in his boat, so he took off his jacket and spread it across her body. Pondering what steps to take, he realized he had to choose between the devil and the deep blue sea.

"It'll have to be the devil," he murmured to himself, making sure his fish knife was at hand in its sheath.

The stranger on the rock had watched how Stefan dragged Annegret from the water and was walking down to the beach. Much to Stefan's relief, the man had put his weapon away. Nonetheless, he stayed alert, not trusting the peace. The best course of action seemed to play the innocent.

"Hey, can you give me a hand? This woman fell into the water, she needs to get somewhere warm immediately," he shouted as he drove the boat into the shallow water, switched off the motor and waited for it to drift onto the pebbles. The screeching sound pierced his good ear and his heart. Under different circumstances he'd never be so heedless with the boat.

"She didn't fall. She jumped."

Stefan hadn't expected such a callous reply. From near he noticed the stranger's fine black suit, almost like a uniform without insignia. Intent on not giving away his acquaintance with the victim, he asked, "Do you know her? Did she attempt suicide?"

"I should hope so. She's a Jew."

"What?" Stefan's chin fell to the floor. "But..."

"Look. You're a fisherman, right?"

"Yes." Flabbergasted, he could not form another word.

"I'm Reichskriminaldirektor Richter, Gestapo. I happen to have found her after she ran away from the nearby munitions factory. She has chosen to kill herself rather than return to work. I think we should respect her choice."

"She's still alive."

"That's rather unfortunate, isn't it? She would be dead if you hadn't interfered with policework," Richter had the audacity to say.

Stefan's head whirled. He didn't understand what was going on. How could this Gestapo officer mistake Annegret Huber for a Jewish slave worker? She didn't even wear the yellow star. Something didn't add up. "Sir, I'm very sorry. It was never my intention to obstruct your work. What do you want me to do now?"

"Take your boat to the middle of the lake and throw her overboard. That will solve our little problem with due elegance."

Herr Richter talked about elegance when planning to kill a woman? "You want me to murder her?"

"Since you were the one who prevented her from drowning in the first place, I reckon it's only fair, don't you think so?"

"No. I can't do that." Stefan shook his head. "She's not a Jew. This is Annegret Huber from the nearby Gut Plaun. I've met her a couple of times in town."

Within the blink of an eye, the revolver reappeared in Richter's hand. "I'm sorry it has to come to this. We need capable fishermen to feed our nation. Unfortunately you don't seem to know what is good for you. It doesn't matter, whether this woman is who you believe she is, or not. She has to die. And now you'll have to die as well. Get in your boat."

Richter motioned with his weapon toward the boat and Stefan used this moment of distraction to launch himself at the older man, knocking his arm upward. A shot bellowed into the air, causing a slew of noises from jolted animals.

Sitting atop Richter, who'd fallen backward under Stefan's weight, he wriggled the revolver from his hand and threw it into the water.

"Why do you want her dead? She's Fräulein Annegret,

owner of Gut Plaun. She's not an escaped prisoner. You're wrong!"

Despite his precarious situation, Richter gave a haughty snort. "I'm never wrong. Get off me and I won't have you tortured before you die."

Red-hot fury short-fused Stefan's rational thinking. He pummeled his fist against Richter's jaw. "I won't let her die."

"You're a fool. Have you thought this through? Defying the order of a Gestapo officer. You'll have to kill me if you want to save her. Do you think you can pull that off?"

Richter's mocking achieved the exact contrary of his intentions, because Stefan knew with sudden clarity that he would do everything to rescue the woman he loved—even kill the Gestapo officer who'd tried to murder her. His hand fumbled for a stone.

"I guess I can," he said, raising the stone and watching with satisfaction how Richter's face contorted at the realization that his time was running out. He bashed the stone onto the side of Richter's head, knocking him out in the process.

He got up, gave the limp body a piggyback ride to the edge of the water, where he dumped him face down. Then he nudged the floating body, observing how it drifted into the deep water and slowly sank to the ground.

Back at his boat, he lifted Annegret into his arms and carried her along the small path to the road, where he hoped to find some means of transportation to return her to Gut Plaun.

42

Dora came into the bedroom with a breakfast tray. "Did you sleep well, Fräulein Annegret? You gave us quite a fright."

"I'm fine, thanks to Stefan who rescued me." She'd been only half-conscious after he'd fished her out of the water and carried her to the car. Richter had left the key in the ignition and it hadn't taken long until they had arrived at the manor.

Frau Mertens and Dora had been out of their minds, fussing over her. Somehow they'd removed her wet clothes and gotten her into bed, putting hot-water bottles around her, before they wrapped her into an eiderdown blanket.

Some time later, the Gestapo had arrived, for the second time that day, and asked questions. She had pretended to be stricken with grief.

"It's so awful. After the incident with Oberscharführer Kallfass, I was hysterical. Horst, God bless him, suggested we go for a walk so I could compose myself." She sniffed for emphasis. "I don't know what to do without him. He was my mentor, my father substitute."

"Can you tell us what happened?" the young officer asked.

"We walked alongside the lake, got up to that rock the youth use as a diving platform, because I wanted to see the reflection of the moonlight on the water." She dabbed at her eyes. "It was so beautiful. I was drawn to the ledge, without noticing it. He came after me, warning me it was dangerous, but I wouldn't listen. Then I slipped and fell. He knew I'm a bad swimmer and didn't hesitate for a moment, before he jumped in after me. The next thing I remember, is that I woke up in the fisherman's boat." She tried a small smile. "Horst was such a good man. I will never forgive myself!"

"Fräulein Annegret, it wasn't your fault," the young man said with empathy.

"If I hadn't gone up there, or walked too near the ledge, nothing would have happened. Why did he have to jump in after me? If he had let me die, he'd still be alive!" She squeezed out tears for good measure.

"You can't think that way, Fräulein Annegret."

Pressing a hand to her forehead, she pretended to be over-whelmed by guilt and grief.

The Gestapo left and questioned Stefan, who corroborated her story, telling them he'd heard the splash and had motored to the place as fast as he could. When he arrived he saw only one person struggling not to drown and dragged Annegret limp from the water.

Several minutes later, after regaining her senses, she had told him about her friend. Despite using his searchlight, he hadn't been able to find any trace of a second person in the water.

They closed the case, considering it a tragic accident and thanked the fisherman for his courageous actions. That had been five days ago and yesterday they had found Horst Richter's corpse. The side of his head had sustained a blow, which must have been caused by hitting something during his dive from the cliff. Apparently this had caused him to be unconscious when he hit the water, with the result that he drowned.

When Margarete finished breakfast, she put the tray aside and stepped out of bed, putting on her dressing gown. A knock on the door indicated Dora was back to retrieve the tray. "Come in."

"Fräulein Annegret, Herr Stober has asked about you. Would you like to see him?"

"Yes, please. I'll receive him in the parlor." Even if Stefan hadn't saved her life, she'd absolutely want to see him.

Less than a minute later, he stepped through the door and her breath caught in her lungs. He was even more ruggedly handsome than she remembered.

"Annegret. I'm glad you're up."

"Thank you again, for what you did." She put her hand on his arm, sensing the electrical charge overleaping. "I guess I owe you an explanation."

"I guess you do."

"Please sit." She motioned to one of the comfortable armchairs and settled on the other one. "It's a long and complicated story. I probably should have told you long ago, but..." She sighed. "Living a lie has become second nature for me."

"This man, he was adamant to kill you. He insisted you were a Jew."

She cocked her head, looking into his wonderful blue eyes, gauging his reaction as she said, "I am."

"I kind of figured." He interlaced his fingers with hers. "You don't have to tell me if you don't want to. It doesn't make a difference to how I feel about you."

His answer had shown her without the shadow of a doubt that he was the man she wanted to spend the rest of her life with, and she actually looked forward to telling him the truth about herself. "I want you to know."

"Then I'm all ears." He settled back into his armchair and didn't interrupt her one single time as she told him her story, starting with the serendipitous bombing that had changed the course of her life and ending with, "I'm sorry for lying to you all this time."

"It was understandable, given your circumstances," he said, taking her hand and rubbing his thumb across the back of it.

"Can you forgive me?" She barely dared to hope he would.

"There's nothing to forgive. I love you all the same."

A long-missed comfort spread through her limbs. "It's such a good feeling to be myself again, at least with one person in this world."

He grinned, grabbed her arm and pulled her onto his lap. "We'll get through this together."

She leaned against him, feeling absolutely carefree in his arms. "Yes we will. We moved a dozen or so women to hide in the woods, hired new stable hands with false work permits, used the Swedish protection passes and yet there's still so much to do. About four hundred remaining Jewish prisoners are running out of time, even with Thomas gone."

"Assuming Lothar Katze will succeed him, I'm sure you can bribe him into new exemptions."

"Yes, but for how long? Until the next overzealous Oberscharführer comes around, eager to prove himself?"

Stefan pressed her tighter against him. "We'll find a way—somehow. First of all, we'll start sabotaging the production in your factory to speed up the end of the war, everything else will fall into place when the time is right."

"I sure wish I had your confidence."

"It can't be long now. Rumors have it the Allies will soon invade France."

"How do you know?" she asked him with wide-open eyes, suspecting she hadn't been the only one with a secret.

"Wouldn't you like to know?" he said with a huge grin, kissing her on her lips. The sweet sensations swept away doubt, curiosity and fear. Whatever happened next, together with Stefan, she'd rise up to the challenge.

A LETTER FROM MARION

Dear Reader,

Thank you so much for reading *The Girl in the Shadows*. If you did enjoy it, and want to keep up to date with all my latest releases, just sign up at the following link. Your email address will never be shared and you can unsubscribe at any time.

www.bookouture.com/marion-kummerow

After finishing the previous book *From the Dark We Rise*, Margarete has become such a dear friend that I couldn't let her go just yet. I felt there was more to her story, and I wanted to give her true love, not a complicated, twisted relationship like the one she had with Wilhelm in *A Light in the Window*.

During my research trip to Plau am See, I was fascinated by the lake. It was such a picturesque, peaceful area. I wondered whether I could make it a more prominent part in the story, since I felt it would give some much-needed serenity to the otherwise grim surroundings. Hence, Stefan, the fisherman.

If you're not completely satisfied with the ending, I have some great news for you: my editor Isobel Akenhead agreed to have a fourth book in the series, because there's so much more to write about Margarete, and now about Stefan, too.

I have big plans for both of them. You may remember that she asked him in chapter twenty-seven if he would help her to sabotage the production in the factory. He agreed, but never followed through.

He certainly wouldn't go back on his promise, so this will be one theme for book four. If you have read my trilogy *Love and Resistance in WW2 Germany*, you'll know that my grandfather was a chemical engineer, inventor, and a Nazi resister, who sabotaged production of radio transmitters for the Wehrmacht, so lots of real-life experiences to write about.

You'll also find out whether Uncle Ernst survived the treatment he received at Thomas' hands.

But enough of what's coming next, and back to the historical details I used in this book.

In reality, the last Jews in the district of Parchim moved to bigger cities in the late 1930s, hoping they would have better chances to survive in the anonymous crowd, as opposed to their home village, where everyone knew everyone else.

The only Jews remaining were the ones imprisoned or used for forced labor, in factories like the one depicted in this story. They were used for lack of other "suitable" prisoners, despite Heinrich Himmler's order on October 2nd, 1942 to transfer all Jews imprisoned in German concentration camps to either Auschwitz or Lublin.

Herr Naumann, who is not a real person, represents the majority of German industrialists who weren't actively anti-Semitic, but used the prevalent ideology for their own profit. They couldn't care less about the race of their workers as long as they worked hard, and for little money.

Lothar Katze, also not a real person, stands for the many Nazi corrupt bureaucrats, who, under the cloak of racial ideology, used their authority to extort the Jews, and those who wanted to help them, for their own benefit. I found it an interesting question, whether a sleazy thug like him is better or worse than a man like Thomas who actually believes in what he does, and considers himself an honest man, because he stands up for his convictions.

Sweden was one of the major steel providers. They walked a very thin line, providing all warring parties with the scarce raw material, while maintaining their neutrality.

Upholding the neutrality, for their own survival, might have been a reason why they didn't readily accept Jewish refugees. According to a statistic of the *Bundeszentrale für politische Bildung*, the German Federal Agency for Civic Education, they accepted less than 4000 Jewish refuges between 1933 and 1945, most of them Danish Jews during a concerted action in October 1943, when Denmark evacuated all their local Jews to Sweden.

You may have heard about escape lines before. Most popular are the ones through Belgium and France or across the Pyrenees into neutral Spain. It is much less known that there were several escape lines in Northern Germany. A person with ties to the Escape Lines Memorial Society in North Yorkshire, UK, advised me there was a successful route running from the German Baltic ports to Denmark and Sweden.

The ports Wismar and Rostock lie both about 150 km or 100 miles from Plau am See, where the book takes place. It is very probable that some fugitives have passed through the area where Margarete lives.

Lufthansa maintained a regular schedule between several German and Swedish cities up until the final days of the war. On their website I found a picture of the JU 52 that I used to describe Margarete's flight to Stockholm, although it's not clear whether they used that type of aircraft on the route to Stockholm.

The protective passports Lars gives her, really existed, although as far as I know they were never used in Germany. Raoul Gustaf Wallenberg, a Swedish diplomat in Hungary, "invented" them to save more than one thousand Hungarian Jews from exterminaton.

You can see the photo of such a "Schutz-Pass" on my Pinterest board: www.pinterest.de/m_kummerow/a-light-in-the-window

There, you'll also find the burgundy-red taffeta dress Margarete wears when she begs Thomas for Uncle Ernst's life.

Again, thank you so much for reading *The Girl in the Shadows*. I hope you loved it, and if you did I would be very grateful if you could write a review. I'd love to hear what you think, and it makes such a difference helping new readers to discover one of my books for the first time.

I love hearing from my readers—you can get in touch on my Facebook page, through Twitter, Goodreads or my website.

Marion Kummerow

https://kummerow.info

 facebook.com/AutorinKummerow
twitter.com/MarionKummerow

Made in United States
Orlando, FL
18 March 2023

31153858R00168